Praise for *Pride and Prescience*

"Thoroughly 'light and bright and sparkling,'" in the best Austen tradition with a dollop of murder and mayhem to leaven the whole. A delight."

—Stephanie Barron, author of the
Jane Austen Mystery series

"Well crafted . . . Bebris works her own brand of Austen magic, whetting the reader's appetite for a sequel . . . Taking a lighter approach than Stephanie Barron's sleuthing Jane Austen series, this one should appeal as much to Regency readers as to Austenites."

—*Publishers Weekly*

"Mannered prose, Regency backdrops, moody country houses, and delightful characterization place this new series high on the to-buy list."

—*Library Journal*

Pride and Prescience

OR, A TRUTH UNIVERSALLY ACKNOWLEDGED

A Mr. & Mrs. Darcy Mystery

Carrie Bebris

TOR®

A TOM DOHERTY ASSOCIATES BOOK

NEW YORK

This is a work of fiction. All the characters and events portrayed in this book are either products of the author's imagination or are used fictitiously.

PRIDE AND PRESCIENCE

A Tor Book
Published by Tom Doherty Associates, LLC
175 Fifth Avenue
New York, NY 10010

www.tor.com

Tor® is a registered trademark of Tom Doherty Associates, LLC.

ISBN 0-765-35071-8
EAN 978-0765-35071-8

First edition: February 2004
First mass market edition: February 2005

Printed in the United States of America

0 9 8 7 6 5 4 3 2 1

For Katherine and James

Acknowledgments

This novel is the work of more than two years, during which my life changed in ways unfathomable to me when I first typed the words "Chapter One." In the period of its gestation, I found myself facing personal challenges of an unexpected nature. Many days, it was difficult to leave the present behind and slip into Regency England to spend time with Elizabeth and Darcy—but once there, it was like entering the home of old friends. I came to understand, more than ever before, Rudyard Kipling's words: "There's no one to touch Jane when you're in a tight place."

There is indeed no one who approaches Jane Austen's ability to help one through a tough time—except the individuals mentioned here. I am indebted to the following people, without whom neither this book nor I would be what we are.

My family, both immediate and extended, for support in forms too numerous and profound to list.

Anne Klemm, a kindred spirit whose friendship has nurtured my writing and my enjoyment of Jane Austen in so many ways—from book discussions and an Austen pilgrimage through England, to brainstorming and critiques. If we were not Jane and Cassandra in a previous life, we were surely sisters.

Theresa Nunemacher and Diane Welch, for the gift of their friendship. And also, along with Alyssa Hoff and Karen Ellsworth, for giving me time and space to write.

Stan! Brown, for helping me find my way back to Netherfield when the path grew dark.

Victoria Hinshaw, Andrew Hughey, Julia Martin, Lisa Bernard, and Peter Archer, for generously sharing their expertise.

Ed Greenwood, for kindness to a fledgling writer.

My fellow members of the Jane Austen Society of North America, for sharing their knowledge of and enthusiasm for Austen and her writing. I especially thank Joan Philosophos and Marsha Huff for their encouragement. Joan, I wish I could give you a copy of this book, but I know you read it over my shoulder as I wrote.

My editor, Brian Thomsen, for helping me turn an idea into reality.

And, of course, Jane Austen.

It is a truth universally acknowledged, that a
single man in possession of a good fortune,
must be in want of a wife.
　　　　　　　　　—Pride and Prejudice, *Chapter 1*

Pride and Prescience

One

*Happy for all her maternal feelings was the day on which
Mrs. Bennet got rid of her two most deserving daughters.*

Pride and Prejudice, *Chapter 61*

On the day Miss Elizabeth Bennet wed Mr. Fitzwilliam Darcy, she did not mind dividing with her elder sister, Jane, the notice due a bride. Indeed, she had been delighted when Jane chose to marry Mr. Charles Bingley in a double ceremony. It seemed only right that two sisters and two men who were themselves particular friends should all embark on their new lives together, and she hoped the event presaged many happy hours spent in each other's company in the years ahead.

Elizabeth did mind, however, sharing the stage with Mr. Bingley's sister Caroline.

The new Mrs. Darcy glanced across the drawing room of Longbourn House. Miss Bingley and her fiancé, Mr. Frederick Parrish, sat beside each other on the sofa, monopolizing the attention of half the wedding guests. Their immediate spectators included two of Elizabeth's younger sisters, assorted aunts and uncles, and Caroline's sister, Louisa Hurst. The couple's chatter had also drawn the observation of others in the room. Mr. Bennet looked on with amusement, her mother with annoyance, her cousin Mr. Collins in uncharacteristic silence, and the Gardiner children in awe. The audience wanted only the addition of the Prince Regent himself to comprise the most unlikely party in all England, but, unfortunately, no one had thought to invite him.

Elizabeth knew little of Mr. Parrish, in fact had never met the American before today. According to Miss Bingley, he was a gentleman of the first consequence. He had one townhouse, two carriages, three tailors, and could walk on water every other Tuesday. He also, anyone within auditory range had been given to understand, was a wealthy landowner, a patron of the arts, and a master of the intricate "ballroom" style of folding one's cravat.

Elizabeth had not yet conversed with Mr. Parrish, and based on Miss Bingley's praise had little inclination to do so. She suspected, however, that of the myriad attributes proclaimed by his fiancée, the gentleman's chief recommendation lay in the simple fact that he had chosen Caroline, from among all the unattached young women of the Polite World, as the object of his affections. How an otherwise sensible-seeming man had allowed that to happen, Elizabeth could only speculate; she attributed it to either a momentary lapse of reason or a prolonged lapse of sobriety.

"Lizzy! Jane!" Mrs. Bennet bustled over to the quiet corner where, beckoned by early winter sunlight edging its way past the draperies, her second daughter had sought a moment's respite from her social duties. Jane, concern clouding her face at their mother's summons, hurried to join them.

Elizabeth sighed at the impending but not unexpected intrusion. She'd known her interlude would prove fleeting on a day such as this; nevertheless, she'd strayed over here to indulge in reflection. After one-and-twenty years, these were her final hours as an inmate of this house, and, though not by nature an overly sentimental person, she'd wanted a chance to bid it farewell in her heart before going away. Fortunately, a very short span of time had sufficed. Her mind had soon wandered to Miss Bingley and other more prosaic thoughts, the interruption of which mattered little. "What is it, Mama?"

"My poor girls, how dare that woman try to spoil your day!" Mrs. Bennet, her bosom heaving and complexion flushed, expressed her indignation with all the wounded vanity the mother of two brides could muster. "To announce her own engagement at your wedding breakfast—"

Elizabeth wished her mother possessed a voice one-tenth its volume. "Mama, everyone here knows this is our day, not hers."

Jane extended a placating hand, as if to literally smooth their mother's ruffled feathers. "I am sure my new sister doesn't mean to draw notice toward herself."

At Jane's defense of Miss Bingley, Elizabeth couldn't stifle a laugh. "Dear Jane, only you could be so generous. She was circulating the news while we were still in the receiving line." Her gaze turned back to the newly betrothed couple. Miss Bingley beamed at something Mr. Parrish said, an expression Elizabeth had rarely seen on the woman's typically haughty countenance. It softened the severe lines of her cheekbones and upward tilt of her chin, lending her an almost pleasant aspect. "Much as I hate to admit it, he seems a good influence on her."

"He's more than that woman deserves," Mrs. Bennet whispered too loudly for Elizabeth's comfort. "And his fortune! Lady Lucas told me he just inherited an enormous sugar plantation in Louisiana. It has a French name . . . Mont-Joyo, or something like that. He's easily worth ten thousand a year. Ten thousand, Lizzy—same as your Mr. Darcy!" Her mother's tone became reverent at the mention of Mr. Darcy. Though he was now her son-in-law, Mrs. Bennet, like many of Darcy's acquaintances, yet found him a formidable man.

Elizabeth observed Miss Bingley listening to Parrish with rapt attention. He cast his fiancée a warm smile, then broadened it to include the rest of his party. *Monts Joyeux.* She searched her rudimentary knowledge of French for a rough translation. Joyful Hills? The image of a home so named somehow suited the attentive, amiable man. But Miss Bingley was another matter. "I'm astonished that she consented to marry an American," she said. "One can't imagine her living in the United States. She'd consider it uncivilized."

"Maybe the size of Mr. Parrish's inheritance influenced her," Jane said. "It must be a very grand estate. I understand, however, that he plans to buy another property here in England." She lowered her voice so that it reached only Elizabeth's ears. "Perhaps Caroline will have her own Pemberley at last, Lizzy, now that she knows she'll never have yours."

Anticipation swept Elizabeth at the mention of Mr. Darcy's home in Derbyshire—now her home, too. Before Darcy became engaged, Miss Bingley had been obvious in her aspirations to one day cross Pemberley's threshold as its mistress. Apparently, she'd experienced more disappointment over failing to secure the estate than its owner, for no sooner had Darcy and Elizabeth set their wedding date than Miss Bingley embarked on a whirlwind courtship with Mr. Parrish. Somehow, in the space of mere weeks, Caroline had managed to win the affections of a very eligible bachelor.

Sensing someone's gaze upon her, Elizabeth raised her eyes to meet those of her new husband. Darcy stood some distance away, enduring the effusive congratulations of Mr. Collins, who had apparently found himself unequal to the effort of holding his own tongue long enough to overhear Mr. Parrish's words, and had therefore chosen to confer upon one of the bridegrooms his felicitations and sagacious marital counsel.

Despite Darcy's diverted attention, the clergyman continued his discourse unabated, completely insensible of the interruption in attendance to his soliloquy.

Though Darcy had cropped his dark brown hair a little shorter than usual for today, unruly curls yet wisped round his head. Short side-whiskers lent prominence to his strong jaw, while the lapels of his double-breasted coat accented the broad shoulders that so capably bore the weight of many responsibilities. Not of brawny build, he nevertheless exuded puissance, the noble virility of a classical marble bust come to life.

He towered over her cousin, his stature enabling her to see every nuance of his countenance. The man who could quell observers with the rise of a single dark brow bestowed upon her a look of infinite tenderness before returning his gaze to Mr. Collins.

"Miss Bingley can have every acre of Pemberley," she said softly. "I have the real fortune."

She glanced once more at her husband. Poor Darcy—stuck in the corner with Mr. Collins, and no end to the interview in sight! Noting that the servants had just laid out the tea table, she headed for it, intending to relieve Darcy's suffering by interrupting the conversation to offer refreshment. No sooner had she poured coffee to take to the gentlemen, however, than Miss Bingley and Mrs. Hurst approached the table.

"I'm positively parched." Miss Bingley took one of the cups from Elizabeth's hands.

Mrs. Hurst took the other. "Yes, it is very dry in this room."

Elizabeth forbore suggesting that perhaps Miss Bingley's thirst derived from having spent the morning talking excessively about herself and Mr. Parrish. Instead, she commented on that safest and most meaningful of all topics—the weather—observing that there had been little rainfall of late.

"A providential circumstance for your wedding," Mrs. Hurst said, "particularly since it was held in the country. Otherwise, you would have risked dragging the hem of your gown through mud on your way into church."

"And what a charming little church—not at all like the large London ones where so many in our circle have tied the knot. Here we could all be so snugly seated." Miss Bingley's voice held all of the usual smugness with which she addressed any of the Bennets. "Altogether a nice little affair from beginning to end. Do you not agree, Louisa? How fortunate you are, Eliza, to have had your mother to guide you in the planning."

Elizabeth ignored the poorly stifled snicker that erupted from Mrs. Hurst. The Bingley sisters had never managed to mask their disdain for her mother, had seldom even tried. In moments of self-honesty, she conceded that their criticism was not without foundation. But their rudeness was. Mrs. Bennet might lack restraint and good judgment, but her silly behavior had at its root the sincere wish of seeing her five daughters securely settled, and maybe even happy. The Bingley sisters, in contrast, had demonstrated by words and deeds that they ultimately had no one's interests at heart but their own.

"Mrs. Bennet must have taken particular pleasure in preparing for today, since she was unable to participate in your youngest sister's wedding," Mrs. Hurst said.

"Yes—how is Mrs. Wickham?" Miss Bingley asked.

"She is well," Elizabeth responded civilly. In other words, Lydia was still infatuated with the wastrel she'd married, and therefore as happy as a flighty, thoughtless, self-absorbed girl can be. Though Elizabeth loved her sister, the remembrance of last summer's scandalous elopement yet pained her, and she felt guilty relief that when Wickham's previous misconduct toward the Darcy family rendered it impossible to include him on today's guest list, Lydia had chosen to remain with her husband at his military post in Newcastle rather than attend the nuptials.

"Have you any advice for those of us who will soon follow

you down the aisle?" Miss Bingley pressed, casting a conspiratorial smirk at Mrs. Hurst. Louisa leaned forward for Elizabeth's response.

"With your own taste to guide you, I am sure your celebration could derive no further benefit from my opinions."

The Bingley sisters returned to their party, where Caroline continued to hold court with Mr. Parrish. The American's distinct accent seemed to entertain its listeners independent of whatever he had to say.

Elizabeth poured more coffee and carried it to Darcy and Mr. Collins. "Forgive the interruption, gentlemen, but I thought you might appreciate something to drink. I've been informed that it's dry in here."

Darcy's look of gratitude had nothing to do with the refreshment.

"Cousin Elizabeth, your eagerness to serve your new husband does you credit." Mr. Collins accepted the coffee but could not leave off talking long enough to taste it. "Do allow me to express once more my most heartfelt wishes for your future happiness. Though, as I was just expressing to Mr. Darcy, it grieves me that you entered into the matrimonial state without his aunt's permission. You will, I am sure, be gladdened to hear that her ladyship still tolerates the mention of your husband's name in her presence, an omen which leads me to believe that if you applied to Lady Catherine with the utmost humility and the deference to which one of her rank is entitled, she may in due course yet condescend to approve the match."

"What a relief! I know not how Mr. Darcy and I will get on until we obtain her approbation."

"Thank goodness you realize the seriousness of the situation. I had feared you were insensible of the grave insult you have paid her ladyship—"

"Mr. Collins," she said as if addressing him in confidence, "I have just come into the knowledge that there is another couple here who could benefit from your insights on marriage." She directed his attention toward the sofa. "Miss Bingley and Mr. Parrish have just announced their engagement, and only moments ago, the lady was seeking my counsel on planning the ceremony. Certainly you—longer married than I, and a clergyman besides—could offer her valuable instruction."

Mr. Collins nodded enthusiastically. "I could indeed. There is so much a betrothed couple ought to consider—"

"And they should consider it all."

"Before I depart, I shall make myself better acquainted with them."

"Why delay?" Elizabeth asked. "There is an empty seat near Miss Bingley. This is the perfect occasion to share your knowledge."

The clergyman wanted no further encouragement. "You are right, cousin Elizabeth. Wisdom can never be imparted too early. If you and Mr. Darcy will excuse me?"

"Of course."

Mr. Collins hastened to Miss Bingley's side, eliciting an expression of horror from that lady and a charge of satisfaction from Elizabeth.

"I had no idea I married a woman capable of such cruelty to another of her sex."

She met Darcy's smile. "I merely thought that someone so desirous of attention and someone so generous in extending it should be united in conversation."

"Somehow, I doubt Miss Bingley agrees."

"I can call him back, if you wish."

"Do not dare."

Spotting Charlotte Collins approaching the tea table, she contemplated how much luckier she was than her friend, in having found a life partner worthy of her respect. Charlotte had gone into her marriage fully sensible of her husband's oddities, and managed Mr. Collins skillfully, but Elizabeth nevertheless preferred her own definition of happiness.

Darcy followed her gaze. "I am glad your friend Mrs. Collins could be here. Have you had much opportunity to visit with her?"

"Very little. I've been trying to devote a bit of time to each of our guests. As a consequence, I feel I've spent the morning talking ceaselessly but saying nothing."

"Then you shall fit right in with the *haut ton*."

She looked up at him, this man with whom she was now joined. "Everyone wants a few minutes with the bride," she said quietly, "and all I want are a few minutes with you."

"Only a few? I had counted on a lifetime."

Her mischievous spirit returned. "Did you not realize? I took you on probation."

"And how have I acquitted myself thus far?" He regarded her with amusement.

"Beyond every expectation. Not that there was ever much doubt of my keeping you, but a man willing for my sake alone to bear the conversation of Mr. Collins has no equal."

Their social obligations compelled them to part. Darcy went to the Gardiners, while Elizabeth met Mrs. Collins at the tea table. She embraced her friend, noting immediately her thickened waist.

"Charlotte, I must tell you again how pleased I am that you managed to come."

"I would not have missed it. Had Lady Catherine withheld permission for Mr. Collins to attend, I would have urgently wished to visit my mother once more before my confinement, or developed a craving for cream that could be satisfied only by the Lucas Lodge dairy. My husband is so nervous about my 'delicate state of health' that he would not dare refuse me."

As Charlotte tucked a stray lock of hair behind her ear, Elizabeth noted that a few strands of grey had emerged amid the auburn since she last saw her friend. "You are feeling well?"

"Very, despite her ladyship's insistence that I behave as an invalid—when I'm not attending to matters she deems more important, of course."

She poured tea for herself and Charlotte. "I wonder that Mr. Darcy's aunt spared her clergyman leave to attend a wedding she herself has denounced."

"I suspect she approved our being present so that she could demand an account of all the sordid details upon our return."

"And what will you report?"

"Let's see . . ." She cocked her head, studying Elizabeth with keen blue eyes. "Mrs. Darcy looked radiant in a full dress of Brussels lace over white silk, with a low yet modest neckline, high waist, short sleeves, and a wreath of orange blossoms securing her veil." Her gaze darted across the room. "Her bridegroom wore a dark blue dress coat, white waistcoat, highly starched cravat, and—" She turned back to Elizabeth. "Really, are gentlemen's clothes half so interesting? What else? The wedding breakfast featured eight courses and three wines. And so on. But those are the particulars her ladyship will enquire about. What she won't ask, but what I shall endeavor to reveal, is that her nephew appeared as happy as his new bride."

"Despite having ruined his great family with disgraceful connections?" Elizabeth mocked Lady Catherine's contemptuous tone. "She will not be pleased at the knowledge."

"I am. I hoped for this event when you visited us last spring, you know. Perhaps in time her ladyship will come to accept you."

"I am told that if I grovel sufficiently, such felicity may be mine."

Charlotte stirred milk into her tea, her expression turning serious. "I shall surely miss your visits otherwise. You must write often, and tell me about your new life. Do you plan a honeymoon trip?"

"Not immediately. Jane and Mr. Bingley have invited us to stay at Netherfield tonight. We'll depart for Derbyshire with Mr. Darcy's sister in the morning. With Christmas approaching, we want simply to get settled at Pemberley before the Gardiners join us three weeks hence. Perhaps we'll go away in spring."

She lingered long with Charlotte, conscious that circumstances surrounding their respective marriages meant that this could be her last opportunity to see her friend for quite a while. Periodically, laughter and exclamations erupted from Miss Bingley's party, drawing their gazes in that direction. Elizabeth had expected the assembly to disperse upon Mr. Collins's arrival, but Mr. Parrish apparently had such a pleasing manner of address that he'd managed to rescue the conversation from the painful death it would have suffered under the clergyman's enthusiastic participation. The American was currently sharing a tale from his homeland, his style quite animated.

"Mr. Bingley's sister has made a good match," Charlotte noted. "It appears she'll enjoy both fortune and affection in her marriage."

"Yes, though one suspects she would have accepted Mr. Parrish for his fortune alone. He certainly seems a better catch than her sister's husband." A quick scan for Mr. Hurst found him dozing on the room's other sofa, an empty sherry glass balanced on his expansive abdomen.

"Her fiancé is certainly a handsome man." In that particular, Elizabeth agreed. Mr. Parrish was tall and slender, with sandy brown hair and an open countenance. "Do you know much about him?" Charlotte asked.

"No more than what Miss Bingley put into general circulation today. She introduced him to me only as 'Mr. Frederick Parrish of Louisiana.' I confess to mounting curiosity, however. Shall we make ourselves better acquainted?"

"By all means."

"Some believe," Mr. Parrish was saying as they approached, "on nights of the new moon, the poor mademoiselle's spirit yet haunts the Place d'Armes."

"Good Lord!" Elizabeth's sister Kitty exclaimed. "I tremble just to hear it! Have you ever seen her apparition yourself?"

"No, Miss Bennet. Nor any of New Orleans's other famous ghosts."

"There are more? Oh, tell us of another!"

Despite Elizabeth's predisposition to think unfavorably of Miss Bingley's betrothed, Mr. Parrish did seem a spellbinding storyteller. Even Mr. Bennet, though some distance away, appeared to attend Parrish's words more closely than those of his own companion. But perhaps that was because her father was presently subject to the befuddled discourse of Mr. Edwards. The elderly vicar who had officiated this morning's ceremony suffered from declining wits, a condition that had led to some fascinating sermons in recent years.

Mr. Parrish rose upon sighting the two ladies. "Please, Mrs. Darcy, take my seat."

His address marked the first time someone had called her "Mrs. Darcy," and she experienced a small rush at the sound of the words. Miss Bingley, however, did not look nearly so delighted by them—unless it had been Parrish's offer of the place next to her that caused displeasure to enter her eyes. No matter. Elizabeth could think of many places, some of them in the barn, where she would rather sit than directly beside Miss Bingley.

She returned his smile. "I would not separate a newly engaged couple for the world." She instead sat down across from Parrish and Miss Bingley to better observe them together. Charlotte took a seat beside her husband.

"Allow me to compliment you on a lovely wedding," said Mr. Parrish. They were words she'd heard often enough today, yet his warm manner made Elizabeth believe he actually meant them.

"Allow me to congratulate you on your forthcoming one. Have you fixed upon a date?"

"Wednesday next, by special license," Miss Bingley declared.

Elizabeth suppressed growing irritation at Caroline's timing. First she had announced her engagement today; now she planned to wed next week. Why must the woman schedule her own nuptials so soon after theirs? Merely to broadcast Mr. Parrish's ability to pay the substantial fee required for the license?

Ruefully, she thought of the idyllic plans she'd just described to Charlotte. She and Mr. Darcy could not with propriety escape attendance at Miss Bingley's wedding simply to advance their own domestic felicity. Now, instead of retiring to Pemberley for the winter, they would scarcely reach it before having to return. "So soon?" she asked, entertaining an irrational hope that she had somehow misheard.

Mr. Parrish regarded Miss Bingley with an ardent look, seeming to draw sustenance from the mere sight of her. "I'm afraid I cannot remain patient any longer than that. Caroline has utterly enchanted me." He turned to Elizabeth. "The ceremony will take place in London. You and Mr. Darcy will attend, won't you?"

Not yet ready to commit irrevocably to altering their Pemberley plans, she hedged. "Provided the weather permits travel."

"A sensible response. Even well-traveled roads can be unpredictable this time of year—I discovered that when I arrived in London last December to my first taste of winter. It took me some time to grow accustomed to your English weather."

"I daresay it's a good deal different than Louisiana. How do you get on now?"

He grinned. "Under an umbrella, most days. That is, when I can see where I'm going through all the fog."

The fog—*that* explained Mr. Parrish's attraction to Miss Bingley. He could not see what he was getting himself into.

"A twelvemonth is a long time to be away from home," Elizabeth said. "Do you miss the States?"

"Not as much as I thought I would. When my father passed away, I wanted a change of scenery, so I came here in search of my mother's relatives in Hampshire. Sadly, I found none living. But I fell in love with the country—and my dear Caroline." He glanced at Miss Bingley once more, his countenance full of more admiration than Elizabeth had ever thought Caroline capable of earning. Miss Bingley, who had appeared vexed that any of Mr. Parrish's attention had been focused on someone other than herself, now allowed a smile to once more cross her features.

"And when will you return to Monts Joyeux?"

"Mr. Parrish intends to sell his plantation," Miss Bingley said quickly. "We'll purchase an estate here in England. Until then, we'll live in town. He's leased a house in Upper Brook Street."

So obvious was Miss Bingley's lack of interest in ever laying eyes on Mr. Parrish's home, that Elizabeth wondered whether his decision to sell it had come before or after their courtship began. She had little time to ponder the question, however, as her Aunt Gardiner soon caught her gaze and discreetly beckoned. Elizabeth made her apologies and headed over to where her aunt and uncle yet stood with Mr. Darcy. His sister, Georgiana, had joined them.

Her husband took her arm. "I have a proposal for you."

"Another one? You've only just made good on your last."

"Not for want of resolution, I assure you."

"Yes, I know—we could have wed weeks ago, had we but considered no one's feelings save our own. Whatever were we thinking? Next time we shall have to do the business in a hasty manner, as seems to be the fashion, so as to trouble as many people as possible."

"Next time?"

"My mother is in such a state of rapture over marrying off two of her daughters on the same day, that I have determined to make this an annual event. Though in alternating years, perhaps I should marry Bingley and you should wed Jane, just to keep the clergyman in a perpetual state of confusion." Indeed, Mr. Edwards had tripped over everybody's names so many times in the double ceremony that Elizabeth could not be certain that the four of them weren't all married to each other.

"And during the years I'm wed to Jane, will she assail my ears with such outrageousness as this?"

"I venture not. Life with her will be orderly, peaceful, and predictable."

"Then I will have none of it."

She smiled up at him, happy that the light teasing which had marked their courtship had extended—at least so far—into their marriage. She didn't know what she would do if her more straightlaced husband ever became impatient with the liveliness of her mind. "So tell me, what is this proposal of which you spoke?"

He glanced at Georgiana and the Gardiners. "Would it disappoint you greatly to postpone our journey to Derbyshire?"

The query came as little surprise. "Until after Miss Bingley's wedding?" She sighed. Much as they longed to reach Pemberley, remaining in Hertfordshire was the more sensible course. "I'm sure Jane won't mind us extending our stay at Netherfield."

"I have a different notion—I thought we could honeymoon in London while we wait. We can go to the theatre, perhaps some museums. You could meet more of my social acquaintance. If we leave within the hour, we can be at the townhouse by dinner."

"And you can have it to yourselves," added Mrs. Gardiner. "Miss Darcy has consented to return to London with us as our guest."

Elizabeth turned to Georgiana in surprise. Since their father's death, Darcy's sister had made London her primary residence. "But the townhouse is your home."

The young woman laid a gentle hand on her arm. "A newlywed couple deserves some privacy. And our family has been just my brother and me for so long that I'm looking forward to getting to know yours better. I'll accompany you to Pemberley after Miss Bingley's wedding, or I can simply travel with the Gardiners. Please say yes, Elizabeth—will you refuse the very first request of your new sister?"

"Of course not." She felt a twinge of disappointment, as she'd been looking forward to settling into her new home with her new husband. The delay, however, would be of short duration, and Darcy had devised a pleasant way to pass the interim.

She turned to him with an arch look. "But it's going to cost you."

"Indeed?"

"Surely you cannot expect your wife to stay a week in London without visiting a shop or two?"

Mr. Gardiner chuckled. "Welcome to the life of a married man, Mr. Darcy. Beware, or she'll make a Grand Tour of every draper and milliner in Oxford Street."

"Nay, I have trunks full of new wedding clothes."

"Where, then?" Darcy asked.

She tilted her chin, her eyes delivering her husband a playful dare. "Can you not guess?"

His gaze narrowed as he studied her. "Will this errand take us to Piccadilly?" he said finally.

"It shall."

"Then it will indeed cost me dearly." He gave her an approving smile before turning to Mr. Gardiner. "Did my wife wish to examine the latest muslins at Grafton House, the expense would be small, for she yet shies from spending my money on herself. Instead, she lures me to Hatchard's bookshop, where I will be tempted to purchase more than she does."

"As I recall, Pemberley's collection is already quite extensive," said Mr. Gardiner. "But the library of a great house can never have too many books."

"Agreed. Particularly if there are any deficiencies that want correction to accommodate my new wife's reading tastes."

"Fortunately, Elizabeth is hardly one to fill your shelves with nothing but gothic romances, as some young ladies would."

While Mr. Gardiner's statement was true, she felt called upon to defend a genre that had provided her many hours' enjoyment. "Though, Uncle, I do take pleasure in them, as in many other things, and will probably add a few to Pemberley's shelves."

"You shall be happy to discover, then, that the library already holds quite a few novels, including gothics," Georgiana said. "We own all of Mrs. Radcliffe's books. My brother has even read *Udolpho*."

"A 'horrid mystery' in every sense of the phrase," Darcy declared.

"But diverting?" Elizabeth challenged.

"Yes," he admitted. "And if you want a trunkful of similar tales, I will happily indulge you."

"What think you, Georgiana?" Elizabeth asked, her gaze never leaving Darcy. "Will I always enjoy such generosity from your brother, or must I seize it while we're still in early days?"

He replied as if they stood alone. "All I have is ever yours."

At last, they took leave of their guests. As their carriage headed toward London, Elizabeth pondered the irony of Miss

Bingley keeping her away from Pemberley just a little bit longer. But then Darcy took her hand in his and gave her a kiss that chased away all unpleasant thoughts.

Let Miss Bingley bask in the glow of her own newfound love. Today Elizabeth could begrudge no one happiness.

Next week, however—that would be another matter. When it came to warm feelings toward Caroline Bingley, even newlywed bliss had its limits.

Two

"*A lady's imagination is very rapid; it jumps from admiration to love, from love to matrimony in a moment.*"
Mr. Darcy to Miss Bingley, Pride and Prejudice, *Chapter 6*

*I*n the privacy of their coach, Darcy enfolded Elizabeth in his arms. He closed his eyes and kissed the top of her head, noting that her soft brown hair still retained the fragrance of orange blossoms. He savored the moment, still amazed by the knowledge that she was his wife now. They had an infinite number of such moments ahead.

"You're sure you don't mind going to London?" he asked.

"Pemberley will still be there in a se'ennight. Besides, much as I adore your sister, I rather like the prospect of having you all to myself."

As much as he adored Georgiana, *he* rather liked that prospect. He tightened his embrace. "I hope you still feel that way when we arrive at an empty townhouse that has just been shut down for the winter. I sent word to the housekeeper that we're coming, but the rider can't be far ahead of us."

"Ah, the inconvenience of Miss Bingley's hasty nuptials expands."

"So you *do* mind. Does it upset you that she used our wedding as a forum for her own announcement?"

"I confess, I was vexed at first. But then I saw them together. Mr. Parrish seems truly besotted with her, and she with him. Have they known each other long?"

He stretched out his legs as far as he could, angling them toward the opposite side of the carriage. "I believe they met at Almack's when we were all in town last winter."

"The infamous 'marriage mart'? Was it love at first sight?"

"I wouldn't know—I avoid the place myself." Most of the *ton* considered Almack's *the* place to meet men and women of proper quality, but he found the club, with its perpetual parade of debutantes seeking husbands, distasteful. Though it was the most exclusive club in London, he declined all invitations to its balls, and had directed Georgiana to do the same upon her coming out.

Her eyes shone with merriment. "Lucky for me, or some accomplished lady with a handsome face would have tempted you long before you laid eyes on my tolerable countenance."

He winced at the memory of the snub he'd incautiously uttered within her hearing the evening they first met—an opinion he'd long since reversed. "Will you never let me forget that most undeserved slight?"

"Never. I delight too much in teasing you about it." Her fingertips gently smoothed his creased brow. "Fortunately, I'm not a vain woman. I doubt Mr. Parrish could have overcome such an adverse start to his acquaintance with Miss Bingley. Not that I can imagine him saying such a thing given how rapidly he formed an attachment to her."

"He does seem devoted."

"Did you know him before today?"

"We met a few times. You will recall that I spent part of last spring at Rosings, so I was absent for much of the official season. He seems an amiable fellow, with exceptionally good manners for an American. I understand he's very well liked in town—more than one lady will be unhappy to hear of his engagement."

"That is usually the case, when a wealthy man weds. You and Bingley dashed countless hopes today. Alas, the cruelty of a double wedding!"

His wife flattered him—Darcy could think of no woman mourning the end of his bachelorhood. "I expect any disappointed young misses will quickly recover."

"I was speaking of their mothers."

The twenty-four miles to London passed quickly, thanks to fair weather and his wife's company. As the carriage pulled up to the townhouse, Darcy wished he could have given his housekeeper and her severely reduced staff enough notice to properly prepare the home for the arrival of its new mistress, but there was no helping that now. Mrs. Hale, he was sure, would have at least managed to uncover the furniture, light fires in the main rooms, and prepare dinner. Once the servants he'd recalled from Pemberley returned, they would have a more comfortable stay.

He assisted Elizabeth out of the carriage, retaining her hand in his as he led her up the steps in the waning winter light. He squeezed her fingers as he opened the front door. "Welcome home, Mrs. Darcy."

They discovered, however, that the home was hardly welcoming. Naught but the sounds of clanking keys and hurried footfalls greeted them in the dim vestibule. A moment later, a very startled Mrs. Hale appeared, lamp in hand. "Who's there?"

"It's only us, Mrs. Hale."

"Mr. Darcy? Sir?" The housekeeper's eyes widened as she took in the sight of her master, accompanied by her new mistress. Her ruddy complexion turned an even deeper shade of red. "I—I'm so sorry, sir—I thought you were going to Pemberley after the wedding? Oh, dear! I must have misunderstood your instructions! Miss Ben—Mrs. Darcy—Madam, forgive me for not having the house done up proper to receive you!"

"Our plans changed unexpectedly," Elizabeth explained.

"I see, madam. . . ." His wife's soothing tone only seemed to fluster Mrs. Hale further as her gaze darted about the house. "Good gracious me. Oh, dear . . . oh, dear . . ." Her work-roughened hand threatened to dislodge the mobcap from her grey head.

Darcy quickly took in the unlit rooms, the covered furniture, his servant's disconcerted state. "Didn't anyone arrive ahead of us to inform you?"

A footman entered from the back of the house. "Sir, I've only just come in—my horse threw a shoe on the road."

No wonder the housekeeper was beside herself. Mrs. Hale took pride in running a well-organized home, and with adequate notice would have striven to impress her new mistress.

. . . as Darcy himself had wanted to impress her. He silently cursed his bad luck. So much for his romantic plan. Elizabeth had seen the townhouse before, when she'd come to London to visit the Gardiners and order her trousseau. But then it had been *his* house; now it was theirs, and he'd hoped for her first night in it to be a homecoming—for her to feel in these rooms that she was a visitor no longer, but in her own space, her rightful place, by his side. He'd wanted the house itself to embrace her as he would, to enfold her in a warm, snug haven in which they could begin their new life together.

Now, due to the perverseness of fate, they would be spending their wedding night in cold rooms dining on leftover mutton.

He turned to her. "Elizabeth, I am deeply sorry—"

She regarded him with amusement. "For what? Shutting

down a house we did not intend to use all winter? Or sending your rider on a horse determined to fling its footwear across the countryside?"

"This is not the welcome you deserve."

"Nonsense. I like what you've done with the place. The furniture all matches now."

"The air in here is so chilly you cannot even remove your wrap."

"It's bracing."

"We have no dinner."

"Mr. Darcy, I believe I am now mistress here. Are you in the habit of criticizing a lady's home and table to her face?"

The mock upbraid jostled off his last shreds of ill humor. He conceded with an exaggerated bow.

"I thought not."

Despite their exchange, Mrs. Hale immediately commenced setting the house to rights. "Light a fire in the drawing room and remove the sheets from the furniture," she instructed the footman. "Madam, if you and the master don't mind waiting up in the drawing room, perhaps your lady's maid can put your chamber in order while I start dinner. The larder's not well stocked, but I'm sure—"

Darcy intervened. Perhaps he could salvage this scheme after all. "Mrs. Hale, we've caught you completely by surprise. Take the time you need to prepare the house. Mrs. Darcy and I will dine out this evening at—" Out of habit he almost said White's, which is where he normally ate when he dined out in town, but he certainly couldn't bring his wife to a gentleman's club. He searched his mind for a respectable hotel, and settled on the most luxurious. It was their wedding day, after all. "The Pulteney."

They remained at the townhouse just long enough to change from their travel attire to dinner dress, then trundled back into the carriage.

"Home sweet home," Elizabeth said as she settled against the bench. "I think we ought to alter our plans yet again, and simply stay the week in this box. I am grown quite attached to it today."

Darcy shifted to relieve the kink in his back that had developed during the ride from Longbourn. "You do not find it a little close?"

"That's part of the charm. The ability to move one's limbs more than a few inches is vastly overvalued."

"And what of the constant motion?"

"Another benefit—it provides ever-changing scenery. What fixed room can compete? Indeed, the more I think upon it, the more my resolve hardens. Economy of exertion, variety of views—I am decided. I shall live in this carriage until we reach Pemberley."

"I do hope you will leave it long enough to join me for dinner."

"If you insist."

Three

"*I hear such different accounts of you as puzzle me exceedingly.*"

Elizabeth to Darcy, Pride and Prejudice, *Chapter 18*

*E*lizabeth glanced round the lobby of the Pulteney, taking in the lavish furnishings and equally opulent-looking guests. Even she, who until now had come to London rarely and stayed with the Gardiners in Cheapside when she did, had heard of the Piccadilly hotel. A year ago she never would have dreamed she might dine here, but a year ago the thought of marrying Mr. Darcy had also been unimaginable. How much her life had changed in a twelvemonth—in twelve hours!

"This is considerably more pleasant than our carriage, is it not?" Darcy asked as they crossed to the dining room.

"Perhaps a degree. Though I had nearly convinced myself that I *wanted* to be traipsing about London instead of comfortably settled at home."

As Darcy enquired after a table, a well-dressed young couple entered the lobby. The gentleman, upon spotting Darcy, guided his companion's attention toward them. The lady smiled in greeting as the pair approached.

"Darcy! I had no idea you were in town." Though the man had a long, narrow face and high forehead, he was not unattractive. His whole lanky frame seemed animated with genuine delight at encountering them. "I'd heard you were off in Hertfordshire getting married." He directed a curious, but friendly, glance at Elizabeth.

She sensed her husband's usual public stiffness relax a bit. Apparently, Darcy shared more than a passing acquaintance with the gentleman. "Yes, I was. Allow me to introduce you to Mrs. Darcy. Elizabeth, this is the Earl of Chatfield and his wife, Lady Chatfield."

The earl bowed. The countess's smile broadened, lighting her bright blue eyes as she addressed Elizabeth. "It is indeed a pleasure to make your acquaintance. My friends shall be envious to hear that I've been introduced to the new Mrs. Darcy so soon."

Elizabeth judged the lady to be about her own age, a few years younger than the earl. She had a delicate visage, small hands, and hair the color of Longbourn's honey. She carried herself with an air of self-possession that Elizabeth associated with those born into privilege, but it was complemented by a natural warmth that made her seem altogether a kind, unaffected person. "The pleasure is mine," she responded.

"Are you in town for Christmas?" asked Lady Chatfield.

"No, only until Thursday week," Elizabeth replied.

"Then I'm delighted we happened upon you here, Darcy," said the earl. "With such a lovely bride to escort around town, I doubt I'll see you at White's this visit."

Darcy acknowledged the possibility as unlikely.

"Say, though—you should pop in to see the betting book," Chatfield said. "Half the members have wagers on whether Lord Griswell's wife will finally produce a son this time around or daughter number seven. Griswell swears it will be a boy, but everyone's betting on another girl just to aggravate the chap. I even put in a wager myself for ten guineas."

"Poor Griswell. You torment him."

"Nay, it's only sport. You should place a wager yourself."

Darcy shook his head. "I am not a gambling man."

"Neither am I. Don't go in for the cards or dice at all. But a small private wager every once in a while is all in good fun. Say, I've seen the name of a friend of yours in the betting book quite often of late. What's the fellow's name? Hurst, that's it! Just last Saturday, he bet a hundred guineas that Frederick Parrish would find his way to the altar before year's end. Parrish, of all people! Even Beau Brummell gave up betting on him marrying anytime soon after he suddenly cried off Miss Kendall last month."

Elizabeth started in surprise at the gossip. Lady Chatfield caught her reaction. "Do you know Mr. Parrish?"

"Only slightly," Elizabeth responded. "We learned today of his engagement to our friend Miss Bingley. They plan to marry next week."

"Really?" Lord Chatfield chuckled. "Capital! Hurst must have had inside information on that one. Well, good for him—makes up for some of his card losses."

"James, sometimes you are too much." Lady Chatfield rolled her eyes, but her gaze held affection when it rested on her husband once more. She turned to Elizabeth. "I realize this is short notice, and you're on your honeymoon. But we're hosting a dinner party Saturday evening, and I'd be honored if you and Mr. Darcy would join us."

Flattered by the impromptu invitation, Elizabeth glanced to Darcy. He nodded ever so slightly, indicating his interest in attending but leaving the decision up to her.

"It will be our pleasure," she responded.

Their conversation ended as the couples were seated at separate tables.

"I hope Mrs. Hale has some apples in the house," Elizabeth said as she examined the menu.

Darcy raised a brow. "And why is that?"

"I need to thank a horse for throwing its shoe. We might not otherwise have chanced upon the earl and his wife."

"I would have left them our cards while we are in town, even if we had not met them here. Their townhouse is but a few doors from ours."

"I like them. Are they intimate friends of yours?"

"Chatfield and I dine together fairly often. We met through White's, before he married the countess. I admire him—he may speak like an idle young buck, but he possesses a strong understanding. He patronizes numerous scientists in the Royal Society."

"Then I look forward to this dinner party even more." Elizabeth brimmed with questions about some of the earl's statements, particularly those relating to Bingley's present and future brothers-in-law. "What is this 'betting book' of which the earl spoke?"

"A tradition at White's—a form of entertainment, really. Members record their private wagers there, in part to keep them honest about payment, but also to impress others with their wit and outrageousness."

"What do they bet on, besides Lord Griswell's children?"

"Anything—politics, the weather, Napoleon's next move." He sipped his wine and shrugged. "Mr. Parrish's marriage plans."

"Miss Bingley's announcement today must have delighted Mr. Hurst. Will his fellow wagerer accuse him of cheating?"

"I doubt it. The bride may be Hurst's sister-in-law, but Parrish's engagement to Miss Bingley happened so fast, who can say whether Mr. Hurst knew any more about it than the rest of us?"

Indeed, Elizabeth silently conceded. Given that all her encounters with the indolent Mr. Hurst had seen him eating, drinking, playing cards, or dozing on the sofa, she believed the proposal could have taken place on his lap without the man noticing. It may well have been a perfectly fair wager.

"Did Lord Chatfield's remark about Mr. Hurst's card losses concern you?"

Darcy shook his head. "Hurst hardly conducts himself like one of those wild dandies who lose the entire family estate in a game of faro. He likely just forfeited a few pounds at whist." He seemed pensive as he took another sip of wine. "Perhaps I should caution you, Elizabeth, that gossip makes the *beau monde* go round. Rumor becomes news, and news becomes scandal, all in just a few retellings by people with nothing better to occupy their minds. Do not believe everything you hear."

She ruefully recalled how she'd once been deceived about Darcy's real character by half-truths someone else had told her. "London society hardly has a monopoly on slander," she said. "Don't worry—I have learned to exercise discernment." She would not allow prejudice, nor the smooth words of another one such as Mr. Wickham, to similarly blind her again.

They spent the greater part of the meal in discussion of more pleasant matters. Darcy expressed a wish to visit the British Museum during their time in London; Elizabeth, an art exhibition. They made plans for their first Christmas together at Pemberley. They spoke of the wedding and their guests— who had said what, who had looked well, who had not. Elizabeth confirmed Darcy's impression that Charlotte was in the way of adding to the number of Collineses in the world.

"Will her mother attend her when the time comes?" Darcy asked.

"Yes, and will stay until the child is a month or two old. Though with Lady Catherine there, heaven knows Charlotte shan't want for advice."

"My aunt is certainly generous with her opinions. Perhaps I should strive to heal our breech directly, so that when your time comes, you, too, may benefit from her instruction."

She called his bluff. "I thought rather to invite my mother to live with us for six months. Women want their mothers at such—Darcy, are you choking on a fish bone?"

In the carriage, Elizabeth yawned. Though the happiest of her life, the day had been excessively long. "To think that when I awoke this morning, I thought merely getting married would occupy my day."

"Me, too." Darcy took her hand and with his thumb traced her wedding band through the glove. "Do you think the house is ready for us yet?"

"Does it matter?"

"Not a bit."

She nestled into her husband's side, resting her cheek against his chest. "Mr. Darcy, take me home."

Four

Darcy had never been so bewitched by any woman as he was by her.

Pride and Prejudice, *Chapter 10*

his one looks innocuous enough." Elizabeth studied the splintered wooden beam. It was a simple, aged pine log, unremarkable but for a star carved into its center. A circle connected the star's five points.

"Lintel, circa 1640," Darcy read from the display card, "taken from the doorway of a Massachusetts cottage. The beam bears a symbol known as a pentagram, evidence of familiarity with witchcraft in New England decades before the infamous Salem Witch Trials of 1692."

His voice echoed in the empty gallery. She and Darcy had come to the British Museum for the afternoon, drawn by the Towneley sculpture collection and a set of medieval manuscripts Darcy had wanted to see. After viewing the old texts, they had wandered into an exhibit titled "Curiosities from the Colonies." This room they had all to themselves. Apparently, none of the museum's other visitors had much interest in New World relics.

In the back of the gallery, they'd discovered a display of

items marked "Mysterious Articles." The beam lay among a dozen or so objects believed to have been used for mystical purposes. She found the assortment particularly intriguing. The shaman's drum, dreamcatcher, totem mask, *vodun* doll, and other eclectic offerings reminded her of Mrs. Radcliffe's novels—symbols of a world in which the supernatural exists alongside the mundane. The fanciful elements appealed to her imagination.

She pointed to another item, a circlet of braided plant roots. "This was believed to ward off illness. Does one wear it, do you suppose? Sleep with it under the pillow? Hang it on the door?"

"Does it matter?" Darcy shrugged. "Superstitious people have all sorts of ridiculous rituals to keep bad luck away. It is not as if the thing actually holds power."

She cocked her head and gave him a wry smile. "Are you sure?"

"I am."

Her lighthearted mood ebbed. He might be certain, but she wasn't. She considered herself a rational woman, one who valued sense above sensibility. She read gothic tales for entertainment not verisimilitude, and believed more strongly in what she could observe than what she couldn't. Yet a part of her occasionally wondered if there wasn't something else out there, forces just beyond conscious perception. Not enchantments, or illusions—the sorcery of Merlin or *A Midsummer Night's Dream*. But a quieter kind of magic, the power that fuels intuition and enables one to take leaps of faith to places reason cannot go.

At her silence, Darcy's expression grew more serious. "Come now, Elizabeth. Do not tell me you believe in fairies and hocus-pocus?"

Reluctantly, she withdrew from her reverie. "I believe warm weather spoils more milk than elves do, and you'll never catch me whistling into the wind to keep witches away."

"Thank goodness."

"But"—she swept her arm toward the display—"does that mean none of this is real? What was it Hamlet said onstage last night? 'There are more things in heaven and earth, Horatio, than are dreamt of in your philosophy.' Do you believe only in what you can see?"

"Excepting God, yes."

"Perhaps I take a broader view."

He raised one dark brow. "Explain."

How to explain what she couldn't quite articulate in her own mind? He'd enjoyed the play last night, told her it was one of his favorites—maybe she should draw an analogy from it. "Have you ever felt your late father's presence at Pemberley?"

"His ghost has never informed me that he was poisoned in the garden," he replied stiffly.

Perhaps referring to *Hamlet* had been a bad idea. She searched her mind for another example. "Do you ever make decisions based solely on intuition?"

"Never."

Exasperating man! And yet she knew him to be telling the truth. Even his first marriage proposal to her—as badly worded and poorly tendered as it had been—revealed the extensive deliberation he'd done before allowing his feelings to override material considerations in choosing a wife. Her husband was a man guided by reason. Rational judgment formed the core of his character, whether or not she agreed with all the conclusions to which it led him.

"I'm only saying that I believe—no, that I acknowledge the *possibility*—that there are elements of this world beyond mankind's ability to comprehend them. Perhaps the people who created these 'mysterious articles' had a better understanding of them than do you or I."

"Elizabeth, look at those items again. They are nothing

more than ordinary objects created by ordinary people in futile attempts to control things about their lives that no one can control. That so-called dreamcatcher is a web of twigs with no more ability to prevent bad dreams than a child's doll; the circlet holds less medicinal value than a good posset. And, far from demonstrating power, the pentagram thing on that beam probably got its owner hanged." He gestured toward another item. "What·is that, resting on the end?"

She looked at the object, a long wooden staff with a fork at one end. The richly hued, flawless oak was so highly polished that she could almost see her reflection in the wood. She glanced at the display card. "A canceling rod," she read, then winced. "Used by village cunning men to nullify spells." She felt foolish speaking the words aloud.

"It's a stick."

She stared at the rod. Intellectually, she knew Darcy was right about it. She no more believed that stick could ward off spells—or believed in spells, for that matter—than she believed in Father Christmas. Incantations were a far cry from the kind of intuitive perception she struggled to define. Besides, she didn't want to quarrel with her husband any longer, particularly on a subject so wholly unconnected with their daily lives.

She cast him a smile. "But you must admit, it's a really shiny stick."

His sober expression lifted and he returned her smile. "That, I will grant you." The tension had passed. As if to physically close the breach between them, he lifted a hand and reached toward her cheek. He stopped himself before actually touching her face—propriety, as always, restraining sentiment in public. But he completed the caress with his eyes. "I do love you," he murmured.

"And I, you." She took his hand in hers. "Though tell me, husband," she said, her spirits once more rising to playfulness, "if you don't believe the slightest bit in magic, how then do you explain love?"

Despite her teasing tone, he regarded her in all seriousness. "Elizabeth, if it is possible that you fell in love with me, married me, will spend the rest of your life with me, then I believe nearly anything is possible."

His hand at her back guided her from the room. "But not magic."

Five

*"I think it no sacrifice to join occasionally in evening engage-
ments. Society has claims on us all."*

Mary Bennet, Pride and Prejudice, *Chapter 17*

*A*t precisely seven o'clock Saturday evening, the Darcys
arrived at the home of Lord and Lady Chatfield. The
butler led them up a grand staircase to the drawing room,
where their hostess greeted them and introduced their fellow
guests. Darcy had told Elizabeth to expect a diverse assembly,
and she was not disappointed. The company included an elderly botanist and his wife, a physicist, an American archeology
professor, a poet, a middle-aged gentleman and his daughter,
and the countess's mother, the Dowager Duchess Beaumont.

The gentleman, she learned, was Mr. Lawrence Kendall.
About fifty years old, he practiced the peculiar habit of some
balding men who think to cleverly disguise their condition by
combing their remaining three strands of hair over the tops of
their scalps. The beefy man made up for his lack of locks with
large jowls that seemed permanently frozen in a scowl. He
nodded at Darcy and acknowledged his introduction to Elizabeth with minimal civility.

His daughter, as Lady Chatfield soon revealed in a whisper,

was the very Miss Kendall whose name had once been linked with that of Mr. Parrish. Juliet Kendall was as thin as her father was fat; high cheekbones fought sharp eyes for prominence in her white face. At perhaps twenty, her countenance had not yet settled into the sourness of her sire's, though her current morose expression indicated that resisting heredity could prove a lifelong battle.

Elizabeth scarcely had time to observe the other guests before the formal promenade to the dining room commenced. As a new bride, Mrs. Darcy was offered the honor of taking Lord Chatfield's arm. Once downstairs, she found herself seated between the earl and Professor Julian Randolph, the archeologist.

She enjoyed the opportunity to converse with Lord Chatfield. When she remarked upon the varied company, he confessed that he liked to invite markedly different individuals to his home to encourage lively exchanges. "Some of the parties we attend are so tedious," he said between spoonfuls of turtle soup from a gold-rimmed bowl. His eyes were merry. "I like to mix things up a bit—seat my mother-in-law next to a naval officer and watch what happens."

Coming from a less affable man, the comment might have made her feel like an actress put onstage solely for the earl's amusement. But he seemed motivated by the desire for all his guests to enjoy the social experiment.

"I see, however, that you have no officers tonight," she observed.

"No, several men of learning instead. Always must have at least one—I discover so many interesting things that way." He gestured toward Professor Randolph, who was fulfilling his conversational obligation to the woman on his right, the botanist's wife. "Randolph is new to my table. Fascinating chap—you must ask him about his specialty."

"I will be sure to enquire. Meanwhile, tell me more of the

other guests. I can see how Mr. Quigley, a man of letters, adds interest to the evening—what of Mr. Kendall and his daughter?"

"That was my wife's idea." His voice lowered to a discreet level. "Miss Kendall has been down in spirits since—well, since last month. The countess thought to introduce her to Quigley, though I fear the effort futile. Kendall is wealthy enough that his only child can marry comfortably where she chooses—I understand she has a dowry of forty thousand pounds, and will inherit her father's entire estate upon his death—but I suspect he intends to solidify his social position through his daughter's alliance with a man of higher rank and fortune than a poet can offer."

Forty thousand pounds!—and the remaining Kendall estate not entailed away on some distant male heir, as Long-bourn was. Elizabeth could scarcely comprehend the ability to bring that kind of fortune to a marriage. Yet it hadn't aided Miss Kendall's courtship with Frederick Parrish; Miss Bing-ley's settlement was half that sum, and carried no promise of future inheritance. With such wealth at stake, what had led Parrish to abruptly drop his addresses to Juliet? Had the charms of his "dear Caroline" distracted him entirely from worldly gain? If so, his devotion to Miss Bingley must be great indeed.

The soup course was nearing its end; Elizabeth would soon be obliged to direct her attention toward Professor Randolph. "And what of my husband and me?" she asked Lord Chatfield as the footmen removed their bowls. "What ingredient do we add to your conversational stew?"

"My dear lady, you were invited simply because we enjoy Darcy's company and wanted to become better acquainted with his wife."

The fish course was served. Elizabeth tasted the whitebait à la diable, wondered hopefully whether her mother was correct in her conjecture that Darcy employed French cooks at Pemberley, and turned to Professor Randolph. He looked young for a scholar, perhaps three-and-thirty, and in robust health. For some reason Elizabeth always pictured academic men as old and doddering, with mortarboards permanently affixed to their heads.

"I went my whole life without encountering an American, and now you're the second I've met this week," she said. "I hope we haven't suffered an invasion while my attention was focused on more domestic matters?"

The archeologist adjusted his spectacles. "No invasion," he responded, "but the state of war between our countries has certainly made it harder for those of us in England to travel home. British seas are no place to speak with an American accent right now."

She regretted having spoken so lightly on such a serious matter. "I imagine not," she said more soberly. "Have you been here long?"

Fortunately, he did not appear to have taken her previous tone amiss. "About a year," he said. "I'd originally planned to stay only through summer, but that, of course, is when the declaration of war came. So here I remain."

"I hope your extended visit hasn't proven too inconvenient. What brought you to England in the first place?"

Randolph withdrew a handkerchief from his breast pocket and wiped a smudge off his spectacles. In the drawing room, Elizabeth had noted that his clothes, though not shabby, betrayed signs of wear and were several years out of fashion. But upon closer view, she believed they had never been *in* fashion—at least, not on this side of the Atlantic. The professor's costume included an extraordinary number of pockets. It was not unusual for gentlemen to have breast or tail pockets in their coats, or fob pockets in their waistcoats. But in addition to these, Randolph's loose-fitting trousers appeared to have at least two pockets of their own, and the unusual cut of his waistcoat hinted at another two pockets on his shirt-front. She wondered if all the pockets reflected American style, his own taste, or an overzealous tailor.

"I accompanied a friend who sought a traveling companion." He replaced both spectacles and handkerchief. "I've also been conducting business of my own—seeking a new post and offering a series of lectures related to a display at the British Museum. It contains numerous artifacts from my private collection."

Elizabeth recalled the gallery she and Darcy had had to themselves the afternoon before. "Just yesterday my husband and I saw a collection of New World antiquities there. Is that the one?"

"Indeed, it is." His face brightened. "The museum curator told me they might close the display due to lack of interest. I'm delighted that you saw it. Did you find it worthwhile?"

She nodded. "Highly intriguing, particularly the 'mysterious articles.' Are those yours, too?"

"Yes. In fact, I specialize in the study of supernatural objects."

Though she'd found their conversation pleasant to this point, she now regarded him with heightened interest. Perhaps this man could answer some of the questions her quarrel with Darcy had raised. "There are enough such things in the world to make a specialty of analyzing them?"

"Mrs. Darcy, every culture in history has believed in some sort of magic. Rain dances, ghosts, second sight, miracles. How many tales of enchantment and wondrous items appear in your English literature and folklore, let alone throughout the world? I but follow the tradition of Arthur's knights, searching the earth for holy grails."

"Do you believe these items truly hold power, or do you study them only as curiosities?"

He sipped a long draught of wine and set the glass down

slowly. "In itself, the fact that their creators and owners believed in their power makes them worthy of study," he said at last. "Familiarity with a culture's beliefs enables historians to better understand the people as a whole."

Randolph hadn't really answered her question. But she hesitated to press the subject, afraid of sounding naïve to the scholar.

He withdrew his pocketwatch to check the hour. The silver timepiece was round and perhaps two and a half inches in diameter. An engraved star adorned the front of the case; a circle connected its five points. As he clicked open the case, she noted some strange characters inscribed inside. They resembled letters, but not from any alphabet she'd ever seen.

"Runes," he said, noting her curious expression. "Characters from ancient times."

The watch reminded her of some of the items she'd seen that morning. "Is that one of your archeological finds?"

"No." He flipped the case shut and returned the watch to his fob pocket. "Nothing so valuable. Merely something I had commissioned for myself."

She wanted to ask what the runes meant, but sensed he preferred to end the subject. "I confess, I've never heard of your pursuit as an academic discipline," she said instead. "Is it a common field of study?"

"Unfortunately, the universities at which I've taught regard my focus as eccentric at best. In fact, one of them even housed me with physicians studying madness instead of with other historians or scientists." He chuckled. "Perhaps someone thought I needed their services."

"You've taught at more than one university?"

"The strength of my more mundane scholarship persuades institutions to hire me on and finance my expeditions, which turn up more ordinary treasures than mystical items. But in the long term, conservative governing boards are reluctant to grant permanent positions to someone with 'strange' interests. So I seem to have fallen into a cycle of joining a new faculty, lecturing for a time, embarking on a university-sponsored expedition, and returning to find that the school wants only the artifacts I've unearthed—not me. While here, I'd hoped Oxford or Cambridge might offer me a post, but so far my work has been greeted with the usual skepticism."

She glanced down the long table to Darcy, who appeared trapped with the duchess in the polite but empty small talk he dreaded. Remembering her husband's response to the museum display, Elizabeth could hardly be surprised that stately academic institutions placed Randolph's studies on the fringes of respectability. Yet surely she was not the only person in all England to find his field of study intriguing. "Have you considered soliciting private patronage?"

He nodded. "I find, however, that without the association of a college to lend my work legitimacy, many potential patrons are more interested in speculation than in scientific inquiry. They seek financial gain, not enlightenment, and expect me to unearth some magical treasure that will make them rich. One exception has been Mr. Frederick Parrish, who sponsored my trip to London purely out of friendship."

Elizabeth was beginning to feel that, in never having heard of Mr. Parrish before this week, she'd been living under a rock. Was there a soul in London unacquainted with him? "I had the pleasure of meeting Mr. Parrish recently. He is a generous man?"

"I have hopes that he will finance my next archeological dig."

She could guess what Miss Bingley would have to say about that.

After dessert, the ladies departed to take tea in the drawing room, leaving the gentlemen to talk and smoke in private. Darcy, as usual, declined to partake of tobacco, but the scientists and the earl lit pipes. The pungent scent drifted into the air, carrying with it a light haze. Lord Chatfield leaned back in his chair, drew a long draught from his pipe, and asked the physicist about an experiment he planned to conduct.

The topic appealed to Darcy after the lightweight conversation of those nearest him at dinner. He rose and stretched, intending to exchange his seat for the one beside Chatfield that Elizabeth had vacated. Kendall's hand, however, closed about his wrist as he tried to pass. The corpulent man had an exceptionally strong grip.

"How is your friend Bingley?" Kendall's low voice carried a belligerent tone; his face appeared flushed. Darcy would have suspected the man had imbibed too much claret, but he knew better. This show was merely the latest display of his congenial personality.

He stared at Kendall's fleshy fingers until they dropped their grasp. "I left him in good health," he said finally.

"I understand he's newly married."

He did not bother answering, nor did a response appear expected.

"Tell me," Kendall continued, "has he learned to think for himself yet, or do you still make all his decisions for him?"

Though tempted to walk away, Darcy forbore. The man obviously intended to speak his mind; to deprive him of the opportunity might provoke a scene right here in the earl's dining room. Of all things, Darcy loathed scenes. "I offer him advice when asked." He spoke in clipped tones.

"And did he ask your advice about his sister's forthcoming marriage?" Kendall snorted. "He probably thinks she made quite a catch in Frederick Parrish."

"I have not concerned myself in the matter."

"Too engrossed in your own affairs for a change? Well, tell little Caroline I rejoice in her nuptials. She and Parrish deserve each other."

As Kendall at last seemed satisfied, Darcy moved away, into the chair he'd sought near the earl. But he found himself unable to focus on the scientific discussion. Instead, he seethed in silence at Kendall's unprovoked diatribe. What had been the man's purpose?

Darcy rarely had occasion to interact with Lawrence Kendall. Though they belonged to the same clubs and knew many of the same people, the difference in their ages and dispositions generally prevented their paths from intersecting. When they did encounter each other socially, as tonight, they had very little to say to one another—which was why this evening's show of spleen on the older man's part had left him baffled.

His knowledge of Kendall came mostly from the gentleman's association with the Bingley family. Charles Bingley's late father had been in business with Kendall; together the two had built a fortune through trade. Near the end of the elder Bingley's life, the relationship had soured. The two men dissolved their partnership, dividing the assets fairly, at least in the eyes of the Bingley family and their solicitors. Kendall, however, unjustly claimed that he had been cheated of his full share—this, after cheating Mr. Bingley through creative accounting for years.

Kendall first came forward with the assertion of fraud shortly after the senior Mr. Bingley's death, and renewed the claim last winter. That second time, Kendall had argued with Charles Bingley so long and so aggressively that Darcy's friend had almost surrendered the assets in question despite his solicitors' advice. Bingley, inclined to assume the best of everyone, began to believe that perhaps an error had indeed been made. Darcy also suspected Bingley's wavering to have been motivated by a desire simply to end the unpleasant conflict. He had urged his friend to stand firm.

That was the last he had heard on the subject, until now. It seemed Kendall yet harbored antagonism toward Bingley. And had broadened its scope to include him as well.

Elizabeth, meanwhile, found herself confronted by the other Kendall of the party. Juliet seemed a pleasant enough young woman as the general conversation drifted among such weighty topics as Lady Edith Carrington's recent presentation at court, and the addition of second flounces to hemlines this season. But no sooner did Miss Kendall learn that the new Mrs. Darcy was sister-in-law to Caroline Bingley, than she maneuvered to sit beside Elizabeth on the sofa for a private tête-à-tête.

"I hear they are to be married Wednesday," she said without preamble, apparently so focused in her own mind on Mr. Parrish's plans that she presumed everyone around her to hold the same individual foremost in their thoughts. She smoothed her skirts, not looking at Elizabeth as she spoke. "It will be a very grand affair, I suppose?"

Elizabeth resolved to say as little as possible on the subject. Even had she possessed the information Miss Kendall sought, she had no wish to inflict additional pain on Parrish's former *inamorata* by feeding her details she thought she wanted to hear. "I'm afraid I have not been privy to their plans." Across the room, Lady Chatfield began to pour tea, a distraction for which Elizabeth was grateful. She rose, stating her intention to head for the tea table.

Miss Kendall, however, would not be dissuaded from her subject as she accompanied her. "The wedding will be the talk of the *ton*, I have no doubt." Juliet accepted a steaming cup from the countess, added a lump of sugar, and stirred absently. "Miss Bingley will want the most lavish affair her brother can afford, and Freder—" She closed her eyes and swallowed. "Mr. Parrish—will acquiesce in every particular." She added more sugar to her tea.

Elizabeth injected a note of levity into her voice. "By the following week, something else will seize society's attention." She sipped from her own cup, seeking a moment's reprieve behind its rim. The earl had indicated Miss Kendall suffered from melancholy in the wake of Parrish's rejection, but Elizabeth thought her eyes seemed unnaturally bright for someone mired in sadness. She attempted to change the subject. "Have you any special plans for Christmas?"

"We played together as girls, you know. Caroline Bingley and me. Dressed our dolls together. Rode horses together." Miss Kendall added another lump of sugar and continued stirring. The silver demitasse spoon clattered against the delicate porcelain. "We haven't spoken in years. Our fathers—well, never mind that. But this is a triumph for her, stealing Mr. Parrish from me. That woman set her cap for him and caught him before I knew what was happening."

Had Miss Bingley actively interfered with the courtship? Given her calculated efforts to discourage her brother's attraction to Jane, Elizabeth couldn't put it past her to have aggressively worked to turn the admiration of a wealthy and not-quite-betrothed bachelor toward herself—especially right after the announcement of Darcy's engagement and the disappointed hopes it represented. If so, Mr. Parrish likely would have been a target regardless of which lady he'd been wooing. Surely Caroline hadn't pursued him solely out of malice toward Miss Kendall?

"That's why she's scheduled the wedding so soon—to spite me." Juliet dissolved a fourth lump in the china cup. The more sweetener she added to her untasted tea, the more bitter her voice became. Her volume, however, remained low enough that only Elizabeth could hear. "She's snickering at me right now, isn't she? Congratulating herself on securing her own happiness and ruining mine all at once." She expelled a short, unconvincing laugh that sounded more like a horse's sneeze than an unaffected expression of mirth. "Well, tell her she failed. After they wed, I will see her unhappy."

Miss Kendall thrust her full teacup onto the table with enough force to topple it off its saucer. Brown rivulets streamed across Lady Chatfield's snow-white tablecloth, rapidly soaking into the fabric and leaving behind a gloppy trail of half-dissolved sugar crystals.

The expanding stain appeared to wrench Juliet from her fixation on Caroline Bingley. Horror spread across her face as quickly as the tea on the tablecloth, and she immediately stammered an apology to their hostess. The countess gently dismissed the accident and summoned a servant to replace the covering.

Elizabeth hoped the disturbance might offer an opportunity for her to slip away from Miss Kendall and into another conversation, but the footman proved too efficient in performing his duty. When the mess had been whisked away, Juliet turned to Elizabeth once more. "I have been standing here realizing I owe you an apology as well," she said, her manner again relaxed as it had been earlier in the evening. "I did not mean to monopolize your attention, nor to speak so warmly on a subject best left undiscussed."

"Think no more of it," Elizabeth said. Though she referred to their conversation, privately she hoped Miss Kendall would also think no more about the forthcoming marriage. By whatever means Parrish's sudden engagement had come about, it had clearly left wounds that would take a long time to heal.

As they walked home, Elizabeth relayed the conversation to Darcy. "Caroline Bingley has cultivated a fervent enemy," she observed.

"Miss Kendall will attract a new suitor before long." He grasped her arm firmly as they passed over an icy spot on the pavement. "Or her dowry will, if she cannot. Once she has the attention of another gentleman, she will forget all about Miss Bingley."

"Let us hope so, before her injured vanity claims another victim. The lady is terribly hard on tablecloths."

Six

*"Happiness in a marriage is entirely a matter of chance . . .
it is better to know as little as possible of the defects of the person with whom you are to pass your life."*
Charlotte Lucas to Elizabeth, Pride and Prejudice, *Chapter 6*

*C*aroline Bingley's wedding indeed proved the talk of the *ton,* an event calculated in all respects to outdo the Bennet sisters' nuptials. Her gown featured more yards of lace, more beads, more ribbon, than Elizabeth's and Jane's combined. Her veil was longer, her brides' cake taller, her wedding breakfast a full twelve courses. The guest list included more "particular friends" than Mrs. Darcy thought it possible for one couple to have; in fact, Miss Bingley seemed to have invited any titled acquaintance whose card she'd ever received.

Elizabeth considered the whole event an exercise in ostentation, from the exotic foreign flowers in Miss Bingley's bouquet—she and Jane had chosen English roses—to the gaudy wedding ring the bride showed off to all. The solid gold band, engraved with a sunburst design, featured an enormous oval fire opal surrounded by six smaller diamonds. The main stone extended all the way to her first knuckle and perched in a setting so high that Elizabeth would have feared catching it on every piece of clothing she owned were the rock adorning her own hand. She much preferred the delicate engraved band Darcy had given her.

Unlike Darcy, Mr. Parrish had chosen also to wear a wedding band. Elizabeth didn't know whether the practice was common among American husbands, but Caroline made sure everyone in attendance was aware of this additional show of Parrish's devotion. For his part, Mr. Parrish appeared to take the matrimonial spectacle in stride. According to Jane, his contribution to planning the event had been limited to selecting the wedding rings and asking Professor Randolph to stand up with him. The latter choice had caused Elizabeth mild surprise—she had not realized, while conversing with the professor at dinner, that he and Parrish had so intimate an acquaintance. Randolph appeared in high spirits, genuinely delighted by his friend's marriage and choice of partner.

It was with relief that she watched the bridal couple quit the Pulteney Hotel, which had hosted the enormous gathering. As the guests dispersed, the Darcys indulged in a much longer and more heartfelt leave-taking of Jane and Bingley. Elizabeth and her closest sister had previously found themselves divided for months-long periods while paying individual visits to friends and relations, but this separation, with each departing for her own new, permanent situation, felt somehow more final. She knew, however, that the two couples would often visit each other's homes.

She and Darcy spent their last London evening in Drury Lane enjoying a performance of *The Rivals*. It was an older comedy, but neither had seen it performed before, and Sheridan's play provided a merrier conclusion to their London interlude than had Miss Bingley's dramatic production. Now Elizabeth looked forward to collecting Georgiana from the Gardiners early the next morning and setting off for Pemberley at last. Christmas was less than a fortnight away; already, cold air nipped fingers and toes, while Yuletide sights and smells filled every shop.

She gazed out the window as their carriage wended from the theatre back to their townhouse through crowded lanes still wet from evening rain. Falling temperatures had turned the damp air into fog, which cloaked the many pedestrians and coaches in eerie greyness.

"Does London never sleep?" she asked. "This seems an extraordinary number of people filling the streets so late at night."

"Late? The hour is just past midnight."

"I think I prefer country hours."

"And here I thought I had married a woman of fashion."

She was grateful for her husband's presence as the driver turned onto a darker, seedier road. Though the members of London's social elite might believe they lived in their own little *beau monde,* in reality their world collided with the city's less desirable districts and denizens at nearly every corner. Fashionable streets lay within blocks of shabbier neighborhoods, and theatregoers could not travel from a Mayfair mansion to Covent Garden or Drury Lane without entering squalid surroundings thick with sights of desperation, sounds of debauchery, and the smells of unwashed bodies and horse excrement.

Fortunately, Elizabeth saw no children begging in the dim, flickering gaslight this evening. The little ones always tugged at her heart, and not a day of their London visit had passed without Darcy stopping the carriage at her behest to press coins into small, cold hands. No, tonight more sinister figures prowled the streets: unkempt wanderers, aggressive panhandlers, scarlet women, dark-clad rogues. Even as she watched, one dagger-wielding ruffian deprived another of his purse, while twenty paces away, a woman with painted lips called out offers that left little doubt of her moral character to a group of intoxicated dandies tumbling out of a gaming hell.

She shuddered and reached forward to draw the curtain, preferring to complete the journey in isolated darkness rather than observe more such sights from the window. No sooner had she grasped the fabric, however, than an inconceivable sight stayed her hand.

"That cannot be Caroline Bingley!" She gasped, staring at a woman walking unescorted along the dirty gutter. Unless the uneven light deceived her—surely it must!—the new Mrs. Parrish ambled toward them down the shadowed street. Despite the chilly mist, she wore no hat, no gloves, and no mantle or spencer over her short-sleeved muslin gown. Indeed, the sole accessory on her person was a bulging reticule that dangled from one arm. She strolled as if shopping on Bond Street in the broad light of day, oblivious to the peril around her.

The woman's face, bearing, and stride in all ways matched those of the former Miss Bingley. But whyever would Caroline Parrish be walking half-dressed down a menacing London street alone on her wedding night?

"Good heavens, it is her." Darcy rapped a signal to their driver. "Stay here," he told Elizabeth as the coach slowed.

The thief Elizabeth had seen earlier, a ragged youth of perhaps fifteen, spotted Caroline's unguarded handbag. He darted toward her, snatching the reticule as he passed. But the strings of the overstuffed bag became wrapped around her wrist. The force of the swiping attempt spun her round, at last making her sensible of her surroundings. She cried out as she struggled with the criminal, but she did not let go of the reticule.

Darcy leapt out of the still-moving carriage. "He has a knife!" Elizabeth warned, but her words proved unnecessary. The criminal, malice radiating from every line of his dirty, pockmarked face, already brandished the weapon in his bony hand. It glinted in the stuttering light.

"Leave this lady alone." Darcy, his back to Elizabeth, faced the ruffian. Her heart hammered so loudly in her ears that she scarcely heard his words. Nearby chatter died as people turned their attention to the evening's latest entertainment.

The young rogue ceased his struggle with Miss Bingley to take Darcy's measure. Darcy made no move forward, but drew himself up to his full height, over a foot taller than his adversary. She could imagine the forbidding expression on her husband's face—the piercing gaze, the impassive jaw. She had seen it before. But would it carry the same power on a dark, dangerous street that it did in a drawing room?

It did, thank heaven. The would-be purse snatcher spat on the ground in an impotent display of resistance, then darted into the mist.

Elizabeth released breath she hadn't realized she held. Praise God the thief had been so young—she doubted even Darcy could have subdued an older criminal with the force of his presence alone. As her husband whisked their friend into the carriage, the surrounding cacophony of begging and bawdiness resumed as if nothing had happened. Indeed, by the standards of these witnesses, nothing had.

Their coachman quickly set the horses in motion. To Elizabeth it seemed they couldn't move fast enough. Once the scene behind them melted into the fog, Darcy directed the driver to Mr. Parrish's townhouse.

The incident had shaken Caroline, but otherwise, as far as could be discerned inside the dark coach, had left her physically unharmed. She sat stiffly beside Elizabeth, clutching the reticule in her lap, and nodded in mute acceptance at Darcy's offer of his cloak.

"Are you all right, Mrs. Parrish?" Darcy asked.

She did not answer, but rather gazed straight ahead as if she hadn't heard the question.

"Mrs. Parrish?" Darcy echoed. She merely pulled the cloak farther round her shoulders.

"Caroline?" Elizabeth tried. Though the two women had never been intimate enough to use their Christian names, she thought perhaps the new bride had not yet grown accustomed to being addressed by her married name.

Mrs. Parrish at last responded. She turned toward Elizabeth and stared at her as if trying to remember something. "Miss Elizabeth Bennet," she said finally. Then she looked at the coach's third passenger. "Mr. Darcy."

Elizabeth regarded her in shocked silence. Had it really taken her that long to realize who they were? The robbery attempt must have unsettled her more than was visible.

Darcy leaned forward. "Mrs. Parrish, did that thief harm you?"

She shook her head slowly. "No, I just . . . No." She straightened in her seat, as if remembering her posture. Her chin recovered its usual tilt. "Thank you, though, for interceding."

Elizabeth waited, hoping Caroline would now offer some explanation of what she had been doing on the street in the first place. Where was her husband? Had the couple gone out together and become separated? Had she fled their house—the marriage? This was all so exceedingly strange.

When no account appeared forthcoming, she ventured the subject herself. "We were surprised to see you as we passed. Does Mr. Parrish wait for you at home?"

Caroline raised a hand to her temple. "Forgive me, Mrs. Darcy," she said, her voice as haughty as ever. "I feel a headache coming on."

The remark silenced Elizabeth as effectively as it no doubt had been intended. She withdrew into the corner of the carriage, the rebuff having smothered all sympathy toward her seatmate. In the year or so she'd known Caroline Bingley Parrish, she'd never aspired to enter the woman's confidence, never wished to number her among intimate friends. But really! When concerned acquaintances rescued one from robbery and who-knows-what-other harm, some word of explanation seemed a not-unreasonable expectation.

She was tempted to leave Mrs. Parrish and her "headache"

to face alone whatever predicament had led to her midnight stroll. Obviously, Elizabeth's concern was neither solicited nor welcome. Yet she sensed something different about tonight's rudeness—that it stemmed not, as usual, from disdain toward herself, but from a desire to keep some private anxiety private. For that she could not fault her.

The fact did, however, set one's mind to wondering what could so trouble a woman who, twelve hours earlier, had declared herself the happiest, most fortunate bride in all England. A glance at Darcy's face revealed that he, too, knew not what to make of their companion's behavior. He started to speak, stopped, then began once more. "Mrs. Parrish, is *everything* quite all right?"

Caroline met his gaze. For a moment, confusion clouded her countenance, and she looked as if she might confide in Darcy. But then her features smoothed and she tilted her chin once more.

"Yes, Mr. Darcy. Quite."

Mrs. Parrish asked to be dropped off at her door, but Darcy insisted on escorting her into the house. Elizabeth concurred, curious to witness the bridegroom's reaction to his wandering wife's homecoming.

Upon opening the door, the butler stepped back, unable to conceal his surprise at the sight of his new mistress standing on the stoop. "Madam! I thought you were within."

Caroline walked past him without a word and climbed the stairs to the drawing room.

"Is Mr. Parrish at home?" Darcy asked.

"Yes—at least, I believe so."

"Summon him."

The butler escorted Elizabeth and Darcy to the drawing room, then continued up to the second story. Caroline waited inside, her back to the door.

It was a good-size room, with furnishings that reflected

French taste. While Elizabeth knew the style was not of Parrish's choosing but his landlord's, the elegant pieces adorned with boulle marquetry and brass inlay seemed well suited to both master and new mistress. A few ornamental items, such as a small wooden statue of an eagle and a heavy earthenware vase, contrasted but did not clash with the main décor. The accents reminded Elizabeth of the American objects she had seen in Professor Randolph's exhibit. She wondered if these mementos of home had been gifts from the archeologist.

Rapid strides on the stairs soon brought Mr. Parrish to them. He raked a hand through elevated locks of hair; his shirt, coat, and breeches appeared hastily donned. His face betrayed utter astonishment. Obviously, their arrival had roused him from bed. "Mr. and Mrs. Darcy." He acknowledged them with a brief bow before quickly moving to his wife's side.

"Caroline?" When she did not immediately turn around, he laid a hand on her shoulder.

"Oh, Frederick!" Mrs. Parrish spoke so softly that Elizabeth heard only with difficulty. "I've had such a fright."

His expression became still more confused, but he drew her into his arms. "Whatever has happened, you're safe now, my love." Despite the presence of the Darcys, Caroline did not resist the tender display. Elizabeth surmised she was still in a state of shock over the robbery attempt.

Nevertheless, the embrace disconcerted their guests. Elizabeth and Darcy averted their gazes, suddenly seized by a compelling mutual interest in a painting that hung above the fireplace. The illustration depicted a large white classically inspired mansion, situated atop a graceful hill, surrounded by magnolia trees and great oaks with Spanish moss cascading from them. Four columns encompassed the two-story house on each side and supported wide porches on both levels. Deep green ivy and bright pink roses climbed the columns to wind through the rails of the veranda balustrade. An engraved plate centered at the bottom of the frame read *Mont Joyau*.

Frederick Parrish's plantation appeared an idyllic, peaceful place. Elizabeth wondered whether he regretted its impending sale. Only the strongest affections toward a spouse could induce her to relinquish such a home. The spelling, she noted, differed from her previous assumption. She would have to ask Darcy about the accuracy of her translation sometime when she wasn't struggling to eavesdrop on a conversation in which she pretended no interest. Unfortunately, she could make out little more than assorted whispered endearments.

She stole a glance at the couple. The embrace had ended, but Caroline yet leaned on her husband's arm for support. "I don't know what came over me—"

"Hush, sweetheart," he murmured, slipping Darcy's cloak from her shoulders and folding it over the back of a chair. "We'll sort it out in the morning. You should rest now." He cleared his throat, signaling that the Darcys could curtail their spontaneous art appreciation. "Pray excuse me while I attend my wife to her chamber."

"Of course." Darcy donned his hat, which in the confusion of their arrival the butler had neglected to take. "We've intruded on your privacy too long as it is."

"No—not at all! I am most grateful for your interest in Caroline's welfare." In the foyer below, the grandfather clock struck half-past one. "I know the hour grows late, but if I might presume upon your kindness further I would like to speak with you before you leave. Meanwhile, my man will see to your comfort."

The butler, apologizing for his forgotten duties, collected their cloaks and Darcy's hat while Parrish escorted Caroline upstairs. Elizabeth easily forgave the domestic's earlier oversight—the reunion had made her and Darcy self-conscious about the propriety of their own presence; the scene had hardly needed a servant in the audience as well.

Now alone in the drawing room, the two of them regarded each other with all the astonishment they'd labored to suppress. "What do you suppose she was doing?" Elizabeth asked.

Darcy shook his head. "I cannot begin to guess. She seemed relieved to return, so I do not think she was running away."

"Then what errand called her out?" She could not imagine any business so vital that it needed to be conducted on one's wedding night. Yet something more than a handkerchief and a few coins had swollen the sides of Mrs. Parrish's reticule—something important enough to be remembered while half her clothes had been forgotten; important enough that she had risked her safety rather than surrender it to a thief. What could the small handbag have contained? Elizabeth glanced to the part of the room where Caroline had stood, hoping perhaps it had been left behind, but the owner had taken the reticule upstairs with her. Just as well—she could never have so boldly invaded the woman's privacy.

Elizabeth also wondered how Parrish had failed to realize his bride's absence. Though society couples commonly maintained separate chambers, Darcy had not left her bed on their wedding night, or any night since. She'd like to think that if she'd slipped out of the house for a moonlight stroll, her new husband would have noticed. The Parrishes seemed equally attached to one another. Surely the marriage had been consummated? Miss Bingley had never struck her as a warm person, but the embrace the couple had just shared suggested the bride was comfortable receiving physical affection from her husband. Elizabeth dismissed any conjecture that fear of marital duties might have inspired Caroline's flight. What, then, had compelled her to rise from bed for a midnight promenade through London?

The butler returned with wine. He set the tray on a small table behind the sofa and poured two glasses from a crystal decanter. Elizabeth and Darcy accepted the glasses but declined his offer of other refreshment. As soon as the servant departed, Darcy rose and moved about the room, his mind apparently too agitated for the rest of him to relax.

"Her manner, when we first discovered her . . ." he said. "She is usually so self-possessed."

"She almost seemed not to know us at first. And then she called me 'Miss Bennet.' Do you think it was merely shock from the robbery attempt?"

"Perhaps. She is fortunate that you sighted her when you did. A woman alone on that street . . ." Delicacy prevented him from finishing the sentence, but he did not need to. She realized full well that Caroline Parrish could have suffered a worse fate than the loss of her reticule.

Mr. Parrish's return suspended further speculation. His face reflected bewilderment equal to their own; lines of care marred his smooth features. "She's resting now." He poured himself a glass of wine and swallowed a fortifying draught. "Said she suffers from a headache, so I didn't want to badger her for details. But can you tell me what happened? The last I knew, Caroline was asleep in this house. How came my wife to be with you tonight?"

"We saw her walking down Bow Street as we drove home from Drury Lane," Darcy said.

"Bow Street? Good God! *Bow* Street? By herself? At this hour?" Parrish combed his hair with unsteady fingers. Apparently, even the American knew the dangers of that district, so infamous that it had inspired the establishment of investigators known as the Bow Street Runners in an attempt to deter crime. "When I think what could have befallen her—what nearly did, for she told me someone tried to rob her?"

"Mr. Darcy intervened. As far as we can tell, she was not hurt."

"Thank heaven you arrived when you did! Sir, please know that you shall always have my deepest gratitude. As do you, Mrs. Darcy. Caroline is fortunate in your friendship."

"We are glad to have been of use," Darcy said.

Mr. Parrish set his glass on the tray and lifted the decanter to refill it. "Did she say anything to explain why she was on that street—any street—in the first place?" His countenance, which had been so happily animated only that morning, now appeared grave.

Darcy declined Parrish's gestured offer of more wine. "No. She volunteered no account, and we did not press her for one."

"How did she seem? Was she—was she quite herself?"

Elizabeth searched for words to accurately describe Caroline's state without further alarming the distressed bridegroom. "When I first saw her, before the robbery attempt, she appeared . . . unaware of the circumstances in which she had placed herself. She progressed steadily down the road, but her gait held no sense of purpose." In her experience, Caroline Bingley did nothing—even take a turn about the room—without purpose. "Afterward, in the carriage, she seemed shaken by her encounter with the thief, but otherwise acted herself."

Parrish nodded pensively and looked to Darcy. "This was your observation as well?"

"It was."

He released a heavy sigh and slumped into a nearby chair. "Caroline told me just now that she cannot recall leaving the house, nor anything about her journey until the moment the thief accosted her. I had hoped you might be able to provide some insight. As it is, I'm not even sure how long she was gone. She must have departed after I fell asleep, for I didn't hear her. What time did you find her?"

Elizabeth sat down across from him. "Shortly after midnight. Perhaps quarter past."

"I don't know what time I fell asleep. Half-past ten?" He glanced from Elizabeth to Darcy and back. "You are wondering, but too polite to ask, if I know whether Caroline was yet awake when I nodded off." He rested his elbows on his knees and rubbed his eyes with one hand. "I know for certain that she fell asleep before me. I then retired in my own chamber. Forgive me if I speak too openly about delicate matters, Mrs. Darcy. I seek only to comprehend what happened to my wife this evening, not to embarrass you."

"I understand." Far from suffering embarrassment, she was grateful to have her curiosity satisfied on this point. She, too, wanted to solve the puzzle of Caroline's actions, and Parrish was right—she never would have voiced such a question. They now knew that Caroline had not deliberately remained awake to leave after her husband retired.

Darcy, however, appeared discomposed by Parrish's candor. He stiffened, and a slight flush of displeasure crept into his cheek. Elizabeth sensed what he was thinking: A gentleman did not allude to certain subjects in front of a lady, and chief among them was whether he had spent the evening in conjugal activities. No doubt he was also contemplating the notorious vulgarity of Americans.

"You say she doesn't recall leaving the house?" Darcy asked. She knew he was trying to steer the conversation back to more appropriate territory.

"Not a moment of it. Somehow she rose, dressed, walked out the door and traveled all the way to Bow Street without consciousness of having done so." Parrish studied his wineglass, tracing the rim with his index finger. "This is probably a question better suited to her brother, but since he is not here and you are, I will ask it. Is Caroline in the habit of sleepwalking?"

"Sleepwalking?" Darcy blinked in surprise, then pondered a moment. "Not to my knowledge. I have been a guest in the Bingleys' home many times, and they in mine. Never have I witnessed or heard of anything like this."

"Back in Louisiana, there was a young woman—Marie Chevenier—who used to sleepwalk every time she visited her cousins on the plantation next to ours. Sometimes she'd wander so far that we'd find her sleeping on our porch early in the morning. They said she never did it at home, only her first few nights in a strange house. I thought perhaps this being Caroline's first night here . . ." An expression of anguish, tempered by hope, flashed across his face.

Elizabeth felt herself moved by the unveiled, unintentional display of Parrish's distress. What an inauspicious start to his marriage!—spending his wedding night talking to near strangers in a desperate attempt to interpret his new bride's peculiar behavior. Sleepwalking may indeed have caused Caroline's bizarre journey; it provided as good an explanation as she could devise. But even if it hadn't, right now Parrish needed to believe it possible.

"I think perhaps you are correct," she said. "Not only is she in an unfamiliar house, but I'm sure the strain of planning such a grand wedding in little over a week taxed her nerves. In a few days she will be fine, and in a month you won't remember this incident, either."

"Do you really believe so?"

"I do." Then, sympathy overtaking self-interest, she added, "May we call tomorrow to enquire after her?" A glance at Darcy revealed his approval. The call would mean changing their travel plans yet again, but it was the proper thing to do. Mr. Parrish needed the support of friends at present, yet would not wish to disclose tonight's events to others. Chance had made them confidantes in the matter; they had an obligation to carry through their involvement.

Parrish's face brightened. "May you? I would consider it the kindest attention. But don't you leave for Pemberley tomorrow?"

"A day's delay is of no consequence," Darcy said. "Besides, we cannot be easy at home until we know Mrs. Parrish is all right."

However true that might be, Elizabeth could not help but feel disappointment settle upon her heart even as she smiled reassuringly at poor Mr. Parrish. She was beginning to think she and Darcy would never reach Pemberley.

Seven

> "And, if I may mention so delicate a subject, endeavour to check that little something, bordering on conceit and impertinence, which your lady possesses."
>
> Miss Bingley to Darcy, Pride and Prejudice, *Chapter 10*

*E*lizabeth slept late the next morning, Caroline Parrish's escapade having kept her awake much longer into the night than she generally retired. She awoke to find Darcy standing before the mirror, tying his cravat. He had already dispatched a servant to the Gardiners' house with a note informing Georgiana of their delayed departure.

"What did you tell her?" She sipped her chocolate in bed, a post-nuptial addition to her morning routine that Mrs. Hale had introduced and to which she had readily become accustomed.

"That we found Mrs. Parrish wandering the streets in a scandalous manner last night, and remain in London to circulate gossip."

She nearly dropped her cup before realizing he jested. As much as she delighted in their banter, it was usually she who initiated its more preposterous turns. "I trust you also included details of the duel you nearly fought with that ruffian, not to mention Mr. Parrish's account of the couple's sleeping arrangements?"

"In the postscript." Having achieved a passable *trone d'amour* with the neckcloth, he abandoned the mirror and came to lean against the bedpost. "I thought Mr. Parrish's intelligence in particular the very thing for a young lady to read before breakfast."

She set aside the cup. "You blushed to hear Mr. Parrish speak of it."

"A good many individuals who purport to be genteel talk too openly about affairs that should remain private."

She sighed dramatically. "Then I suppose I should withdraw the notice I sent to the *Times* announcing the reason we arrived late for last night's curtain."

"No, let it run. I am sure the *ton* will be fascinated by how long it took you to dress your own hair."

She gasped in mock outrage and tossed a pillow in his direction. "Take the blame for that upon yourself." Her hair had been perfectly arranged when she gave Lucy the night off.

He caught the missile and returned her mischievous grin. "With pleasure."

They arrived at the Parrish townhouse sometime later to find Caroline gone out and her husband struggling to suppress his irritation.

"Riding, of all things! When she ought to be resting after last night's episode!" Mr. Parrish practically flew about the drawing room in agitation. "I left the house for only an hour—to consult the apothecary for a draught to help her sleep more peacefully tonight—and when I returned she'd accepted an invitation to go riding and already departed. Not in a carriage, mind you. On horseback!"

Despite his incensed tones, Elizabeth understood that deep concern for Caroline's welfare fueled the exclamations.

"She's a good horsewoman, but she was in such a state last night . . . ," Parrish continued more calmly. "Thankfully, she took my most docile·mare."

"Mrs. Parrish is indeed an accomplished rider," Darcy assured him. "I have seen her handle a horse many times. A trot down Rotten Row won't tax her abilities."

"The airing may even do her good," Elizabeth offered.

"Let us hope so, though I still cannot fathom her motive for accepting such an impulsive invitation. I don't even know with whom she rides—an 'old childhood friend,' she told my man on her way out the door."

"All the better," Elizabeth said. "Time spent in the comfort of familiar company cannot help but soothe her nerves."

Some of the tension seemed to leave Parrish's face. "I pray that you are right. But here you are come to call on us instead of at last departing for your own home, and I utterly forget my duties as a host. May I offer you some refreshment?"

A sudden commotion in the entrance hall prevented any reply. The three of them hurried to the staircase. Below, two footmen were assisting Caroline into the house.

"Unhand me! I can walk by myself!" she insisted, even as she leaned heavily on their arms for support. Her bonnet was askew and set far back on her head, as if a sudden storm had tried to blow it off. Several locks of hair had sprung free of their usually meticulous arrangement and hung unevenly at the sides of her face.

"Good God!" Parrish hurried down the stairs, Darcy and Elizabeth not far behind. "What's happened now?"

"Her horse bolted, sir," said the footman on Caroline's left.

"I can speak for myself, too!" She angrily shook free of his grasp. "Get out of here before I dismiss you for insolence!"

The servant looked from wife to husband. Parrish took Caroline's arm in his own. "Thank you for assisting Mrs. Parrish, Thomas. I will speak with you later. You, too, John."

At his master's command, the other footman, older and stouter than the first, released his hold on Caroline but lingered close until it was certain that Parrish's support was enough to keep her on her feet. Darcy took a few steps forward, but Mrs. Parrish indeed seemed capable of standing for herself.

As the servants departed, all realized two additional people stood crowded in the vestibule—Juliet Kendall and a maid. Miss Kendall appeared exceedingly uncomfortable, as if trying to shrink herself so as not to take up any more space in Parrish's house than necessary.

Surprise, panic, and irritation flashed across Parrish's face in rapid succession. "What the devil are *you* doing here?" he growled.

She flinched and took a step back. "I merely wished to assure myself that Caroline got home safely."

His expression darkened. "You? *You* were the 'friend' who invited my wife to go riding? What was your purpose?"

Elizabeth dearly wanted to learn the answer to that very question herself, but doubted Parrish's tone would elicit a full explanation. He looked as if, were his wife not leaning on him for support, he would have lunged across the room to throttle his former sweetheart.

"I wanted to wish her joy in her new marriage."

"I'll bet. And did you express this sentiment before or after you spooked her horse?"

Juliet paled at Parrish's accusation. "I did nothing of the sort! Hecate bolted all by herself—I have no idea why." She backed up another step, bringing herself against the door. Her maid stepped in front of her as if to physically shield her from the force of his anger.

"Get out of my house," Parrish hissed. "Whatever your previous relationship with Caroline may have been, your history with me renders further association between you inappropriate. As of this moment, my wife has dropped her acquaintance with you."

Miss Kendall left without another word. Parrish closed the door behind her. "I beg your forgiveness for that display," he said to the Darcys. He seemed more himself again. The flush receded from his face; both his countenance and his voice returned to their usual pleasing natures. "Her sudden appearance here—her desire to court my wife's friendship—it's not just awkward but suspicious."

Elizabeth silently concurred. The last time she'd seen Juliet Kendall, the woman hardly appeared disposed to wish the new Mrs. Parrish joy. She wondered at the jilted Juliet's real motive for suggesting the outing.

Caroline had been uncharacteristically silent during the exchange. She now sagged against her husband, apparently having forgotten her earlier insistence that she required no one's aid. Parrish and Darcy helped her up the stairs and into the drawing room, where she sank into the chair nearest the door. She removed her errant hat but appeared unconcerned by the state of her hair.

"You should retire to your room," Parrish said.

She started to nod, then seemed to change her mind. "No, I think I'll just stay here awhile."

"Surely you at least want to freshen your toilette?"

Again, she seemed on the verge of assenting to her husband's suggestion, then resisted. "And ignore our guests? Whatever will the Darcys think, now that they have become such frequent visitors?" Despite the words, Elizabeth could detect no sarcasm in her tone.

"We are concerned for your well-being," Darcy said. "Are you recovered from this morning's excitement?"

"Yes. It was an alarming ride, but I managed to hold on

until one of the servants overtook me and got the horse under control."

"Do you know why it bolted?" Elizabeth asked. Not much of an equestrian herself, she thought this seemed unusual behavior for an allegedly docile mare.

Caroline shook her head. "One minute I was leaning over a bit to hear something Miss Kendall was saying, and the next I was flying through the park."

"My dear, you needn't talk about this now," Parrish said. "Are you sure you don't care to rest?"

Elizabeth sensed they had overstayed their welcome, and a glance at her husband revealed that he was of like mind. They took their leave of the Parrishes, who let the butler show them out. As they donned their mantles, one of the servants who had accompanied Caroline passed through the entrance hall.

"A word with you?" Though voiced as a question, Darcy's manner made it a command.

"Yes, sir?"

"I understand you saw Mrs. Parrish's horse bolt this morning?"

"I did, sir."

"Have you any idea what agitated the animal?"

"No, sir. I had a pretty good view, too—the ladies had told me and Miss Kendall's maid to drop behind some while they talked. They had the horses walking real slow so they could ride close to each other. Then of a sudden, Hecate just took off like someone stuck a needle in her."

"Was there any movement on the part of either lady that could have startled the horses?"

The footman thought for a moment, then shook his head. "They were just riding along. Mrs. Parrish leaned toward Miss Kendall, like she wanted to hear better, but it wasn't a quick shift."

Elizabeth, though she could visualize the scene, couldn't fathom the topic of conversation between Caroline and Juliet. What an interesting tête-à-tête that must have been!

"Do you know what they were talking about?" she asked. It was an intrusive question, one she would hesitate to ask Caroline directly. But Juliet's solicitation of Caroline's company surely related to the riding mishap somehow. To believe otherwise was to trust too much in coincidence, particularly in light of Juliet's bitterness the last time Elizabeth had seen her.

The footman's eyes grew wide at Elizabeth's query. "Oh, no, madam—I would never eavesdrop on Mrs. Parrish!"

"I would never suggest that you might," she reassured him. "But sometimes servants do overhear things even when trying not to. If perhaps that were the case, it surely couldn't be held against you. We seek only to protect Mrs. Parrish from any sort of future incident."

"As I said, madam, the ladies were fifty yards or so ahead of me, and they had their heads together pretty close. I couldn't have listened to their conversation if I tried."

"Did the two of them seem cordial toward each other?"

"Mrs. Parrish, she seemed more reserved than usual at first. But Miss Kendall appeared very kindly disposed."

"At any point in the outing, did you see Miss Kendall touch Mrs. Parrish's mare?"

"She arrived at the park on horseback and never dismounted. The lady did compliment Hecate—called her a beautiful mare—and stroked the horse's mane. But she held her own reins the whole time they rode together."

"What about Miss Kendall's maid?" Darcy asked. "Was she ever near the horse?"

"No, she hung back with me."

"Has Hecate ever done this before?"

The servant shook his head. "She's as tame a mount as you'll ever find. Mrs. Parrish has ridden her a few times and never had any trouble with her 'afore. She did seem a bit skittish this morning, but Mrs. Parrish, she's a fine rider and had her well in hand. Just don't know what happened."

They dismissed the servant and went outside to their waiting coach. The footman's description of the meeting puzzled her. She'd hardly describe Juliet's attitude toward Caroline as "kindly disposed" a mere week ago when she'd vowed to see Frederick's new wife unhappy. What had been her true motive for the outing? Had Miss Kendall in fact caused the horse to bolt in hopes that an accident would ensue?

"What do you make of these events?" she asked Darcy as he handed her into the vehicle.

"A freak occurrence. While I can't account for Miss Kendall's interest in meeting with Mrs. Parrish, I think the horse must have been startled by a small animal or something. It does not take much to spook some horses. I do find it surprising that the servant had to check the mare, as Bingley's sister definitely knows how to handle a mount, but perhaps the animal resisted the commands of an unfamiliar rider."

"I'm not so sure." She settled into her seat, suppressing a shiver as she drew her cloak more tightly around her shoulders. Unbidden, the memory of Lady Chatfield's tea-stained tablecloth flashed across her mind. "Will you require the carriage any more this afternoon?"

"It is yours if you want it." He sat down beside her and drew her toward his warmth. "Where do you plan to go?"

"I think it's time I called upon Miss Kendall."

Eight

"Detection could not be in your power, and suspicion certainly not in your inclination."

Darcy, writing to Elizabeth,
Pride and Prejudice, *Chapter 35*

$\mathcal{T}$he Kendalls lived in a well-appointed townhouse just off Hyde Park, with furnishings that revealed their comfortable financial status. As she waited in the parlor for Juliet to receive her, Elizabeth mused that the import business, in which the Kendalls had been in partnership with the Bingleys, certainly had its material advantages when it came to decorating a home. The satin wallpaper, French furniture, and silk-embroidered draperies had no doubt been obtained at a fraction of their usual cost. An Italian marble mantel dominated the room, framing the fireplace with images of Roman deities in high relief. Jupiter and Juno, Diana and Cupid, Janus and Mercury, Vulcan and Vesta kept watch over the parlor, their stony gazes evaluating all who entered.

Darcy had not been pleased with Elizabeth's decision to call here, and his displeasure had increased when she insisted on coming alone. He objected not on the basis of the riding incident but on the Kendalls' history with the Bingleys. He'd explained the animosity between them and discouraged her from further developing an acquaintance with a family at odds with their closest friends. Yet Elizabeth could not shake the sense that Miss Kendall was somehow responsible for Caroline's wild ride. She wanted to speak with Juliet, to see if her instincts would prove reliable. The young woman had been surprisingly candid during their previous conversation about her feelings toward Caroline; perhaps Elizabeth could spur additional revelations—such as the motive behind the strange meeting—simply by providing a sympathetic ear. To do so, however, she needed to approach Juliet alone, not in the company of her often intimidating husband.

Miss Kendall greeted her with the usual polite pleasantries. She was honored by the call, flattered that the new Mrs. Darcy took interest in her, looked forward to calling upon her if she remained in town. But the words held a certain edge to them; in manner and tone, Juliet seemed more the acerbic woman Elizabeth remembered from the Chatfields' dinner party than the timid miss who'd cowered in the Parrish vestibule that morning. Keen eyes took Elizabeth's measure, as if assessing her value as an acquaintance. Value toward what purpose? Elizabeth could not guess, but her back straightened in reflex.

At Juliet's invitation to sit, she chose the chair nearest the fireplace. Though a blaze burned in the hearth, the air held a chill made more frigid by her hostess's demeanor. She ignored Jupiter's gaze as she settled in front of him and Juliet perched on the seat opposite. After several minutes of small talk, which seemed to bore both women in equal measure as they danced around the subject hanging unspoken between them, Miss Kendall herself brought the conversation round to the morning's ride.

"Did you leave Mrs. Parrish in good health?" The benign enquiry, voiced so commonly as part of society's standard prattle, from Miss Kendall sounded like someone had wrested it out of her.

"Yes. By the time my husband and I departed, she appeared to have recovered from this morning's events." Elizabeth paused, debating how best to proceed. Appealing to her vanity seemed the best course; she would make this a conversation about injuries done to Miss Kendall. "And yourself? I hope you were not harmed by the incident?"

"I am perfectly well, thank you."

"Thank goodness. One of the servants said you were riding fairly close to Mrs. Parrish when her horse bolted, and I feared the proximity might have endangered you. Though you seemed fine when you accompanied her home, I wanted to ascertain for myself that all was well."

"You are kindness itself, Mrs. Darcy. I assure you, I suffered no physical harm. While Caroline lost control of her horse, I managed to maintain command of mine."

Outside, a passing cloud darkened the winter afternoon, bathing the room in shadows pierced by the flickering firelight. The unsteady illumination seemed to animate the Roman deities, lending them airs from mysterious to mischievous. Elizabeth ignored the impish look Cupid cast her way and focused on the task at hand. "You must have excellent equestrian skills. I confess, I am no horsewoman. In fact, I'm having trouble understanding what caused Mrs. Parrish's misadventure."

Miss Kendall shook her head. "I've no idea. Perhaps Hecate objected to Caroline. The mare did seem unusually skittish. No horse is completely predictable, especially in the hands of an unfamiliar rider, but Hecate is well trained. I've ridden her myself."

Her last statement seemed a calculated reminder of her previous relationship with Hecate's owner. "It must have been difficult for you to see Mr. Parrish's new bride in a seat you so recently occupied," Elizabeth said. "I must admit I was all astonishment to hear that the outing took place at your solicitation. Not many women would demonstrate such a generous, forgiving nature."

Now it was Miss Kendall's turn to pause. She picked a nonexistent piece of lint off her skirt and stared at her fingers as she rubbed them together slowly. "I thought the sooner I saw her in her new situation, the better."

Elizabeth thought it a reasonable excuse for the invitation. Yet what had the pair been discussing so closely? Dare she ask? She had the opportunity now; she might as well seize it. "And were you able to enjoy the easy conversation of old friends?"

Juliet lifted her chin and finally met her gaze. "No, I'm afraid not." She rose abruptly. "Pray forgive me, Mrs. Darcy, but I suddenly find myself wearied by the day's events. Surely you understand?"

Elizabeth understood perfectly—she had pushed too far, too soon in their acquaintance. "Of course." She rose to take her leave. "I'm unsure how long my husband and I will remain in town, but I hope to have the pleasure of your call at some point in the future."

"The pleasure will be mine," Miss Kendall said, but her flat tone did not match the words.

The interview was at an end, and Elizabeth knew little more than she had before she arrived. Beside her, the fire popped, and Janus mocked her with both his faces.

Nine

> "Reconciling herself, as well as she could, to a change
> so sudden and so important, fatigue . . . made her at length
> return home."
>
> Pride and Prejudice, *Chapter 36*

*E*lizabeth poked at her eggs, the tines of her fork piercing the soft whites now grown cold. Snow the day before had further delayed a return to Pemberley, and now she and Darcy waited for a servant to return with word of road conditions before deciding whether to set out this morning or remain still longer.

She hoped they could quit London presently. They'd made the most of their time in town, engaging not only in entertaining diversions, but also undertaking errands and other business. Elizabeth had visited Oxford and Bond streets to order new draperies, wallpaper, and additional appointments for the summer breakfast parlor and long gallery at Pemberley; Darcy had managed a few visits to the Haymarket Room to improve his mastery of fencing under Domenico Angelo's instruction. But London, for all its excitement, had grown tiresome after the repeated postponements of their travel plans, and both longed to leave.

"If we don't go today, perhaps we should just spend

Christmas here." As much as she'd prefer to be in Derbyshire, at least they could settle into the townhouse and begin holiday preparations instead of endlessly expecting to depart.

Darcy set aside the *Times* and motioned the footman to refill his coffee cup. "I thought you wanted to be at Pemberley?"

"I do. I'm just trying to be practical." She glanced to the window. Light snowflakes merrily bobbed through the air, oblivious to the disappointment their presence caused those on the other side of the glass.

"Leave practical to me. If Pemberley is where my wife wants to spend Christmas, we will get there."

"If we stay here any longer, we really ought to invite poor Georgiana to come back."

His brows rose. "Are you saying the honeymoon is over?"

"Certainly not. I think only of your sister's comfort. Though she and the Gardiners report they are having a lovely visit, one is never as completely at ease in someone else's home as in one's own." She pushed aside the plate of cold food and set her napkin on the table. Perhaps she would write a letter to Charlotte this morning.

"Precisely why we should preserve our plan to celebrate Christmas in Derbyshire. London is home to too many—a noisy, crowded boardinghouse compared to the tranquility of Pemberley."

"Yet you maintain this townhouse, and permit Georgiana to pass most of the year in it."

"Out of necessity. Business often calls me here, and the city offers cultural and educational opportunities unavailable in the country. It also provides more varied society."

She cast him an arch look. "Now it is my turn to ask if the honeymoon is over—I hope you don't grow weary of my company already?"

"Quite the reverse, Mrs. Darcy. Once we do reach Pemberley, I may never wish to leave it again."

They were interrupted by the entrance of a servant. "A letter for you, madam. Just arrived—the rider waits for a reply."

She exchanged a puzzled glance with her husband. Whatever could be so urgent? As she reached for the note, she recognized the handwriting immediately. "It's from Jane." She broke the seal and quickly scanned the contents. "Caroline Parrish has suffered an accident. A surgeon has seen to her injuries but Jane and Bingley desire our counsel. They ask us to meet them at the Parrishes' townhouse as soon as possible."

She looked into her husband's face, which mirrored her own concern and confusion. What could have happened that required their opinion on the matter?

He turned to the servant who had brought the letter. "Tell the messenger we will meet them directly."

The Darcys arrived to find Parrish, Jane, Bingley, and the Hursts all gathered in the drawing room. Parrish, his face in profile, stared outward as he leaned against the window. He had been speaking softly to Bingley, who stood beside him, but stopped as the butler entered with Elizabeth and Darcy.

As soon as the servant departed, Jane, her face more grave than her sister had ever seen it, immediately crossed the room and took Elizabeth's hands in her own. "I'm so glad you are come. The most shocking thing has happened—we don't know what to make of it."

Elizabeth glanced from Jane to the others. Bingley stood stiffly, his normally carefree countenance clouded by anxiety that matched his wife's. He exchanged a glance with Parrish, who pushed away from the window to stand with a defeated posture. Louisa, hands in her lap and fingers unconsciously playing with her rings, studied the floor. Mr. Hurst sprawled on the sofa, a degree of seriousness quickening his usual bored expression. An unnatural silence hung in the air as all seemed reluctant to speak of the situation that had brought them here.

Jane drew her toward the sofa. "Come sit down." Elizabeth, her curiosity mounting, sat beside Jane as advised.

Darcy followed her to the sofa but remained standing. "Mr. Parrish? Bingley? Could someone tell us what has transpired?"

Parrish cleared his throat. "Forgive me. I still find it difficult to give voice to this incident. Early this morning, my cook found Mrs. Parrish lying on the kitchen floor with two knife wounds."

Elizabeth gasped and looked to Jane, who nodded in confirmation of the incredible news. "Is she—will she recover?"

"The surgeon thinks so. Her injuries are painful but not very deep. She's resting now."

Her mind struggled to comprehend the intelligence. Caroline Parrish had been attacked in her own home? "How—Who . . .?"

Darcy's hand touched her back. "Has a constable been summoned?" London's feeble police force wasn't renowned for its competence, but Elizabeth supposed the assistance of some authority figure was better than nothing.

"He's been here and gone. Pompous lout." Parrish crossed to a vacant chair and slumped into it. His red eyes and accompanying dark circles testified to a long night with little sleep. The once lighthearted American seemed to have aged years in the two weeks Elizabeth had known him. "He declared that all the evidence points to a desire for self-destruction."

She could scarcely believe the words. "A suicide attempt?"

Darcy's unguarded expression revealed equal bewilderment, but he quickly recovered his composure. "What led him to such a conclusion?"

"The location of the wounds—her wrists. And we found the knife still in her hands."

"Perhaps she struggled with her attacker and wrested the knife from him before losing consciousness," Jane offered.

"Perhaps," Parrish said flatly. But no one, Jane included, appeared to think that explanation probable.

"What has Mrs. Parrish said?" Darcy asked.

"She was unconscious when the cook found her. She roused briefly while the surgeon attended her injuries, but had no recollection of events. She's been sleeping since."

"Did the surgeon also believe her wounds to be self-inflicted?"

"He was too tactful to say so outright, but I sensed by his manner that he did."

A small cry from Louisa Hurst drew the party's attention toward that quarter. "This is all just too terrible." She dabbed dry eyes with a handkerchief to underscore her distress. "The scandal! That horrible constable and the surgeon are no doubt even now gadding about town trumpeting the news. None of us will be able to show our faces in society again."

Ah, yes—the scandal. Of course that would be uppermost in Mrs. Hurst's thoughts while her sister lay bleeding into her bandages. Elizabeth was no stranger to the disgrace into which younger sisters could plunge their relations, but she liked to think that even during the Wickhams' elopement she'd maintained concern for Lydia's well-being along with the family's reputation. But then, she'd always known the Bingley sisters to demonstrate different priorities. She wondered anew that Charles, whose face registered a blend of sadness and disgust at Louisa's outburst, had sprung from the same stock.

After an embarrassed silence, Darcy continued as if the utterance had never taken place. "What were your own observations last night?" he asked Parrish.

"Very few, I'm sorry to say. Professor Randolph joined us for dinner but did not stay late. Once he departed, Caroline retired early—as you know, she hasn't been feeling quite herself these past few days. I grew restless and went down to White's, where I wound up in a political debate the others wouldn't let drop. By the time I returned, it was nearly five in the morning, and I no sooner reached my bedchamber than

Cook discovered Mrs. Parrish on the kitchen floor. I sent one man for the surgeon, another for the constable, and did my best to staunch her wounds while awaiting their arrival."

Bingley, who had been slowly shaking his head in disbelief during Parrish's narrative, threw himself into a chair and rubbed his forehead. "I just don't understand this. Less than a week ago, my sister was the happiest woman on earth, and now she's tried to—to—it's so awful, I can't even say it!"

"It was even worse to behold," Parrish said quietly.

"What did you mean about her not feeling quite herself lately?" Bingley asked. "Has she been ill?"

"There have been episodes—" Parrish looked to Elizabeth and Darcy. "Your friends can bear witness. Caroline's behavior has been erratic. Sleepwalking, losing control of her horse, trouble remembering events."

"Good grief! Why didn't you tell us?"

"I hoped it would pass, or that things were not as they seemed. But this latest incident . . ." He leaned toward Bingley, elbows on his knees, fingers forming a pyramid. "Charles, I understand this is information a family wouldn't wish to share with a young woman's suitors. But Caroline is my wife now. I need to know—has she a history of unusual actions? Behavior that suggests a troubled mind?"

"No—I tell you, this is not like her at all. I am most distressed!"

"As am I. It grieves me to see—" Parrish cut his words short at the butler's entrance. Not, Elizabeth supposed, that there were many secrets about the household's mistress unknown to the servants at this point.

"Professor Randolph has arrived, sir."

"Show him in."

Elizabeth wondered that Parrish would welcome the intrusion into their family council of a person so unconnected to Caroline. The expressions of the others revealed they were of like mind. The unfortunate professor therefore entered a room oppressively silent.

He appeared, however, not to notice. He nodded in brief acknowledgment to the assembly, then crossed to their host. "I came as soon as I received your summons. What has happened, and how can I help?"

That Parrish had actually requested Randolph's presence amazed Elizabeth still more. They must be intimate acquaintances indeed for Parrish to reveal to him the details of Caroline's recent behavior. Perhaps Parrish sought the moral support of his own friend in the midst of this conference with his new wife's family.

As if answering the unspoken question, Parrish addressed the party. "I asked Randolph to come because I value his opinions and connections as a man of science. Though he has not directly studied nervous disorders, he has colleagues who specialize in that field, and may know of someone who can help restore my wife to herself."

"You are most welcome indeed, sir," said Bingley. "I hope my sister benefits from your attention."

"Though I've not yet heard the particulars, I hope I may be of service."

Randolph listened solemnly to Parrish as he described Caroline's unusual activities and demeanor since the wedding. When the narrative concluded, the professor, like Parrish, enquired whether Bingley or the others were aware of previous occurrences. All denied knowledge of any such behavior until now.

He pondered their replies a moment. "Has the lady resided in London long?"

"Off and on since our father's death a couple years ago," Bingley said. "Before her marriage, Caroline stayed with our sister, Louisa, and Mr. Hurst in their townhouse when she wasn't helping me oversee domestic matters at Netherfield. That's my country household."

"Did London agree with her?"

"Oh, yes!" said Mrs. Hurst. "She's quite popular here in town—you saw how many friends attended the wedding. When she stays with us, not a day goes by without an invitation arriving, or Caroline making a social call."

"And Netherfield—was she comfortable there?"

Bingley suddenly appeared uncertain. "She always seemed so to me."

Louisa cleared her throat. "She did find the society a bit—shall we say—confining."

"I don't know why," replied Bingley. "She never complained about country society during our visits to Darcy's estate."

Elizabeth bit her lip and deliberately avoided making eye contact with Jane.

"Have you had many callers here since the wedding?"

"A fair number," Parrish said. "Most of my wife's friends are in London presently, and I haven't discouraged visitors as I didn't want anything to appear amiss."

Randolph removed his spectacles and wiped them with a handkerchief. "From what you have told me, and from my own observations yesterday at dinner, I think perhaps Mrs. Parrish is simply suffering from nervous exhaustion resulting from the excitement of the wedding and the weight of her social obligations. My advice is to remove her from London to a quieter setting where she can catch her breath."

"Such as Netherfield?" Bingley asked.

"Actually, I have another suggestion." He returned the eyeglasses to his face, where they immediately slipped halfway down the bridge of his nose. "Mr. Parrish's plantation, Mont Joyau. It's a beautiful setting. Very peaceful, and at this time of year the weather will be far more pleasant than at Netherfield. New Orleans is close enough to offer interesting society, amusements, and other benefits of a large city as she feels up to circulating, yet she won't be in the middle of the bustle as she is here."

"Mont Joyau?" Parrish perked up; some of the defeat left his countenance. "Mont Joyau—of course! I like that idea, Randolph. I should have thought of it myself. What better place to mend one's spirit? Caroline could see where I grew up. And I could roam its fields once more before selling it."

"Mont Joyau holds an additional advantage," Randolph continued. "I have a colleague, Dr. Lancaster, who lives in New Orleans and specializes in nervous disorders. He would be able to assist and perhaps hasten Mrs. Parrish's recovery."

"Indeed?" Parrish's brows rose. "I had no idea you were so well connected, Randolph."

Elizabeth studied once more the Mont Joyau painting above the fireplace, trying to imagine the former Miss Bingley living in Louisiana. She doubted the lady would like it one bit. The place seemed too foreign, too *alive* for a woman whose blood, though not blue, ran cold as ice. The fair English rose—for so Caroline perceived herself—would wilt in the American South. She would find the landscape too exotic, the weather too hot, New Orleans too primitive, society too uncultured. Though as for that last point, perhaps the sheer wealth of Parrish's fellow plantation owners would prove enough to overcome her snobbishness.

A frown creased Bingley's brow, indicating his equal lack of conviction that Caroline would thrive in the new environment. "It's so far away."

"Consider the distance a benefit," said Randolph. "Mrs. Parrish will be able to retreat completely from whatever it is here that weighs so heavily upon her. The change of scene will do her good—after all, doctors recommend warm destinations as the cure for many ailments. Instead of the south of France, she'll see the French Quarter."

"But at least southern France is civilized," Louisa sputtered.

"The people she'd encounter in Louisiana—the—the— *darkies* she'd have to oversee as servants, for heaven's sake! My poor sister!" She sniffed and dabbed at her eyes again with the handkerchief. "The conditions would be barbaric."

"This *is* my home we're talking about," Parrish said in a tone far more civil than would have been justified.

Louisa's hands fell to her lap, but she otherwise gave no indication that she'd heard him. Elizabeth grew embarrassed on Mrs. Hurst's behalf, since the woman hadn't the sense to feel shame herself. As for Louisa's anxiety, Elizabeth imagined Caroline would have little trouble adjusting to the experience of ordering slaves about.

Darcy broke the dead silence. "With all respect to you, Mr. Parrish"—he acknowledged him with a bow before turning his attention to the professor—"will not the unfamiliar setting add further strain to Mrs. Parrish's nerves? To be apart from everyone she knows excepting her husband, in a place she's never visited before?"

Randolph chuckled. "I believe it's called a honeymoon, Mr. Darcy. And contrary to your concern, I'm suggesting that's just what the lady needs—to be away from all the familiar people and pressures, in a place where she can relax and ease into her new life."

"Even so, would not the journey itself unduly tax Mrs. Parrish? Can her nerves withstand the privations and confinement of life aboard ship for a prolonged period of time?"

"Though it's a major voyage, I believe she would be more comfortable and able to rest better aboard a ship than if she were to undertake an overland trip by coach to a warmer climate. Once she's on the boat, it needn't repeatedly stop to change horses or subject her to a different inn every night."

Parrish rose. "You have convinced me, Randolph. And I think the sooner Caroline and I set out, the better. Are we all in agreement? Bingley?"

"I—I'm not quite—that is—" Bingley's gaze darted to Darcy. "She's my sister—I cannot be objective. Do you think this is best?"

"No." Darcy gestured toward the painting. "While I believe Mont Joyau holds all the advantages enumerated by Professor Randolph, I think a trip and extended stay there also pose disadvantages for Mrs. Parrish that exceed the benefits. The hardships of an ocean voyage, the prolonged isolation from her friends, the foreign environment—I cannot think upon these factors but as obstacles to her recovery. I would much rather see her recuperate at Netherfield, or even Pemberley, where she can rest among friends in a place already comfortable to her."

At Darcy's implied invitation to Pemberley, Elizabeth forced her lips into a bright smile . . . and inwardly cringed at the thought of Caroline Parrish moving into her home for a prolonged convalescence before she herself had even settled in as mistress of the estate. Only her love for Jane, whose heart would be made easier by Bingley's relief at the arrangement, could make such an ordeal bearable.

Parrish's countenance froze, suggesting he was equally enamored of the suggestion. First his home had been insulted by Mrs. Hurst, and now someone not even of the family presumed to know better than he what was best for his wife. "As newly married couples all, I'm sure we do not wish to intrude on each other's privacy to such an extent. Mr. Darcy, I appreciate your apprehensions and your offer of hospitality, but I'm sure my wife will be quite all right at Mont Joyau. The plantation has been in my family for generations; the mansion boasts some of the most comfortable and luxurious-rooms in Louisiana. It's hardly the savage wasteland some of those present seem to think it is."

"I assure you, Parrish, no one here intends you or your home disrespect," Bingley said quickly. "I think only of my sister's well-being. It would be no intrusion to have you and Caroline stay with us in Hertfordshire for as long as necessary. Indeed,

Jane and I would be pleased to have you as our first guests. While I am only a tenant at Netherfield and cannot rival your long family history at Mont Joyau, you'll find it a pleasant estate. Of course, Caroline is your wife and you can take her where you will. But truly, I shall be disappointed if you do not come."

"And what of the opportunity for Randolph's friend Dr. Lancaster to treat her?" Parrish asked. "Who can aid my wife"—he cast a look of appeal at Mrs. Hurst—"*quietly*—at Netherfield?"

"The need for discretion is not lost upon any of us," Darcy said. "Perhaps, Professor Randolph, you can write to your colleague for advice while we search for a physician here in England whose secrecy can be trusted. Meanwhile, Mrs. Parrish could begin her recovery at Netherfield."

"I can send a letter this very morning if need be. But Mrs. Parrish will benefit far more from Dr. Lancaster's direct observation than his interpretation of my notes. And corresponding across the ocean will take months—if the missives even arrive, with the seas in a state of war."

"All the more reason for Mrs. Parrish not to travel upon them."

Parrish scanned the room as if seeking another ally. His gaze lighted upon Mr. Hurst, who had for the most part spent the discussion silently liberating Parrish's sherry from the crystal decanter on the table beside him. "Mr. Hurst, we've not yet heard your opinion on the matter. Caroline has spent a lot of time in your home up till now. Where do you think she can best recover?"

Hurst shrugged. "One house is as good as another. Though perhaps she oughtn't come back to Grosvenor Street with us."

Had Hurst been listening at all? Who had suggested Grosvenor Street? The whole idea was to get Mrs. Parrish out of London. Elizabeth pitied Frederick Parrish. 'Twas difficult to know the right course of action with conflicting advice all around.

"Perhaps a compromise might be reached," she offered. "Before subjecting Mrs. Parrish to a long journey, why not see if a short stay at Netherfield suffices? If not, then undertake the more involved trip to Louisiana."

Jane's countenance, which had been clouded by the dissent in the air, brightened. "Yes! Maybe Caroline's condition is not as bad as it seems and she needs only a short respite."

"Should that prove true, no one would be happier than I." Parrish released a heavy sigh and shrugged in resignation. "As much as I wish to share Mont Joyau with Caroline, I have no desire to go against the wishes of all her family. Charles, Jane, I gratefully and humbly accept your hospitality."

Bingley beamed at Parrish's decision. "Splendid! Jane and I will depart this afternoon to prepare for your arrival. Bring Caroline as soon as she is ready to travel."

"Mrs. Hurst and I will come, too," Hurst said quickly. "For support, you know."

For the wine cellar, more likely, Elizabeth longed to say.

Bingley, however, expressed pleasure at Hurst's suggestion. His gaze swept the others. "Here's an idea—why don't we all remove to Netherfield? Caroline can spend Christmas surrounded by those who love her."

Christmas with Caroline Bingley Parrish. Oh, joyous thought. Elizabeth met Darcy's eyes, in which she alone detected the chagrin that matched her own as their plans to spend Yuletide at Pemberley slipped completely and finally from their grasp. Of course they must go. Every proper sentiment dictated that they defer their idyllic dream to the greater and very real needs of others close to them.

Jane's expression was all sympathy. Elizabeth knew her sister would prove the bright spot in this whole scheme. She would think upon the visit as going to support Jane. Better yet, of celebrating the holidays with Jane.

"We would love to join you," she said.

Ten

"I hope," said she, as they were walking together in the shrubbery the next day, "you will give your mother-in-law a few hints, when this desirable event takes place, as to the advantage of holding her tongue."

Caroline Bingley to Mr. Darcy,
Pride and Prejudice, *Chapter 10*

*E*lizabeth inhaled deeply, drawing the crisp country air into her lungs to refresh both her body and her spirit. Though London offered diversions and an atmosphere unique in all England, her honeymoon there had confirmed that she was a country girl at heart. The slower pace gave one time to think, to notice one's surroundings, to gain an intimate understanding of self and others, instead of getting lost in the perpetual whirl of the *ton* and its activities.

If she could not enjoy the tranquility of her own home, visiting Jane was the next best thing. Netherfield Park offered not merely the companionship of her most beloved sister, but also extensive walking paths. Elizabeth took great pleasure in walks; only the most disagreeable weather prevented at least one outing each day. Sometimes she preferred to go by herself and be alone with her thoughts. On other occasions she welcomed company, as today when Jane joined her.

The Bingley sisters walked when it suited them: namely,

when a brief stroll offered the opportunity for a private tête-à-tête or, in their maiden days, a chance to show off their forms to best advantage before eligible gentlemen. Since they had thus limited their excursions at Netherfield to the immediate environs of the house, Caroline had allowed many of the park's more distant paths to continue unmaintained—a condition left by the previous tenant—during the year she'd governed her brother's housekeeping. The garden paths near the house remained tidy, but disuse had caused the more remote trails in the rest of the park to grow further untamed. Elizabeth and Jane had to watch their footing as they traversed the grounds lest they catch a toe on a rock or root.

Jane had modest plans for restoring the paths; indeed, three new gardeners had already begun. Their work, however, left something to be desired. Hired shortly after Bingley's engagement, they eagerly sought to please their new mistress and proceeded immediately to address her general remark about tidying the paths. Figuring that if a dirt path was adequate, a brick one was better, they undertook to surprise Jane and their new master while the head gardener was away purchasing bulbs for autumn planting. Their inexperience, however, led the trio to lay the bricks rapidly, in unfavorable weather, and without proper foundation, edging, or slope to facilitate drainage. The resulting path was a gauntlet of hazards. Shifting had started as soon as cold temperatures arrived, and uneven bricks competed with icy pools to upset the unwary. The "improved" path was now the most treacherous one on the estate.

"The poor lads meant well," Jane said. "Mr. Smyth wanted to dismiss them when he returned and saw what they'd done, but Bingley interceded. They're all three of them orphans, perhaps fifteen or sixteen, with nowhere else to go, and winter was coming."

Elizabeth smiled at Jane's charity. Leave it to her sister and Bingley to hire three new gardeners in the fall, and inexperienced boys at that. Fortunately, snow had put a temporary halt to their overzealous efforts to please their benefactors.

Jane described their plans for spring plantings. Bingley hoped to purchase an estate of his own soon, so he and Jane did not wish to invest much time or capital in the enhancement of interim surroundings. But while Netherfield was theirs, she wanted to make it a home, and she shared her ideas for the house and grounds as they walked. It was a more pleasant topic than the unspoken one that weighed on both their minds.

Though she tried to focus on Jane's words, Elizabeth's thoughts defiantly kept returning to Caroline Parrish. Yesterday's family conference at the townhouse troubled her in a way she could not pinpoint, leaving her mind restless as she sought to define the vague sense that something more than frayed nerves propelled the recent events surrounding the former Miss Bingley.

Elizabeth so loved life that she found completely alien the notion of taking one's own. To intentionally end the adventure of daily existence was to close a book before reaching its last page. Even for those in dire worldly straits, she considered suicide not taking arms against a sea of troubles, but a cowardly refusal to face them. Yet to all appearances, Caroline Parrish had made such a choice, a choice Elizabeth believed to be as contrary to Caroline's nature as it was to her own. Whatever faults comprised Mrs. Parrish's character—and they were numerous—weakness was not among them. With a backbone of brass and a core of pure selfishness, Caroline was not likely to give up easily what she believed life owed her. Especially not less than a week into a very advantageous marriage.

"You are pensive this afternoon."

Jane's gentle chide drew her from her reverie. She smiled apologetically, realizing she'd given up all pretense of listening to Jane's discourse. "My thoughts keep straying to your sister-in-law."

"As do mine. I pray this visit to Netherfield proves beneficial for Caroline."

"And short?"

Now it was Jane's turn to look guilty. "I am certain we all wish for a swift recovery."

Elizabeth would have laughed at her sister's equivocation had the subject not been so serious. "She's friend to neither you nor I, but I do believe Darcy gave Bingley sound advice. She's better off here than traveling to America. Such a trip seems imprudent for many reasons, not the least of which are Caroline's own inclinations. I did not want to injure Mr. Parrish's feelings by saying so, but his wife never appeared interested in Mont Joyau even before all this started."

"Those were my impressions as well. And the mere trip here wore her out so—Mr. Parrish says she's been sleeping since we arrived. Poor man! He looks exhausted himself."

They reached a fork in the path and decided upon the branch leading back to the house. "Perhaps Mrs. Parrish will feel up to joining us for dinner, or at least having visitors to her room," Elizabeth said. "I would like to hear her explanation of what happened, though I doubt she'd confide the details to us."

"She won't talk to Charles or Mrs. Hurst about it. Only Mr. Parrish. Who can blame her? How mortifying to have so many people know that one's nerves have frayed to the point of—to . . . to *that* point. It feels indecent even for you and I to discuss it between ourselves."

"Well, someone ought to discuss it, if we are to learn what really happened." Since the family council at the Parrish town-house, no one had said a word about the suicide attempt. The subject was like an elephant in the middle of the parlor; its presence dominated the room but nobody would acknowledge it.

Jane regarded her quizzically. "What do you mean?"

"Has Caroline ever impressed you as a woman with fragile nerves?"

"No. Quite the opposite. But I suppose anyone's inner fortitude can fail under stressful circumstances."

"Yes—circumstances like the death of someone close, or the loss of a family fortune, or some other calamity. But marrying a kind, handsome, rich man at a wedding designed to be the social event of the season? Unless her nerves broke because all her dreams have been realized and she has nothing left to which to aspire, I fail to see a convincing cause for such an extreme action as attempting to take her own life."

"But she was holding the knife when their cook found her in the kitchen."

"All the more reason to question. Would she choose such a painful, violent method of death? Or one so untidy? She would be too conscious of the fact that her body would be found in a stained gown. And to perform the act in the kitchen? I doubt Caroline Bingley Parrish had ever entered a kitchen before in her life. Would she end her existence in one? In a place where she would be discovered not by her husband or even her lady's maid, but one of the lower servants?"

Jane stopped and looked her full in the face. "What are you saying, Lizzy? That both the constable and the surgeon are wrong?"

She had no real answer for Jane. What *was* she saying, after all? Only that the explanations they'd been offered seemed too facile given Caroline's character and her own half-realized perceptions. But of what value were indistinct apprehensions?

"I don't know. Just that it's all very puzzling." The sound of horses drew her attention toward the house. A familiar carriage approached the front gate.

"Lizzy! Jane!" cried the well-known voice from within. "I came as soon as I heard you were here!"

Elizabeth sighed. There would be no enticing Caroline Parrish out of her chamber today. She and Jane fixed smiles on their faces and went to meet the latest arrival.

"Mama!"

"Now, Lizzy, explain this to me again. Why are you and Mr. Darcy not at Pemberley?"

Elizabeth shifted in her chair, unwilling to lie to her mother outright but unable to prevaricate much longer in the interest of saving Caroline Parrish from becoming the subject of what would surely develop into the most rapidly circulating local gossip since Lydia's elopement. Why she cared about Caroline's reputation in the neighborhood, she couldn't say; the new Mrs. Parrish certainly didn't deserve protection among people she'd openly disdained time and again. Perhaps Elizabeth shielded her for Jane and Bingley's sake. Or Mr. Parrish's. She met the gaze of the latter gentleman across the drawing room, where he sat between the Hursts and Professor Randolph. His eyes pleaded for discretion.

Darcy, apparently sensing her discomfort, intervened. "Coming here was my idea. Elizabeth and I will be off to Pemberley soon enough. My sister, in fact, waits for us there."

"Oh, I see." Mrs. Bennet nodded knowingly. "Of course." Darcy's statement had clarified nothing, but her mother held him in such awe that she either didn't notice or didn't dare voice the question a fourth time. "Well, I'm sure you will be quite comfortable here. Netherfield may not be as grand as your own estate, but it is a fine house. And Jane, you are now mistress of it! I'm so happy for you, darling—mistress of

Netherfield! What a fine situation for my daughter!"

Jane smiled self-consciously, clearly embarrassed by her mother's effusions before her new family. "Yes, Mama. But we won't be here forever, remember."

"I know, I know. But that will be still better—an estate of your own! Mr. Bingley, when are you going to stop sitting on your inheritance and purchase a home for my daughter to live in?"

"Quite soon, madam. As soon as we find one we like well enough."

"The Gouldings just quit Haye Park. How perfect that would be, Jane—having you continue to live so close! And in such a large house! You would need a steward for certain. Pemberley has a steward, does it not, Mr. Darcy?"

"It does."

"Mr. Bingley, you must promise to hire a steward for your new estate."

"If it's big enough to warrant one, I will."

"Then you must buy one big enough. You can afford it on your income."

Louisa Hurst muffled a snicker and scanned the room for someone to temporarily fill Caroline's place in the catty coterie they formed whenever Mrs. Bennet was present. Finding no one to share her amusement, she had to settle for playing with her bracelets to demonstrate her superiority above the older woman's conversation. Mr. Hurst, apparently bored, rose and headed for the sherry decanter.

Mr. Parrish, however, was all politeness, listening to Mrs. Bennet with either real or well-feigned interest. "Why, Charles, I thought your talk of purchasing an estate was just a long-cherished dream, not something you intended to act upon presently," Parrish said. "Perhaps we should tour some prospects together . . . once other affairs are settled. Mrs. Bennet, do keep us informed of other houses that become available.

Your knowledge on these matters can aid our search tremendously."

Mrs. Bennet glowed at the compliment. "I will indeed, sir. One hears of so many country houses changing hands these days. It's a sad business—all these reckless gentlemen losing their fortunes by gambling."

The rattle of the sherry decanter drew Elizabeth's notice away from her mother's penetrating social insights. Mr. Hurst had dropped the stopper on the floor. As he stooped to pick it up, his hand shook. She observed him with disgust. Were he not a gentleman, he would be considered a drunkard.

Her mother continued her discourse unabated. "I'm so glad my three married daughters have sensible, respectable husbands. Well, Lydia's husband, Wickham, was perhaps a bit wild before their marriage. But such an agreeable young man, and so handsome! He's in the militia, you know, up in Newcastle, so I haven't seen my Lydia for months now. Lizzy, you should invite them to visit you when you get to Derbyshire."

Elizabeth didn't know which topic of her mother's conversation was more indecorous: the references to Bingley's income or the praise of Lydia's scapegrace spouse. To relieve her own humiliation, she changed the subject entirely. "I believe Papa aspires to come peruse Pemberley's library. How is my father?"

"Oh, the same as ever. I tried to persuade him to come with me today but he would be obstinate and refuse. Said I should give you a few hours at least to get settled before calling. The very idea! That your own mother should have to stand on ceremony when it comes to waiting upon her daughters. He says such things just to vex me, I'm certain. What that man does to my poor nerves! So you and Jane will have to come to Longbourn tomorrow to see your father if you don't want to wait for him to get round to calling here.

Bring your husbands, and we'll have a family dinner. Oh—I suppose we're all family now, aren't we? Why don't you all come? Mrs. Parrish, too. Where is she, by the way? I want to wish her joy."

"I thank you."

All turned toward the doorway at the sound of Caroline's voice. The speaker ignored their looks of surprise and ambled to the nearest unoccupied chair, upon which she seated herself with her usual grace and smoothed the skirt of her silk dress. The dark green lace-trimmed gown was too elaborate for the informal afternoon gathering, an uncharacteristic faux pas. Elizabeth suspected the costume's chief endorsement lay in the matching spencer that hid Caroline's wrist bandages from view.

Mr. Parrish crossed to her immediately and raised her hand to his lips. "My dear, how delightful that you could join us. I didn't expect to see you this afternoon."

"I grew weary of my chamber's four walls." A small ringlet escaped her otherwise perfectly coifed hair; she withdrew her hand from her husband's to tuck the wayward strands behind her ear. Her wedding ring caught a ray of sunlight, momentarily splaying prismatic beams onto the far wall. "I didn't realize we had company."

Louisa smirked. "Mrs. Bennet has just invited us all to dine at Longbourn tomorrow." Glee flashed across her countenance as she anticipated a clever barb in response.

"Indeed?" She turned to Mrs. Bennet with a face that reflected naught but sincerity. "I thank you for my share of the invitation, but I'm afraid I feel a trifle indisposed of late and must decline." Amazingly, no hint of sarcasm tinged her words.

Louisa poorly masked her disappointment, fixing her mouth in a false smile. "I thank you as well, but if Caroline cannot go, my place, of course, is with my sister."

"Of course." Mrs. Bennet appeared less than distraught at being relieved of entertaining the extended Bingley clan. "Perhaps another time."

"I look forward to it." Again, Caroline's demeanor gave every indication that she actually meant the words. Whatever the woman's other problems, recent events seemed to have softened the sharper edges of her manner.

Jane rang for tea. At her summons, two housemaids appeared almost instantly, bearing trays laden with china cups and demitasse spoons, milk, sugar, tarts, macaroons, petit fours, crumpets—everything but tea. When Jane gently drew their attention to the omission, they nearly knocked each other down in their rush to retrieve the forgotten beverage.

"They're new," Jane said apologetically. "Sisters. Neither of them has any experience, but they just lost their father and needed the work. They're very eager to learn. I'm sure once they've been here a little while . . ."

Mrs. Hurst rolled her eyes.

"Now, Jane," said Mrs. Bennet, "mind you keep a close rein on those servants or they'll take advantage of your generous heart."

Mr. Hurst, muttering something about it being a shame to let the crumpets go cold while they waited, ambled over to the trays. "What's this? They also forgot butter knives! Hmmph! Well—no matter." Not to be detained any longer, he pulled out a pocketknife and proceeded to slather butter over two crumpets.

The maids returned, each with a teapot. They served the tea, then waited on the party so attentively that barely could anyone sip a drop without one of the girls warming the cup with more. The minute anyone finished a tart or other treat, the plate appeared at his or her elbow for another. Mrs. Hurst found the excessive courtesy irksome; Jane seemed embarrassed. The rest of the company looked upon it with mild amusement, except for Mr. Hurst, who was simply pleased to be able to so thoroughly indulge his fondness for petit fours at so little trouble to himself. Mrs. Parrish appeared insensible to the spectacle, eating lightly and saying little.

The conversation meandered through the usual polite talk. Mrs. Bennet dominated it, with the Bingley sisters nodding encouragement but contributing rarely. Louisa played with her bracelets, while Caroline repeatedly spun her new wedding ring around her finger and occasionally slid it up as far as her first knuckle. Elizabeth wondered if she was trying to draw attention to the ostentatious ornament or merely enjoying its novelty.

Once the weather had been thoroughly discussed—it was eventually decided that snow would indeed fall again before Christmas—Mrs. Bennet delineated the movements and activities of everyone in the neighborhood during the past fortnight, most particularly what all their acquaintance had said about the Bennet double wedding. Mrs. Whitingford had declared it the loveliest ceremony she'd ever had the pleasure of attending, while Mrs. Farringdale had expressed the hope that her own daughter would someday marry so well. The latter sentiment did more to placate Mrs. Bennet's indignity over a past perceived insult to Jane than five years of apologies ever had.

"Ha! Who's on the shelf now, I ask you? That milk-and-water miss never could hold a candle to you, Jane, and now her mother realizes it and don't know what to do with the girl."

"Miss Farringdale is perfectly pleasant, Mama," Jane said, ever charitable in her defense of their sex.

"Hmmph. The only thing that could improve that young lady's disposition is a larger dowry. Mrs. Parrish, I believe you've met her. Do you not agree?"

Caroline, though she had appeared to follow the conversation, stirred as if awakened from a light slumber. "I'm—I'm sorry?" She blinked twice. "Of whom do we speak?"

"Miss Farringdale. You know, that insipid girl with the pale complexion who—"

"I am sure your assessment is accurate." Caroline raised a hand to her temple. "Forgive me. I suddenly have a headache."

Parrish was at her side in an instant. "I'll help you back to our room. You never should have left it, my dear. You need your rest."

"You are right." She rose and leaned heavily on her husband's arm. "It was good to see you, Mrs. Bennet. Excuse my hasty departure. I wish you all a good evening."

Elizabeth stared after her. *It was good to see you?* Caroline must have hit her head when she fell to the kitchen floor.

Eleven

> "I did not know before," continued Bingley immediately,
> "that you were a studier of character. It must be an amusing
> study."
> "Yes, but intricate characters are the most amusing."
> Mr. Bingley and Elizabeth, Pride and Prejudice, *Chapter 9*

*L*ate afternoon sunlight lanced through the conservatory
windows, enveloping Elizabeth in its warmth. She
basked in the sensation, having missed the feel of the sun on
her skin during her time in London. She suspected, with the
air growing colder as each day of December passed, that the
greenhouse would quickly become one of her favorite rooms
during her stay at Netherfield.

One of the properties she most appreciated about the hot-
house was its fragrance. The conservatory served as a permanent home for exotic plants, a winter shelter for less hardy
cultivars, and a nursery for seedlings awaiting spring planting. One corner hosted a small potted herb garden that
enabled the cook to use fresh flavoring for winter cooking
rather than relying on dried herbs—a treat that a previous
tenant had implemented and Bingley's staff had continued.
The resulting blend of aromas created a heady perfume that
she inhaled deeply.

Long shadows stretched across the floor; the first day of

their Netherfield sojourn was ending. She wondered how many more would pass until she and Darcy could leave, but was determined to make the best of this visit while it lasted.

She wandered through the room, admiring a collection of tropical flowers. Bingley's head gardener was a gifted grower—no wonder he was so frustrated with his inexperienced new assistants. As she passed a group of tall plants with particularly thick foliage, she sighted Professor Randolph at the end of the conservatory.

He stood just beyond a cluster of rue, so engrossed in snipping some bright green leaves off a plant in the herb garden that he did not look up until she greeted him.

"Oh! Mrs. Darcy!" He pushed up his spectacles, almost wounding himself with the small pocketknife in his hand. "I didn't hear you approach."

"I am sorry to disturb you."

"Nonsense! Nonsense!" He folded up the knife and slid it into his trouser pocket. "I was just gathering some spearmint leaves for Mrs. Parrish."

"I wasn't aware she had a partiality for mint. Perhaps Jane should inform the cook."

He withdrew a handkerchief from one of his breast pockets and carefully folded the leaves inside. "Hmm? Oh—it's not for her to eat. It's for her to smell. I thought it might aid her recovery—many believe the scent sharpens mental powers."

"Really? I had no idea it possesses medicinal properties."

He tucked the handkerchief back into his pocket. "A little bit medicine, a little bit magic."

"Magic—you mean luck?"

He shrugged. "Many of these plants are more powerful than you might imagine in the hands of an adept herbalist."

"Another specialty of yours?"

"No, no. I'm just a dabbler myself. As an archeologist, most of my knowledge is of things long dead."

"Well, I am sure Mr. Parrish appreciates your help with his wife. Have you had much opportunity to observe her yet?"

"A little. She has demonstrated reluctance to converse with me, and won't discuss her injuries at all. Mr. Parrish's presence seems to encourage her cooperation, however."

"She is fortunate in his devotion." The sun dropped behind the horizon, casting the room in dusky twilight. She shivered, suddenly chilled.

Randolph glanced out the windows, into the darkening night. "The days are growing short. Winter solstice is next week."

"So is Christmas."

Her statement received no response. Having fallen into a reverie, he stared at the waxing moon that had already started to rise.

"Professor?"

He shook himself. "Pardon me? Oh, yes—Christmas. We all certainly look forward to that."

She soon left him in the conservatory and went to dress for dinner, contemplating his casual remark about herbal magic and his greater awareness of the winter solstice than Christmas. She was beginning to consider Professor Randolph one of the most intriguing members of her acquaintance.

"What do you read, Mrs. Darcy?"

"*The Italian.*" With little reluctance, Elizabeth closed the volume and set it aside to grant Mr. Parrish her full attention. Between her own scattered thoughts and the light conversation of others in the drawing room, she'd had trouble concentrating on the book and had persevered only to have some occupation from which she could easily withdraw when Darcy was ready to retire for the evening.

"Ah! A fellow admirer of Mrs. Radcliffe." Parrish grinned

and seated himself on the other end of the sofa. "I thought I was alone in that guilty pleasure among this company."

She glanced round the room. Randolph and Parrish had just abandoned the card table, where the Hursts, Jane, and Bingley still played loo. Darcy sat at the desk penning a letter to Georgiana. A sense of déjà vu seized her as she recalled a similar scene from her first visit to Netherfield, only this time Caroline was not present to laud Darcy on the speed of his writing and evenness of his lines. The lady in question had not left her chamber since her afternoon headache came on, but now, according to her husband, at least slept peacefully.

"Why do you say so?" she asked. "Because no one else is presently reading?"

"Two reasons. First, I thought my partiality outdated—Mrs. Radcliffe has not published a new novel for some years. I wonder that you have not read this one before now."

"Oh, I have. I chose it because it is an old favorite."

Parrish picked up the volume. As he thumbed the pages, she noticed the ring on the fourth finger of his left hand. Similar in style to Caroline's, the wedding band lacked gems, but its engraved sunburst detail marked it as a companion piece. Her chest tightened at the sight of it—a reaction, she supposed, to the strong attachment it symbolized. Double-ring wedding ceremonies were rare. The display of loyalty was especially moving in the face of such early and unexpected marital challenges.

"Elizabeth is too kind in her excuses," Bingley called from the card table. "She rereads the book because my library lacks many alternatives. I apologize, my new sister, for not yet amending that deficiency."

Darcy blotted his paper. "Such endeavors take time to carry out properly, Bingley. First find your family a permanent home. Then start collecting books to fill it."

"Again the subject of an estate arises! It seems none of

my friends will rest until Jane and I quit Netherfield."

"It's not every day a man gets to spend a fortune," Parrish said. "Perhaps they want to experience the thrill vicariously. Or they can't stand the thought of all that money just lying around."

"Well, it's in the five percents, so it's hardly just lying around. But I do realize land would make a better investment. Now that my mother-in-law and closest friend are in collusion—an event I thought I'd never see—I'll quickly indulge their hopes as well as my own. Jane, shall we visit Haye Park tomorrow on our way to Longbourn?"

Jane expressed delight at the prospect. Elizabeth mused that Haye Park might prove a little too close to their mother, but kept the thought to herself. Instead, she returned to the book discussion.

"You said you had two reasons for surprise at our shared enjoyment of Mrs. Radcliffe's novels. What is the other?"

"I feared my tastes unrefined. Novels are entertaining but hardly hold the intellectual weight of poetry."

Professor Randolph took a chair beside the fire. "There is nothing wrong with reading simply for pleasure." He leaned back and stretched out his legs.

"I agree," said Darcy, "though Mrs. Radcliffe and her imitators do give 'pleasure' a curious form. Readers come to their novels *wanting* to be scared, wanting to lie awake at night wondering what that noise was on the other side of their own doors."

"Nonsense, all of it," Mrs. Hurst declared. "An utter waste of time."

Elizabeth, despite the reverence in which she held Mrs. Hurst as an authority on the meaningful employment of one's time, forbore enquiring whether it was gothic romances in particular or reading altogether that she held in disdain. "Professor, do the tales have any merit, in your estimation? I speak not of literary merit, but credibility. Of course they are works of imagination, but . . ."

"But could supernatural events really occur in our world? Right here, in King George's England?" Randolph chuckled softly. "They do every day, dear lady. But most people look right past them, seeing only what they want to see, believing only what they wish to be true. Even for those who delight in stories like Mrs. Radcliffe's, the otherworldly must always be a foreign thing, something that happens somewhere far removed from one's present place or time."

"To think otherwise causes one too much discomfort?"

"Precisely. So they block their own awareness and use science to explain anything impossible to ignore. Educated people, at least. Reason has become the new god among the upper classes. Your lower classes, your unrefined societies, these are far more likely to accept the presence of the preternatural in their daily lives—to believe in miracles, or ghosts, or magic."

Darcy stopped writing in midstroke. "Oh, come now. When one of my tenants tells me his neighbor has cursed his cattle, am I to accept this accusation as the cause of his animals dying? Is it not more likely that some disease has stricken them?"

"Whence does the disease derive? And why has it stricken only his herd and not those of other farmers?" Randolph shrugged. "It may indeed have occurred naturally. I merely point out that it's your illiterate tenant who considers more explanations than you do."

"But your 'mysterious articles,' at the museum," Elizabeth said. "Some looked quite valuable, like they were created by or for people of great means."

"Indeed, they were. Most of them date back to times when belief in magic was more common and embraced by wealthy and poor alike. The more recent items belonged to exceptional individuals attuned to the presence of the extraordinary in our world."

"In other words, modern people who still believe in hexes and sorcery?" Darcy asked.

"You say that in a tone laced with ridicule. But I have seen enough evidence of such things that I cannot deny their existence. Why, just last month, an aristocratic lady of whom you have all heard, but whose identity I shall protect, pointed out to me the unusual cornerstone of her country house. Inscribed beneath the date were some Latin phrases. The lady told me that according to family legend, the mansion had been built on land that had once been a druid grove. Romans seized it, razed the trees, and erected a fortification on the site. Within a year of its completion, every occupant was dead of a mysterious fever. More soldiers came. They, too, died, and the fortress was abandoned. The elements wore it down, but in Henry the Sixth's time a new manor was raised. Fever plagued its occupants for decades, claiming heirs one by one. The family, in danger of its lineage ending, leveled the building.

"Again, the site lay unused for many years, but eventually the land passed to a younger son who wanted to develop the property. He constructed the residence that stands there today and, with the help of a local wisewoman, inscribed and laid the cornerstone himself. At the time I spoke with the current mistress, the house seemed to have escaped the doom of its predecessors. No fever had troubled the family for five generations.

"She and her husband, however, were improving their estate and the stone was part of a wall scheduled to be removed. 'Revise your plans,' I urged her. 'Don't disturb the cornerstone. Those words are a charm—the stone protects the occupants of this house.' She didn't heed my advice, and within a week of its removal her eldest son took to bed with a putrid fever. The stone was quickly set back in place, and he recovered."

"This, you call evidence?" Darcy folded his letter. "I call it coincidence. Certainly not the result of some old druid's spell."

"Not a spell, necessarily. While it's possible that the druids themselves laid a curse, it also may be that the Romans incurred the wrath of higher powers to whom the grove had been consecrated."

A prickling sensation danced across the back of Elizabeth's neck. She couldn't decide whether Randolph was the most insightful or most insane person she'd ever met. "It does seem odd that so many people succumbed to fever, over so many years, in the same place."

"Not at all," Darcy said. "People die of fever all the time. Next the professor will tell us that the Black Death was caused by someone picking flowers in a faerie glen." He passed wax over the candle flame until it softened, and sealed his note. "With all due respect to you and your studies, Randolph, I remain unconvinced."

Randolph half-smiled. "Most people do. 'Tis my lot in life, it seems, to stand accused of tilting at windmills."

Parrish, who'd been following the discussion closely, cast a look of apology at his friend. "I'm afraid I have to side with Mr. Darcy. Much as I enjoy a good story, tales of spells and spirits are really just flights of fancy." He handed Elizabeth's book back to her.

She accepted the volume in puzzlement. Of all the people in the room, she'd expected Parrish to come to Randolph's defense. "I thought you were a patron of the professor's work?"

"I am. Magic so permeates life in New Orleans, from slave *vodun* to high society séances, that one can't help but take at least a passing interest in it. But Randolph's studies appeal to me for their entertainment value, not for any practical purpose. I don't believe the artifacts themselves hold any power. Rather, I'm intrigued by their histories. I support his work for the same reason I buy Mrs. Radcliffe's books—amusement."

Poor Professor Randolph—surrounded by skepticism from all quarters! Elizabeth quite felt for the man. She regretted having told Darcy earlier this evening about her encounter with Randolph in the conservatory, sure that the conversation she'd repeated had further prejudiced her husband against the archeologist.

Randolph fished in his waistcoat pocket and withdrew his pocketwatch. The star symbol on the outside caught the fire-light as he clicked it open to consult the time. Remembering the runes inscribed within, Elizabeth longed to ask him about them further. But she held her tongue, not wishing to expose him to additional ridicule from their present company.

Bingley also seemed to take compassion on the professor. "Darcy, I wouldn't cling to my cynicism so stubbornly for all the world," he declared. "In fact, I've half a mind to ask Randolph here to inspect my new estate for evidence of curses and charms before I commit to its purchase."

"If he actually discovers any, then I will have him to Pemberley for the same."

Twelve

"You either chuse this method of passing the evening because you are in each other's confidence and have secret affairs to discuss, or because you are conscious that your figures appear to the greatest advantage in walking."

Darcy to Elizabeth and Miss Bingley,
Pride and Prejudice, *Chapter 11*

Elizabeth stared at the oak beams above her head, willing herself to fall asleep before the clock struck another hour. Slumber eluded her tonight, though she could not identify why. Darcy, his arm wrapped around her possessively, dozed beside her, oblivious to the insomnia that plagued her.

The sound of footsteps in the hall caught her ears. 'Twas late for even servants to be about. The light steps passed her door, then seemed to backtrack and pass again. Curious, she disentangled herself from Darcy's embrace and slipped on her dressing gown. She padded to the door, eased it open, and peeked out.

Caroline Parrish paced the hall. She was oddly dressed—wearing nightclothes, but with the addition of shoes and a spencer. Insensible to Elizabeth's observation, she approached her own door, stopped short, then retreated toward the central staircase. Three times she repeated the ritual before pity moved Elizabeth to intercede.

"Mrs. Parrish," she whispered, stepping into the hall and

closing her own door behind her so as not to disturb Darcy. "Are you all right?"

Caroline halted midstride and regarded Elizabeth uncertainly, as if trying to identify her. Though candles in sconces lent the hall but dim light, the two women stood within a few feet of each other—close enough that Elizabeth could discern several black smudges on Caroline's nightdress. At that proximity, Elizabeth should have been instantly recognizable to Caroline.

"Mrs. Parrish? It's me, Elizabeth Darcy. Do you need something?"

Caroline simply stared.

"Mrs. Parrish?"

Caroline did not even blink. Indeed, she seemed even more dazed than when Elizabeth and Darcy had found her wandering Bow Street. Was she sleepwalking? Perhaps she had become disoriented and was unsure which door was hers.

"Come." Elizabeth beckoned. "Let's return to your chamber."

She took Caroline by the hand, noting that her usually well-manicured fingernails were broken and dirty—another sign of the toll her illness had taken upon her. What was happening to this woman? The Caroline Bingley that Elizabeth had known just a week ago would have meticulously maintained even the smallest aspect of her appearance till her dying breath.

Mrs. Parrish allowed herself to be led like a child to her room. When Elizabeth knocked softly on the door, Caroline grasped her arm tightly. The strength of the grip surprised her.

"It's all right," Elizabeth said. "This is your chamber."

The door opened. Mr. Parrish was dressed in his shirtsleeves. "There you— Mrs. Darcy!" The startled gentleman quickly recovered himself. He glanced at his wife, then back to Elizabeth. "Forgive me—I did not expect to find you at my door at so late an hour."

"I discovered Mrs. Parrish wandering in the hallway."

"Darling, I was just coming to look for you." Parrish took both Caroline's hands in his and drew her into the chamber. "Have you been sleepwalking again?"

Caroline nodded vaguely.

"She may be yet," Elizabeth said. "She hasn't spoken a word to me."

"Well, she's safe now." Parrish studied his wife a moment, anxiety stealing into his gaze. He then half-closed the door so that Caroline could not overhear them. "I can see that even here at Netherfield I need to keep a closer eye on her. Thank you, Mrs. Darcy."

She left the unfortunate couple to themselves and returned to her own bed. Darcy rolled over and spooned against her. "Where did you go?"

"Mrs. Parrish was sleepwalking again."

"Is she all right?"

"I believe so."

His arm tightened around her. "You seem to have become her guardian angel."

She would have laughed at the irony, were the situation not so serious. Caretaker of Caroline—what had she done to deserve that?

Grey clouds hung heavy in the sky, cloaking the landscape in shadow. Bare trees, some scantily clad in tattered leaves tenaciously clinging to their branches, stood as forlorn sentinels along the roadside, while brown patches of dead grass poked through a thin blanket of snow like strands of hair straying through a moth-eaten wool cap.

Elizabeth tucked her lap blanket around her knees and rested her boots atop the hot brick on the carriage floor, grateful for the warmth that crept into her toes. The three-mile ride to her parents' house seemed long this bleak afternoon, though whether because of her mood or the scenery, she couldn't say. She leaned back, impatient for their trip to end, depressed that familiar landmarks indicated they'd traveled less than a mile.

Bingley and Jane had set out earlier to tour Haye Park, leaving her and Darcy to follow in their own coach and meet them at Longbourn. Darcy had proven a quiet companion on the journey, no doubt overwhelmed with delight at the prospect of spending a full afternoon conversing with her mother. Perhaps she would take pity on him and suggest an after-dinner walk to interrupt the visit. Or perhaps not. She remained a bit vexed with him for last night's discussion with Professor Randolph.

Darcy was Darcy—logical to the very center of his being, firmly rooted in reality—and she wouldn't change him for anything. He'd had to grow up more quickly than she, losing his mother as a boy and his father as a young man barely past his majority. Such a childhood left little time for imaginative play, as he prepared to take on the responsibilities of a great estate and those who depended upon it for their livelihoods. While he respected her mind, he had the advantage of her in education, having studied with private tutors and later taking a degree at Cambridge. As a male, he moved in a world to which she had no access—a world of business and solicitors and politics and law. All of these things made him the man he was, the man she'd chosen to wed. She trusted him to make wise decisions, to know the right answers at times when she did not.

On most matters.

But, God bless him, must he always be so very sure of himself? Must the truth as he saw it and The Truth invariably be one and the same?

"You were unkind to Professor Randolph last night."

His face registered surprise at the admonishment. "How so?"

"You dismissed his work as silly in a roomful of people who are practically strangers to him."

"Am I to pretend belief in the ridiculous?"

"No. But we're surrounded by ridiculous people. Most of the *ton* lead ridiculous, useless lives spent in dissipation and selfish pursuits. Just look at some of the people right there in the drawing room with us. Has Mr. Hurst ever exerted himself beyond running trump in a game of whist? He is fortunate to have been born a gentleman, because I don't think the man could survive if he ever had to support himself. Yet we tolerate him, and others like him, because he has money and social standing. At least Randolph spends his time seeking to understand something beyond himself."

"Perhaps I spoke too strongly—I did not mean to make him uncomfortable. However, if his studies are legitimate, he should be able to defend them without considering the debate a personal attack."

"Darcy, sometimes your manner lends the air of a personal attack to an observation on the weather. You can be very intimidating, you know, especially to strangers." Not wishing to upbraid him too severely, she lightened her tone. "Though, of course, you never frightened me."

"Does anything?"

She pondered the question a moment as the carriage turned at a bend in the road. "The thought of someone close to me suffering injury. And you?"

He was equally reflective. "The same. Or losing my mental faculties, like we fear Mrs. Parrish may be in the way of. I sincerely hope the professor's efforts prove beneficial in that regard."

"See—even you think some part of his knowledge holds merit."

He shrugged. "I have more faith in folk medicine than in folklore. If he wishes to perfume her with spearmint, I do not see the harm." He smiled. "Though I believe Mrs. Parrish prefers French scents."

"Enough of Mrs. Parrish. Though I pity her circumstances, I look forward to a day spent free of her." Beyond her own wish to escape Caroline's presence for a time, Elizabeth took comfort in the small size of today's party, as it meant her mother would have only Darcy and Mr. Bingley to whom to expose herself.

"But you and Mrs. Parrish have become such intimate friends, strolling Netherfield's halls during the night."

"Oh, yes," she said dryly. "If our acquaintance continues to warm so quickly, we'll be using Christian names by this afternoon."

"Pray, what bosom confidences have you lately exchanged?"

"She has related to me every particular of Mr. Parrish's assets."

His brows rose. "Indeed? And what have you told her in turn?"

"That you snore."

They passed a few more minutes in light conversation before the coach suddenly slowed. "Sir?" their driver called from without. "I think you'll want to take a look ahead."

Darcy stuck his head out the window to peer down the road. Elizabeth's heartbeat accelerated as their vehicle came to a halt altogether. "What is it?" she asked.

He brought his head back in and looked at her. His face had drained of color. "Bingley's carriage overturned."

Thirteen

"Nothing therefore remained to be done but to . . . throw
into the account of accident or mistake whatever could not be
otherwise explained."

Pride and Prejudice, *Chapter 17*

A sickening sensation overwhelmed Elizabeth at the
sight of the mangled carriage. Though Darcy commanded her to stay back while he checked inside for Jane and
Bingley, her legs shook so badly she could not have approached
anyway. She at once couldn't bear to look, and couldn't bear *not*
to look, at the splintered wood and twisted metal wrapped
around a large tree. So her gaze ricocheted from the barouche
to the surrounding terrain as she swallowed bile and took deep
breaths of cold air, struggling to block out the smell of blood
and the pained screams of writhing horses.

Their driver grasped her elbow to steady her and suggested
she return to their own coach. She refused. "Go assist Mr.
Darcy." Jane and Bingley needed his help more than she did.
She hoped.

"They are not inside." Darcy quickly cast his gaze around
the accident site. "Over there! They must have been thrown
from the carriage."

Jane and Bingley lay near a copse of tall evergreen trees, the lowest branches having obscured sight of them from the road. They were alive—unconscious and cold, but alive. Elizabeth blinked back tears of relief at the discovery. Bingley's driver, crushed beneath the wreckage, had not been as fortunate.

"Jane? Jane?" She grasped her sister's hand, willing her to awaken.

Jane stirred. Without opening her eyes, she slowly lifted a palm to her crown. "My head . . ."

"Hush, dear Jane. It's all right." She choked down a sob. "You're going to be all right."

Darcy roused Bingley, who also complained of a headache. Otherwise, though battered and bruised, the couple appeared to have escaped serious injury. Elizabeth and Darcy assisted them into the coach while their driver attended Bingley's driver and horses. The unfortunate servant he discreetly wrapped in a blanket and secured to the back of the coach. One of the animals suffered two fractured legs and had to be shot; the other three appeared frightened but unharmed once disentangled from their harnesses.

Jane shivered, prompting Darcy to remove his mantle and drape it over her shoulders. She huddled into it. "I feel as if I'll never be warm again."

"We will get you home as quickly as possible," Darcy said. "Others can come back and see to the wreckage. Was there anything in the carriage we should retrieve before leaving?"

"Perhaps Jane's reticule," Bingley said.

Jane shook her head. "It holds nothing that seems of any value to me right now. Let us please just leave this place."

"We shall." Darcy looked out the window. "My driver has almost finished securing your team to our coach."

"What of our driver?"

Darcy hesitated. Bingley had already been told the servant's fate, but Jane had not. His silence proved answer enough.

"Poor man." Jane's face, already ashen, somehow lost still more color. Elizabeth knew her sister felt responsible for the death simply because it occurred on a journey undertaken for her pleasure. "What a dreadful way to die. I hope he did not suffer."

"It appears he died quickly," Darcy said.

"He was in our employ only a fortnight. His mother is a widow—he was supporting her. I shall have to write her with the awful news. Charles, we must send her something."

"Of course." Bingley dabbed at a scrape on his forehead.

Elizabeth approved of the gift; she would have done the same thing. But how had the horrible event occurred in the first place? "Can either of you tell us what happened?"

"I think we lost a wheel," Bingley replied. "Since Jane and I were within the barouche, we couldn't see exactly what occurred. The carriage must have hit a rock or something in the road because it suddenly shifted. The disturbance spooked the horses. They took off in a gallop—or as close to one as they could come with the carriage careening behind them. The next thing we knew, we were rolling over."

"That's when we hit the tree," Jane finished. "And that's the last I remember."

Elizabeth again expressed gratitude that the couple had survived the ordeal relatively unscathed. Darcy echoed her sentiments, then left to speak with their driver.

"I noticed some wild-looking tracks maybe a hundred yards back, sir," Elizabeth heard the servant say. "I didn't see a wheel along the road, but I wasn't looking for one, either."

Her husband's footsteps retreated and soon faded beneath the sounds of the driver finishing with the horses. Above, grey clouds thickened with the threat of more snow, and an icy gust of wind flapped the coach's window curtain. Jane coughed and burrowed into the borrowed mantle. Bingley suppressed a shiver, leading Elizabeth to insist he take her lap blanket, which he'd refused previously. They needed to get Jane and Bingley warm and comfortably resting.

Whatever was Darcy doing out there?

Darcy followed the erratic wheel tracks to their source, wanting to see for himself the object that had caused Bingley's carriage to lose a wheel. They proved difficult to discern, despite their aberrant appearance compared to the straighter lines striping the path. Hoofprints and grooves from his own coach, and others that had preceded Bingley's, obscured the marks, which had not been deep in the cold earth. The light dusting of snow covering the surrounding ground had melted on the highway under the weight of traffic.

Rocks and other obstacles in the road were no unusual thing for this thoroughfare or any other. Dips and ruts pocked the lane; stones, pinecones, and twigs studded it. But an observant driver should have spotted and tried to avoid an object large enough to damage the carriage. The failure of Bingley's driver to do so earned him a share of responsibility for the accident—a large enough share that he, Darcy, hoped it would mitigate the guilt his new sister-in-law clearly felt over the man's death. So, though aware of the necessity of haste in returning to Netherfield, he'd stolen these few minutes to seek proof of the driver's own carelessness before additional travel on the road obliterated the evidence altogether. The peace of mind it afforded his friends would advance their recovery as much as any surgeon's visit.

He reached the point where the crooked grooves gave way to straight. No obvious instrument of destruction presented itself. A few larger stones littered the path, but none substantial enough to wrench a properly secured wheel from its axle.

He shook his head in disgust. Bingley's coachman must

have practiced sloppy maintenance in addition to inattentive driving. The couple's practice of hiring help based on need rather than competence had nearly cost them their own lives.

The wheel he found several yards away, having flown from the force of its removal. He left the heavy part where it had landed and returned to his own coach with long, quick strides. He'd seen enough.

A light snow had started to fall by the time the party returned to Netherfield. A coach with an unfamiliar crest stood in front of the house, but Elizabeth barely spared it a glance in her haste to call assistance for Jane and Bingley. She entered the hall to find Mr. Parrish descending the staircase.

"Mrs. Darcy! I thought you were all gone to Longbourn?"

"There has been an accident—Mr. Bingley's carriage overturned."

He took the remaining steps two at a time. "I hope he and Jane weren't injured?"

"Not seriously. At least, I don't believe so. But they need help coming in the house. If you could find a footman—"

"Only lead the way, and I'll aid them myself. We should send for a surgeon. Do you have one in the neighborhood?"

"An apothecary. Mr. Jones."

"You," he addressed the parlor maid who had suddenly materialized at Elizabeth's announcement of the accident. "See that Mr. Jones is summoned immediately."

Parrish accompanied Elizabeth outside. The snow was falling faster now, great, heavy flakes that stuck where they landed despite the wind. A blanket of white already covered the drive and steps.

Darcy and his driver had helped the couple out of the coach. Jane leaned heavily on Darcy's arm, Bingley on the servant's. Darcy's face bore an annoyed expression that

Elizabeth attributed to the snowflakes pelting him.

Parrish loped down the great stone steps. "Forgive my manners, Mrs. Bingley, if I violate propriety. But I cannot stand on ceremony when I see a lady in need. Will you allow me to carry you into the house to save you further exertion?" He looked to Bingley. "With your husband's permission, of course?"

"Please—if Jane does not mind. Get her out of this weather. I wish I could carry her myself."

Parrish regarded Jane expectantly. She nodded her assent. He lifted her easily, her slight frame scarcely encumbering his strong arms. As if bearing no more than a doll, he whisked her up the steps and into the hall.

By this time, Mrs. Hurst awaited them. Behind her, doing their best to appear unobtrusive, several other servants had congregated in the corner.

"What is all the commotion?" Louisa demanded. Upon sight of Jane, she looked beyond the door. "What has happened? Where is my brother?"

"They suffered a carriage accident," Parrish said as Bingley straggled in. Darcy, his gaze darting about the hall as if seeking something, braced him with a hand at his elbow.

"Gracious! Charles, are you all right?" She darted toward Bingley, brushing against Parrish hard enough to displace his footing. He maintained both his balance and a firm grip on Jane.

Mrs. Hurst's behavior made Elizabeth all the more grateful for Parrish's genuine solicitude toward her sister. Even as he stood waiting for Louisa to complete her effusions over Bingley, his face betrayed no sign of impatience or physical strain at the continued burden of supporting Jane. Clearly, she was in good hands, not to mention strong arms.

Elizabeth looked round for Mr. Hurst, hoping he might call off his wife so Jane and Bingley could proceed to their chamber and get on with the business of recovering. That gentleman, however, remained absent. Apparently, news of the accident—by now in general circulation throughout the house, judging from the number of servants who had suddenly found chores urgently requiring their presence in the entry hall—had proven unable to rouse his interest, or at least his person, from whatever critical occupation presently engaged him.

A glance upward, however, revealed a face. Caroline Parrish stood on the balcony two stories above. Her countenance, though difficult to read at this distance in the grey light slanting though the windows, displayed agitation. She wrung her hands, working her wedding ring up and down her finger, as she observed the scene below. She yet wore nightclothes, though they had changed from the plain white shift of the night before to a lacy gown that fluttered in the wind sneaking through the open front door. The updraft also caught her unbound dark hair, tousling it about her shoulders.

"I heard the carriage draw up at least ten minutes ago," barked a bellicose male voice from the drawing room. "How long am I to be kept waiting?"

With a start, Elizabeth recalled the strange coach outside. She searched her memory until she recognized the tones. They belonged to Mr. Lawrence Kendall, Juliet's father.

"As I said, sir, Mr. Bingley will receive you at his first opportunity," the housekeeper replied.

Bingley, who'd been about to ascend the stairs, paused as he listened to the exchange. His fingers tightened around the newel post. He suddenly looked even more exhausted than before.

Parrish stared at the drawing room door, looking for all the world like he'd just as soon avoid Kendall himself. Recalling Juliet's resentment, Elizabeth was unsurprised that Parrish would wish to dodge the man who might have become his father-in-law. He carried Jane toward the steps. "Let's get you upstairs."

"Please wait a moment," Jane said, her gaze on Bingley.

Kendall's voice again issued from the drawing room. "You

told me he was not expected home until after dinner. Is he deliberately avoiding me?"

"He's back early, and I've been in here attending you the whole while. I'll inform him directly that you are come."

"Do that."

Mrs. Nicholls emerged looking like she'd just been released from Newgate.

"Nicholls, is that Mr. Kendall?" Bingley asked.

"Wishes to see you on a business matter, sir." The house-keeper spoke slowly as she took in the crowded hall, her master's disheveled appearance, her mistress aloft in Parrish's arms. A look of reprimand dispersed the lower servants. "I told him you was gone for the day, but he insisted on waiting."

Bingley released a deep sigh. "Show him to the library. Then devote your attention to Mrs. Bingley's comfort."

Darcy motioned for him to continue up the steps. "You need not subject yourself to his tiresome claims right now. I will greet him on your behalf and advise him to postpone his visit until a more favorable time. Or better still—to conduct all further business through your solicitors."

Bingley shook his head and embarked on a slow shuffle across the hall. He favored his right leg. "Thank you, but you know nothing short of an audience with me will appease him. I'd best conclude the unpleasantness as quickly as possible." He stopped. "I would not object to your company, however."

"Of course."

"Charles?" Anxiety clouded Jane's features. "Please—will you interrupt your interview when Mr. Jones arrives so he can examine you?"

"As soon as he has attended you, my dear."

The response seemed to appease her. Parrish mounted the staircase, with Elizabeth close behind. Her gaze lifted once more to the balcony.

Caroline was gone.

Fourteen

"Bingley has great natural modesty, with a stronger dependence on my judgment than on his own."
Darcy, writing to Elizabeth, Pride and Prejudice, Chapter 35

$\mathscr{D}$arcy had harbored no intention of letting Bingley enter the library alone. His friend had trouble resisting Kendall's aggressiveness on a good day; he was presently in no state to deal with the man.

Though at the moment fatigue and pain robbed Bingley of his usual easy demeanor, the accident had rendered his appearance even less formidable. His undone cravat hung loosely about his neck; dirt streaked his white shirt; wet patches darkened his blue coat; his trousers bore several long tears. The scrape on his forehead had started to bruise, and half-melted snow yet coated his hair.

"Do you not at least wish to change your attire?"

Bingley glanced at his clothes and grimaced. "Truly, Darcy, if I climb those stairs, I don't think I possess the vigor to come back down. Perhaps my state will convince Kendall that he arrives at a poor time to discuss business."

Or encourage him to press his advantage. Darcy handed his hat to a tarrying servant and stopped before the hall mirror to restore his own appearance. He brushed the snow from his shoulders and re-laid the folds of his cravat. Then he mentally braced himself for the encounter ahead.

The ill-mannered gentleman paced the library, the change of rooms having done nothing to improve his mood. "About time," he muttered as Bingley entered. Toward Darcy he directed only a scowl.

"To what do I owe the honor of this visit?" Bingley dropped into the chair behind his desk. Darcy remained standing near the door, planning to involve himself only if called upon by necessity or a direct invitation from Bingley.

"My solicitors have prepared an amended accounting of company assets at the time your father and I dissolved our partnership." He withdrew a packet of papers from his breast pocket.

Again? Darcy reminded himself to stay silent. How many times were they going to revise the same figures?

Kendall laid the papers before Bingley. "The numbers differ widely from those your father presented to me. His records failed to include receipts from an entire shipload of goods from Italy and Spain."

Frowning, Bingley skimmed the pages. "We've discussed this before. You signed away the rights to that cargo in exchange for a flat sum when the partnership ended."

"Yes, we *have* discussed this before. I told you—we thought the ship lost." Kendall spoke as if addressing a boy in short pants. "By the time it came in, your father and I had settled affairs between us. He kept the cargo for himself. But half of it is rightfully mine."

"According to the terms of the agreement—"

"The agreement be damned! He tricked me into signing it—pressured me to resolve our business 'in a timely fashion' because of his poor health."

And, Darcy knew, because the elder Mr. Bingley realized he

was being cheated by Kendall. For years, Kendall's accounting had been suspect, leading his partner to finally undertake a quiet audit. The inspection revealed embezzlement. Mr. Bingley, battling illness, chose to dissolve the partnership rather than challenge Kendall. He'd wanted the business settled before his death so that Kendall would have no opportunity to further rob his children of their rightful inheritance, and had been willing to assume a loss on the missing ship rather than leave any of his affairs unresolved. To everyone's surprise, the ship had come in after his death. It bore a rich cargo, though Darcy suspected Kendall's years' worth of stealing more than exceeded his "share" of the single ship's profits.

Bingley cast Darcy an uncertain look. Accounting had never been his strength, and Kendall had rearranged the figures so many times that he'd begun to lose faith in his own understanding of his father's records. Darcy stepped forward, picked up the papers, and, without examining them, handed them back to Kendall.

"Whatever the circumstances, the pact bears your signature. You agreed to the terms it stipulates. You have no legal claim to that ship's cargo."

"I have a moral claim to it!" Kendall's spittle flecked Darcy's cheek. "He cheated me! And his son continues to cheat me!"

That Kendall had the audacity to accuse the Bingleys of his own crime turned Darcy's stomach. "Charles Bingley has already granted you more consideration and dealt with you more patiently that I would have under the same circumstances. Your claims are groundless, your arguments repetitive, and your manner unbecoming a gentleman. I see little point in continuing this interview."

"Not that it's any business of yours, but I've come here today to spare your friend the embarrassment of a public appearance in court." He leaned over the desk. "That's right,

Bingley—if I can't get satisfaction from you, we'll see what Chancery has to say about your father's swindling." He tossed the papers down. "Keep these. Study them until you know to the halfpenny how much you owe me. Note that the record now includes interest. Yes, interest! I demand not only the money rightfully owed me, but interest on it for the years it's been denied."

Bingley again turned to Darcy. Was it injury, Kendall's threat, or merely the poor light that caused his friend to look so pale? The room had darkened considerably since they entered it. Without, the wind howled.

Darcy knew Kendall's threat was groundless. Bingley could produce the evidence he needed to win any suit the crooked businessman might bring against him—he had the audit results safely locked away in the top drawer of his desk. The drawer also held a pistol, which Darcy was tempted to flash if Kendall continued to abuse his weakened friend. "If the lord chancellor even hears your case, I am sure justice will prevail."

Kendall grinned malevolently. "And that's a big 'if'—isn't it? You know how long cases can languish in Chancery. I can tie up your friend's assets for years while we wait for our day in court. It will cost him more to pay his solicitors than to simply hand over the sum I demand now."

"Enough." Darcy had tolerated as much of Kendall's bullying as he intended to. "Mr. Kendall," he said quietly, "Mr. Bingley has in his possession evidence that you cheated his father for years by embezzling money from the firm. Unless you want *those* papers produced in court, I suggest you drop your empty claim forthwith, because with proof of your guilt in hand he has no intention of capitulating to your attempts at extortion."

A fleeting expression of panic overcame Kendall's features as he glanced from Darcy to Bingley, but his countenance immediately hardened once more. "You're bluffing."

"I am not." Darcy strode to the door and opened it wide. "There is nothing more to say. Now depart."

Kendall's bravado continued strong. "There is plenty more to say—but I shall save it for the lord chancellor." He stopped at the door, leaning his mottled face so close that Darcy could smell tobacco on his breath. "You can protect your friend from his own inexperience," he hissed. "Your solicitors may manage to protect him from the entanglements of Chancery, and his ill-gotten fortune might protect him from his conscience. But none of you can protect him from me. Not forever."

"It would have been a dramatic exit, had Kendall not been forced to immediately return and ask for shelter until the storm breaks." Darcy tugged at his cravat to loosen the knot, then slipped it from his neck.

Elizabeth watched his reflection in the vanity mirror as she unpinned her hair. The blizzard had resulted in two unplanned overnight visitors at Netherfield tonight, the other being Mr. Jones. The apothecary had dutifully braved the elements to reach his patients and, to the relief of all, had recommended only blancmange and rest to expedite a full recovery for Jane and Bingley. After the day's excitement, he'd given them some laudanum to help them sleep more soundly. Unfortunately, upon completing his ministrations he, too, had found himself stranded by the blinding snow. He'd proven himself a more pleasant guest than Kendall, however, whose company in the drawing room after dinner had inspired the whole household to retire early for the evening.

"Nothing undermines a good threat like immediately begging a favor." She picked up the silver brush, a bridal gift from Georgiana, and absently turned it over to trace the engraving of her new initials with her fingertips. "What do you think he meant by it?"

Darcy shrugged. "Probably nothing. He was just trying to salvage his pride after being so dismissed."

"If you do not take care, he may threaten you, too." She shook the brush at his reflection. "Abandon Bingley," she commanded with mock gravity, "lest the wrath of Lawrence Kendall fall upon thee!"

"I shall take my chances."

She ran the brush through her hair, counting the strokes. "Have his claims any merit?"

"None. The most reprehensible part is that he accuses the late Mr. Bingley of unethical conduct, when he himself was stealing from his partner for years."

"I can understand Mr. Bingley's desire to end their relationship quickly when his health failed. He undoubtedly hoped to spare his son any legal entanglements with such a disagreeable man. When Charles inherited, Kendall would have dominated the new partnership." She divided her hair into three locks and began working them into a braid.

Darcy approached behind her, meeting her gaze in the mirror. He stayed her fingers, grasping them in his warm, strong hands. "Leave it unbound."

Fifteen

> Elizabeth had hoped that his resentment might shorten his
> visit, but his plan did not appear in the least affected by it.
>
> Pride and Prejudice, *Chapter 21*

*T*he wheels spun rapidly, their spokes creating the illusion of
backward movement as their rims bit into the light snow.
One pair followed the other in perfect alignment, creating two single
tracks that snaked along the ground behind the carriage.

Something small and round fell and rolled to the side of the
path.

The symmetry ended. The left rear wheel wobbled. It gripped
the axle at an angle and held for what seemed an impossibly long
time. Stop! *she* wanted to cry. Stop the carriage!

But the driver could not hear her silent plea. The barouche sped
on. The wheel flew off. The horses snorted and whinnied in panic.
The vehicle tumbled—

Elizabeth jerked awake. Her heart raced as if she'd been
running. Her breathing came in short, labored gasps. She lay
still a moment, every muscle tensed, until she recognized the
dimly lit room as her chamber at Netherfield.

She inhaled a deep breath and slowly released it. Beside
her, Darcy slept peacefully, unaware of her disturbed slumber

or the howling wind outside. The waning firelight played across his sinewy body, but her mind was too unsettled to take pleasure in studying him.

For the third time tonight, she'd woken from the same nightmare. Vivid images of Jane and Bingley's accident repeated themselves in eerie detail. Though she hadn't witnessed the event in person, she'd seen more than enough of it in her dreams. For some reason, however, she never saw the victims, only the vehicle. Considering the driver's fate, she was grateful for the censorship.

Somewhere in the house, a clock struck two. She rolled to her side and closed her eyes, but sleep eluded her. The dream had left her body too restless, her mind too anxious. The accident was over, her sister and brother-in-law were safely recovering, yet a vague sense of dread suffused her.

Something was wrong. Was it Jane? Had her sister suffered worse injuries than Mr. Jones realized? Was she in pain right now?

Elizabeth rose and found her dressing gown. She could not rest until she checked on Jane and assured herself that she was all right. Barefoot, she padded to the door, swung it open silently, and slipped out.

The hallway was deserted; even the servants had long since gone to bed. Most of the wall sconces had been extinguished, leaving just enough light to safely negotiate the passage. She contemplated returning to her room for a candle but decided against it. Best make this a quick errand and return to bed.

She had barely started down the hall when the creak of a door stopped her. She thought at first her own door had been caught by a draft caused by the strong winds outside, but then recalled that it had opened soundlessly for her. No, someone else was up and about. Could it be Jane, seeking something to relieve her own or Bingley's discomfort?

The noise had seemed to come from downstairs, although

the weather made her uncertain. The snow had changed to sleet, which now pelted the windows in an angry barrage. She shivered and pulled her dressing gown about her more tightly as she headed down the staircase.

A faint light crept out of the library, and along with it, the wood-against-wood sound of drawers sliding open. Her fellow nocturnal wanderer must be Bingley, though she wondered what business couldn't wait until morning. Perhaps he, like herself, suffered a sleepless night and sought to make use of the time.

She would ask him if he left Jane resting comfortably. But as she neared the doorway, she realized Bingley wasn't in the room at all. Lawrence Kendall sat behind the desk rifling through a pile of papers and ledgers.

She caught the gasp that nearly escaped her and stepped into the shadows. She could still see Kendall, but was, she hoped, hidden from his view.

Unlike her, Kendall was dressed save a neckcloth and coat. His attire suggested to her that this was no impromptu snooping sortie, but a deliberate, planned invasion. He scanned the papers quickly, casting each aside after a few moments' perusal. The ledgers he also flipped through rapidly, skimming a few pages in front, middle, back. The more records he went through, the more deeply he frowned. "Where is it?" he grumbled. "Where the bloody hell is it?"

He stuffed the papers into their portfolio and shoved it, along with the ledgers, back into one of the desk drawers. He then tried to open another drawer but met resistance. He tugged and rattled the drawer around in its housing, but his efforts yielded only noise. "Damn you, Bingley," he muttered. "Where's the key?"

His gaze lit upon a letter opener, which he attempted to use as a lock pick without success. Finally, he pushed himself away from the desk in disgust.

Elizabeth, her heart suddenly pounding, backed away from the library door. Where to go? She couldn't possibly make it up the stairs before Kendall came out. Her gaze darted about the hall until she spotted the drawing room door standing open.

Grateful for the impulse that had led her to undertake this foolish mission barefoot, she scurried into the drawing room and pressed herself against the wall. Seconds later, Kendall emerged from the library. She held her breath as he mounted the stairs. Not until she heard his footsteps recede into the guest wing did she dare move.

The wind moaned. She wanted to do the same. Should she wake Darcy and tell him what she'd just seen? Would Kendall return tonight with better break-in tools to find what he wanted? Before she proceeded any further, she looked to the top of the staircase to make sure Kendall was indeed gone.

Caroline Parrish met her gaze.

Clad in a gauzy white shift and flickering shadows, she gripped the balcony balustrade as she looked down into the entry hall. Though Elizabeth thought they had made eye contact, Mrs. Parrish seemed insensible to Elizabeth's presence. She rocked slightly, alternately pushing away from the rail and pulling herself toward it. The weak candlelight prevented Elizabeth from reading her expression closely, but she presented a haunted mien.

Caroline shook her head repeatedly, muttering something. Elizabeth could not discern the words with accuracy from this distance, but she thought she heard "no" more than once.

Was Mrs. Parrish sleepwalking again? Still worse to contemplate, might she finish the act she'd attempted in London by hurling herself onto the marble below?

"Caroline?" Elizabeth stepped forward.

Caroline's rocking ceased immediately as she caught sight of Elizabeth. She backed away from the rail, wringing her hands.

"Mrs. Parrish, let me take you to your room." Elizabeth ascended the stairs, but stopped midway when Caroline shook her head. "Caroline," she said gently. "It's only me, Mrs. Darcy. Let me help you."

Caroline stared at Elizabeth a long moment. She slowly raised her left hand, cupped, palm toward herself, as if to beckon. Elizabeth advanced. But then Caroline turned suddenly and fled down the corridor. Her rapid footfalls made no sound.

Elizabeth hurried up the remaining stairs, arriving at the top just in time to see Mrs. Parrish's door close. She blinked, unsure what to make of the incident. Was encountering Caroline in the corridors to become a nightly ritual? She shuddered as a draft caught the back of her neck. A gust of wind beat against the windows.

She scanned for signs that Lawrence Kendall yet moved about, but saw no one else as she returned to her chamber. With great relief, she closed the door behind her and sagged against it.

"I was about to come looking for you."

Her hand flew to her chest until she realized the hushed voice beside her belonged to Darcy. She slumped against the door once more and released her breath.

He took her fingers in his and led her back to the bed. The sheets still held his warmth. "I apologize," he whispered. "I did not mean to startle you. But what errand called you out of our room at this hour? Have you followed Caroline Parrish's lead and taken up nocturnal wandering?"

"More than you know. I just saw her in the hall." She nestled against him and described her recent adventure. As she spoke, her muscles relaxed. Mr. Kendall seemed less menacing in the safety of her husband's embrace.

Darcy, in contrast, tensed as she related the tale. At its conclusion, he left her side and slipped into his breeches.

"Where do you go?"

"That man cannot be trusted until morning. I know where Bingley keeps his key. I am going to move the documents in that drawer to a safer location until he can attend to them. Someplace Kendall won't think to look."

"Where?"

He kissed her. "Under our mattress."

Sixteen

"Nothing was to be done that he did not do himself."
　　　　　　　　Mrs. Gardiner, writing to Elizabeth,
　　　　　　　　Pride and Prejudice, *Chapter 52*

*I*t seemed she had just settled back into slumber when
Darcy's urgent voice penetrated her consciousness.
"Elizabeth!"

She burrowed further into the bedclothes.

"Elizabeth!"

This had better be important. "What?" she whispered without opening her eyes.

No response. She rolled to face him and forced her lids
open. He lay fast asleep.

She held perfectly still, listening for the voice again. Had
she only imagined it? Had Darcy uttered her name in his
sleep? Had someone called from the hall? She would have
testified under oath that a voice had come from within their
chamber—indeed, from right beside her. An unsettling
thought gripped her: Was someone else in the room?

She held her breath and peered wide-eyed into the shadows.
The wan firelight revealed no other person. Only the sound of

sleet yet pelting against the glass disturbed the night.

The voice must have come in a dream. She sighed and curled into a ball, wondering what time it was and whether she was destined to get any rest before dawn. At this rate, she'd appear a sorry sight in the morning. The wind howled, mocking her sleeplessness.

Despite the heavy counterpane and her husband's proximity, a shiver seized her. The fire sputtered. She lay in bed, the knowledge that she should add a log to the hearth battling reluctance to leave her cocoon to do so.

She forced herself from beneath the blankets. To delay would only permit the room to grow colder. The floor chilled her toes as she neared the fireplace. For a dying flame, the smell of smoke hung strong.

A basket of extra wood stood beside the hearth. As she reached for a log, she blinked back the sleepy haze that clouded her vision. Or at least she tried. But she could not clear her gaze.

Because the smog wasn't in her head. Nor, a glance revealed, did it come from the fireplace.

Smoky tendrils snaked in beneath the door.

She dropped the log. "Darcy!"

She rushed to the door, tested its panels for heat. Mercifully, her touch met cool wood. "Darcy! I think the house is on fire!"

He was at her side before she finished the words. She tried to yank the door open but he restrained her panicked movements. "Slowly!" Though his command suggested composure, his tone revealed alarm that matched her own.

Together, they cautiously opened the door. Smoke swirled in the hallway. It seemed to come from the room across the hall. Jane and Bingley's room.

Elizabeth started forward. Darcy stopped her. "Rouse the others and the servants. Send someone to help me but do *not* follow me in there yourself. Get out of the house."

Every instinct urged her to run straight to Jane. But she

realized it would take stronger arms than hers to help Darcy get the couple to safety, and many hands to keep the blaze from engulfing the house.

She sprinted down the hall and pounded on the next door. "Fire! Wake up! Fire!" Mr. Hurst answered with greater speed than she would ever have thought he possessed.

"Quickly! Go to Bingley's room and help Darcy!" Without waiting for a response, she crossed to Parrish's door.

The American answered before she even knocked. "I heard your cry. But I can't find Caroline—she's not in our chamber!"

Elizabeth glanced toward the staircase where she'd so recently seen the elusive Mrs. Parrish. There was no sign of Caroline, but she saw that Darcy had already dragged Jane into the hall and gone back for Bingley. Jane wasn't moving. *Dear God, let it be only the laudanum.* Hurst slung her over his shoulder while Louisa fluttered around uselessly.

With the door to Bingley's chamber open, the hallway was rapidly filling with smoke. In just a few minutes more they wouldn't be able to see a thing. "Ring for the servants while I wake the others," she said. "Then I will help you look."

She left the family quarters and dashed up the side staircase. She had no idea who occupied which guest suite, and so just pounded on each door in succession. "Fire! Help!"

Randolph came into the corridor immediately. "What can I do?"

"Go downstairs. See whether Darcy has gotten Jane and Bingley to safety. Then help Mr. Parrish find his wife."

Lawrence Kendall made no offer of aid, just fled down the steps as fast as his boots could carry him. Mr. Jones had the presence of mind to grab his medical bag. "I have a feeling I'll be needing this," he said as they descended the stairs.

When they reached the landing, so much smoke filled the air that she could barely discern the servants who had formed a bucket brigade and already worked to douse the flames.

Had Darcy gotten Bingley out yet? And Caroline—where was she? She headed toward the mayhem, but Mr. Jones caught her arm. "Where are you going?"

"I promised Mr. Parrish I'd help him look for his wife."

"He has probably long since found her. Doubtless, they wait with the others outside. Where you should be."

"But Darcy—"

"Will vivisect me if I allow you to remain in this house a moment longer. If you must help someone, come with me to attend your sister."

She did not need further prompting to seek out Jane. Her lungs burned as she and Mr. Jones groped their way down the final flight and across the entry hall. Coughs wracked her, slowing their pace.

At last they reached the door and burst into the night. Icy pellets stung her, rapidly drenching the thin shift she wore. The stone steps froze her bare feet.

The lawn was pandemonium. Servants raced about everywhere. Some of them carried buckets toward the house, while others carried valuables out. She saw no sign of Darcy or the Bingley family.

"Mrs. Darcy, thank heaven!" Her lady's maid appeared at her side and wrapped a blanket around her shoulders, rescuing her from both the elements and indecency. She handed another to Mr. Jones, who also wore only nightclothes. "I've been waiting here for you, just a-praying you'd come out soon!" She bent down and slipped a pair of unfamiliar shoes onto Elizabeth's feet. "I hope these fit—they're mine. I couldn't get to your chamber for any of your things."

"Lucy, I can't take your shoes from you!" The servant probably had just the one pair.

"Oh, not to worry, madam. One of the men brought me a pair of Wellingtons from the barn. I'm sorry I don't have a pair for you, too, sir, but there are more boots and blankets in the carriage house. That's where Mrs. Bingley and the others are gathered."

Elizabeth gratefully pulled the blanket about her more tightly. "Lucy, you are a godsend. Is Jane all right? What of her husband?"

"I think they're fine, ma'am. But they sure will be glad to see Mr. Jones."

The trio made their way to the carriage house with as much haste as the weather allowed. Elizabeth felt sorry for Mr. Jones having to walk through the slush with no shoes, but the apothecary uttered not a single complaint. He did, however, immediately procure some boots when they reached shelter.

To her overwhelming relief, she found Jane and Bingley both conscious. They spoke groggily, the effects of the drug and the accident and fatigue still evident. Coughing spasms seized them as smoke worked its way out of their lungs. But they were alive and safe once more. Mr. Jones moved one of the lanterns to a nearby crate and began to examine his patients for the second time that day.

The Hursts sat on the back of their coach, huddled beneath separate blankets. Mr. Hurst wore a pair of borrowed fishing waders beneath his nightclothes, lending him an absurd appearance that Elizabeth wished she were in a better mood to appreciate. Ever the lady, at least in her own mind, Louisa had taken the time to don her dressing gown and a pair of now-soaked slippers before fleeing the house.

"Where is everyone else?" Elizabeth asked. "Where's Mr. Darcy?"

Mrs. Hurst sneezed and looked about for a handkerchief. Spotting none, nor an appropriate substitute, she self-consciously dabbed at her nose with the corner of the blanket. "After we got Jane and Charles here, he left. I think perhaps he's helping Mr. Parrish look for Caroline."

"And Professor Randolph?"

"Also looking for Caroline."

"Mr. Kendall?"

"Right here, Mrs. Darcy," boomed a voice from within Kendall's coach. The gentleman had drawn the curtain across the window. "Thank you for the enquiry. I didn't know you cared."

Odious man.

Elizabeth took her sister's hand. "Dear Jane, what a wretched day you've had. First the carriage accident and now this! Have you any idea what happened?"

"No." A coughing spasm seized her. "I was sleeping so soundly," she continued when she could speak once more, "that I didn't even know we were in danger until I woke up and found Mr. Hurst carrying me outside."

"And I woke up beside her—slung over Darcy's shoulder," Bingley said. "Slept right through a fire in my room, but this weather sure is rousing."

As if in confirmation, Louisa sneezed again. Mr. Jones nodded toward the assorted footwear someone had piled in the corner. "I suggest you trade your slippers for something dry."

She cast him a look colder than the draft that threatened to extinguish the lanterns. "Servants' boots? No, thank you." She shuffled to the doorway, where, with great exertion, she slid one of the doors partly open. Darkness still gripped the sky.

"Does anyone happen to know the time?"

"I think it's about five, ma'am," Lucy answered. "Perhaps half-past. Mrs. Nicholls says she was already awake when the bell rung."

Elizabeth joined Louisa and squinted into the blackness. She wished the sun would rise, that the storm would abate, that *something* would happen to end this gloomy night that seemed intent on stretching to eternity. Confusion gripped the entire grounds of Netherfield. People dashed about everywhere, yet she looked in vain for the one face she most longed to see. Where was Darcy? Though she knew he was quite capable of taking care of himself, she could not be easy until she saw him again.

"I don't know what's wrong with that Mr. Parrish," Louisa muttered. "He's doing an abominable job of caring for my sister."

Elizabeth longed to respond that it was Caroline herself who continually presented poor Mr. Parrish with the most obstacles to that goal, but she knew her point would not carry. "He seems to be trying his best," she said.

"An Englishman would try harder." Mrs. Hurst returned to her coach and asked her husband to hand her inside where she could sit more comfortably. "Mrs. Darcy, if your maid is done attending you, perhaps she could fetch me a hot brick. My own maid seems to have disappeared."

"A hot brick?"

"Yes, for my feet."

Elizabeth blinked. "I'm sure there are plenty in the burning house. Would you like some tea as well?"

"That would be lovely."

Elizabeth met Lucy's gaze. The maid regarded her uncertainly. She had served her only a short time, since Elizabeth's engagement, and had not yet learned to read her mistress's moods.

"Lucy, without getting in the way of anyone working to put out the fire, please enquire among the servants whether anyone has injuries requiring Mr. Jones's attention. Also ask whether anyone has seen Mrs. Parrish or my husband. If you happen to encounter Mrs. Hurst's maid, kindly relay her requests."

"Yes, ma'am." With a relieved expression, Lucy set off.

The apothecary finished his ministrations and, aided by Mr. Hurst, moved the weary couple to the relative comfort of the Darcys' coach. Jane and Bingley each rested against one side and stretched their legs the length of the padded seats.

Elizabeth sat on the coach floor for a time, holding Jane's hand and speaking with her softly, but her thoughts were too scattered and her heart too anxious to attend her own conversation. Fortunately, her sister soon drifted back into slumber. Bingley followed shortly.

She left the coach and wandered restlessly about the carriage house. She longed to *do* something. She'd promised Mr. Parrish she'd help look for Caroline, and Darcy's prolonged absence distressed her more each minute. Mr. Jones observed her agitation without comment, but his expression clearly discouraged her from succumbing to the impulse to leave this sanctuary. Who was he, though, to stop her? A man, just a man, with no real power over her save his own disapproval. And how often did she let mere disapproval by an outsider sway her actions?

She pulled the blanket more tightly around her shoulders, preparing to go back outside. Darcy had told her to get out of the house, and she would honor his wishes in keeping her promise to Mr. Parrish. She would begin her search on the grounds—perhaps Caroline had exited the mansion but didn't know where the rest of the family had gathered.

If, however, in the process of seeking Caroline she learned that Darcy had not yet made it out of the burning building, the fires of hell itself would not keep her from going back in after him.

Ignoring Mr. Jones's objections, she slid open the door to find Lucy just returning. She quickly drew the drenched maid inside. "Lucy, what have you learned?"

"No one's seen Mrs. Parrish, ma'am. Mr. Parrish is a-looking everywheres for her. He says you should stay put. The professor's helping him look." She blew on her hands through chattering teeth. "Only one person's hurt so far. One of the maids—nobody I talked to seemed to know if she's an upstairs or downstairs maid, but anyways she's in the barn with some bad burns."

Elizabeth retrieved a dry blanket and draped it across Lucy's shoulders. "And my husband?"

Lucy bit her lip. "He's still in the house, ma'am. Directing everyone putting out the fire."

Her heart dropped to the pit of her stomach. Darcy being Darcy, of course that's where he was. She should feel pride, but all she could muster was anxiety for his safety.

Mr. Jones picked up his medical bag. "Can you lead me to the maid?" At Lucy's affirmation, he turned to Elizabeth. "Mrs. Darcy, your husband needs to focus on what he's doing, not worry about you running around putting yourself in danger. And I need you to keep an eye on Mr. and Mrs. Bingley for me. Can I trust you to stay here?"

Elizabeth wanted to shout in frustration at being forced to inaction. Instead, she muttered an ungracious "Yes."

The apothecary and Lucy departed. Elizabeth checked on Jane and Bingley. The couple slept fitfully. She tucked Bingley's blanket more securely around him and stroked Jane's furrowed brow until it smoothed.

Mr. Hurst's snore came from the next coach, followed by an unladylike sneeze. "Mrs. Darcy?" Louisa called. "I don't suppose your maid remembered the hot brick?"

She could not bring herself to dignify the question with a response. Mr. Jones was right—he *did* need her to watch over Jane and Bingley in his absence, because the rest of these selfish people could not be relied upon to do so.

She regarded Mr. Kendall's carriage. No doubt he slumbered, too. Why let a little thing like someone's home burning down interrupt a good night's sleep? All his earlier snooping and skulking that night, not to mention his hasty escape from the house, had probably worn him out.

The image of him fleeing down the staircase intruded into her mind once more. She hadn't credited the corpulent man with such speed. His coattails had actually flown behind him as his boots clattered in double time. She rolled her eyes in disgust. Yet something besides contempt nagged at her recollection.

Boots. Coattails.

At the time the fire broke out, Mr. Kendall had been fully dressed.

Seventeen

"I confess myself to have been entirely deceived in Miss Bingley's regard for me."
Jane, writing to Elizabeth, Pride and Prejudice, Chapter 26

Elizabeth stared at Mr. Kendall's coach, wishing she could see inside to confirm her mounting suspicions about its owner. For Kendall to have been dressed when she'd sounded the alarm, he had to have been awake when the fire broke out. According to Lucy's earlier time estimate, it had been perhaps half-past four when she and Darcy had discovered the blaze and awakened the household. That was more than two hours after she'd seen Kendall in the library.

What had he been doing that whole while? Had he returned to the library and broken into the desk—only to discover that the papers had been moved? And to what act could his resulting ire have led him? Unable to steal them, would he try to destroy them?

She crossed to the carriage and knocked on the door. "Mr. Kendall?"

A heavy sigh issued from within. "Yes, Mrs. Darcy?"

"Might I have a word with you?"

The door opened. As she had thought, Kendall wore the

same attire he'd had on in the library. He scowled at her. "What is it, Mrs. Darcy?"

Now that she had commanded his attention, she didn't know what to say to elicit more information about his movements in the past few hours. She could hardly interrogate the gentleman like the criminal he was. "I—" She grasped for an excuse to have initiated the interview. "Many of us left the house so quickly that we are without proper clothing for outdoors. I wanted to enquire whether you need a blanket to keep warm."

"I am fine."

"Yes, I see that you are dressed."

His cold expression caught her breath. Suddenly she realized her foolishness in approaching him like this alone. She already knew him to be a sneak and a thief. Were he also an arsonist, that made him a very dangerous man indeed. She took an involuntary step backward.

"I stayed up late to write letters and fell asleep in my clothes. Is there anything else, Mrs. Darcy?"

Before she could reply, Lucy slid open the door and Mr. Jones burst into the carriage house. In his arms he carried the injured maid.

Relieved by the excuse to end her conversation with Kendall, Elizabeth hurried to spread some blankets near one of the lanterns. She wondered at the apothecary's decision to transport his new patient through the inclement weather rather than treat her where she'd already found shelter. The carriage house must offer superior lighting or comfort to that of the barn.

When he settled the maid onto the blankets, Elizabeth inhaled sharply. Though dressed in the coarse woolen uniform of a scullery maid, the woman was no servant.

"Mrs. Parrish!" she exclaimed.

"My surprise was as great as your own," said Mr. Jones.

"How she came to be wearing these clothes, one can only imagine. My questions to her have gone unanswered."

Elizabeth removed Caroline's wet shoes and tucked a blanket around her legs. Mrs. Parrish cradled her left hand against her chest, swaying forward and back in a self-soothing rhythm. She fixed her gaze on Elizabeth and murmured something indistinguishable.

Elizabeth leaned in more closely. "What did you say, Mrs. Parrish?"

"My hand." Her voice was barely audible. "Please look at my hand—"

"Caroline!" Louisa shouldered her way past Elizabeth to capture Mrs. Parrish in an embrace that suggested all the warmth of the air outside. "My dear sister, I've been positively beside myself!"

Caroline winced as Mrs. Hurst pressed against her injury. "Louisa."

Elizabeth straightened and backed away from the effusive reunion. "She told me she wants you to examine her hand," she relayed to Mr. Jones.

"I tried to do so in the barn, but she resisted. Perhaps now that she's among friends she'll allow me to treat the burns." The apothecary withdrew bandages and a small tin from his medical bag. "Would you assist me, Mrs. Hurst? I could use someone to hold the lantern close."

"I'm sure Mrs. Darcy can handle it." Louisa retreated a few steps to hover behind Mr. Jones. She addressed the maid. "Fetch my sister some more appropriate attire."

"Lucy, please see if you can locate Mr. Parrish and tell him his wife has been found," Elizabeth said. "Mrs. Parrish's wardrobe needs can wait. Her present clothing, though beneath her station, is at least warm."

Louisa gasped. "Surely you cannot be suggesting that my sister remain dressed in that—that garment?"

"I do more than suggest." As Lucy departed, Elizabeth lifted the lantern and brought it near Mr. Jones, who had politely busied himself during the exchange by beginning his examination. "Unless you care to trade gowns with her?"

Mrs. Hurst gaped. In the welcome silence that followed, Elizabeth turned her back on her and observed the apothecary's ministrations. Caroline's hand glowed an angry red from palm to fingertips. Blisters swelled the base of her fingers.

"Mrs. Parrish, can you tell me how you hurt your hand?" Mr. Jones opened the tin. A pungent scent met Elizabeth's nostrils.

"I—I don't remember." Caroline raised her right hand, which appeared uninjured, to her temple. "I fear another of my headaches has come on."

The apothecary dipped two fingers into the tin and scooped up a dab of salve. When he touched the unguent to the burn, Caroline flinched and whimpered.

"There, now, Mrs. Parrish. This ointment will help soothe the pain. Just let me remove your wedding ring to aid circulation. . . ." Mr. Jones tried to slide off the ring, but it held fast on her swollen finger. He worked some salve under it, tried twisting it slowly, but the ring would not budge. Caroline mewed and shut her eyes against the pain.

"Stop tormenting her, you country bumpkin!" Louisa jerked Caroline's hand out of the apothecary's grasp, eliciting a cry from her sister. "Caroline, the minute this storm lets up, we are summoning a surgeon from London. Someone who knows what he is about."

Elizabeth's face warmed with the embarrassment Mrs. Hurst should have been feeling. Mr. Jones was a capable medical man, who had seen her family through illnesses and injuries since she was a child. "Mr. Jones, I appreciate the care you have given my sister and her family tonight. We could ask for none better."

The apothecary returned the tin to his medical bag, rose

stiffly, and handed Elizabeth a roll of cotton cloth. "Perhaps Mrs. Hurst would prefer to bandage her sister's injury herself. It should be covered lightly. I will go check on Mr. and Mrs. Bingley."

Elizabeth offered the bandage to Louisa, silently daring her to take it. Mrs. Hurst snatched it up and proceeded to make a bungled attempt at covering the burn. She first applied the dressing so loosely that it fell off the hand, then pulled it so tight that tears sprang to Caroline's eyes, all the while loudly criticizing the inferior supplies of country doctors. Eventually, Elizabeth took pity on Mrs. Parrish—and everyone else in auditory range—and offered to perform the task herself.

"If you insist." Louisa shoved the bandage back into Elizabeth's grasp.

Elizabeth studied Caroline's hand before applying the bandage. On the palm side, blisters and swollen tissue almost eclipsed the ring. If only they could remove it, Caroline's pain might lessen and her injury could heal more quickly. "Mrs. Parrish, would you like me to try one last time to take off your ring?"

Caroline squeezed her eyes shut but nodded.

"You're as bad as that bumbling apothecary," Louisa snapped. "Leave it be."

The carriage house door slid open, arresting further debate. Mr. Parrish and Lucy entered. Behind them, early streaks of dawn revealed that the storm had at last abated.

"Caroline! Thank heaven you are safe!" Parrish hurried to his wife's side. His hair was soaked; rivulets of water streamed down the greatcoat he'd obtained at some point since Elizabeth had last seen him. "I've been searching everywhere for you."

He reached for her hand but stopped when he saw the injury. "Oh, darling—you've been hurt!" He looked to Elizabeth, his expression seeking an explanation she could not supply.

"Mr. Jones has just finished treating her hand," she reassured him.

Parrish sat down beside his wife, put his arm around her shoulders, and drew her to his side. "You're safe now, darling." Caroline rested her head on his shoulder.

At the tender display, envy touched Elizabeth's heart. The Parrishes were safe; she could only pray that Darcy was, too, and that at the end of this awful ordeal she would know the solace of her own husband's embrace. As if reading her thoughts, Lucy departed again with the stated intention of learning more about Darcy's progress against the fire.

Parrish watched Elizabeth finish dressing the burn. "Thank you, Mrs. Darcy, for taking care of my wife. You are a good friend to her."

Elizabeth shrugged, disconcerted by Parrish's gratitude. Despite having been thrown into Caroline's company more often in the past fortnight than she'd ever thought herself capable of enduring, she'd developed no further attachment to Jane's new sister-in-law than she'd harbored previously. The solicitude she'd shown Mrs. Parrish was simply the concern she'd feel for any fellow human being in similar circumstances. "I'm sure she derives more comfort from your presence than anything I could do."

Indeed, the patient soon dozed off in her husband's arms, a fitful slumber that paralleled Elizabeth's own agitation. Mr. Parrish pulled her against him more securely and whispered something indiscernible in her ear. Her troubled features smoothed and she relaxed into his side.

Parrish's face, however, became graver as he studied his wife. He opened his mouth several times as if to say something, but shut it again with his thoughts unuttered. Finally, he spoke. "Mrs. Darcy, have you any idea how my wife burned her hand?"

Elizabeth confessed ignorance.

He glanced about the carriage house, at Mr. Jones resting just outside the coach occupied by Jane and Bingley, at the other carriages with their silent inmates. "I have been contemplating the question as I sit here," he continued in low tones. "I have also been wondering what caused tonight's fire. I—I do not like the direction my thoughts are taking."

A chill traveled down her spine. Mr. Parrish hinted at an idea that had grazed the edges of her consciousness, suspicions so unpleasant she'd dared not articulate them even in the privacy of her own thoughts. The location and nature of Caroline's injury, her reluctance to tell Mr. Jones how she'd burned herself, her unknown whereabouts at the time the fire broke, her wandering earlier that night and other strange behavior . . .

"Do you grasp my meaning, Mrs. Darcy? Pray tell me I needn't say more."

She understood. But could so distasteful a thought be true? Had Caroline started the fire? Inconceivable notion! "Perhaps you draw conclusions from mere coincidence," she tried to reassure him.

"I want more than anything to believe that. But your sister and her husband—indeed, the whole household—could have died in this blaze. I—" His voice broke. "I no longer fear for only my wife's safety."

Parrish's speculation provoked disquiet within her, the same uneasiness she'd experienced upon waking from her repeated dreams of the carriage accident. Never had Netherfield seemed such an ominous place as it did tonight, an abode of mishaps and misfortune. They had been here but two days and had known scarcely a moment's peace of mind. Or did the howling storm and her own flagging reserves only make it seem such?

"Mr. Parrish, doubt feeds on exhaustion. When we have all had a chance to recover from tonight's events—"

"While still more mysterious accidents occur? To turn a blind eye is irresponsible." He smoothed Caroline's hair, stroked her cheek. "I don't want to believe my wife capable of the unthinkable. Yet I know my feelings for Caroline cannot help but cloud my judgment. I am in need of advice, Mrs. Darcy. You have a quick mind and a compassionate heart. What do you think I should do?"

Elizabeth studied Caroline in silence, the fatigue of a long, sleepless night settling upon her. She could think of little beyond crawling into a warm, dry bed with her husband and sleeping for two days straight. "We need not decide anything in this moment. Let us ponder the situation when our minds are clearer and we know more particulars of the fire."

It was an evasive answer to a serious question, but she could spare no further energy on the Parrishes and their problems. Not until she beheld Darcy safe once more.

Surely the blaze was under control by now. Where was he?

Eighteen

"I have no idea of there being so much design in the world as some persons imagine."

Jane to Elizabeth, Pride and Prejudice, *Chapter 24*

*D*espite weariness that seeped down to his bones, Darcy strode to the carriage house with rapid steps. The flames were out, the house saved, the servants organized, the landlord summoned. He now sought a few precious minutes with Elizabeth before sending her and the others off to the sanctuary of Longbourn while he continued to oversee details of the fire's aftermath. He wished he could have relocated the party sooner, but no one could be spared to drive them, and the weather and darkness had rendered the roads too hazardous to attempt travel anyway. Even now, in full but dreary daylight, the memory of yesterday's carriage accident made him hesitant to let Elizabeth undertake even the short distance without him.

"The landlord will be furious, I suppose?" Randolph kept pace with Darcy's long strides. Once Caroline Parrish had been found, the professor had appeared at Darcy's side, offering to help in any way necessary and working ceaselessly until the last ember died.

"I have met Mr. Morris only once, but he seems a reasonable

man. Accidents happen." So did intentionally set blazes, but Darcy was keeping those suspicions to himself. When Bingley's chamber had at last been cleared of both smoke and people, he had sifted through the ashes and found no evidence of arson. Yet he could not overlook Lawrence Kendall's earlier threat against Bingley, or Elizabeth witnessing him riffling through Bingley's records. How far would he go to destroy proof of his larceny?

They reached the carriage house. Elizabeth, who had been standing outside watching the mansion, came to him quickly the moment her eyes lighted upon him. Her sweet face held an expression of relief that surely matched his own. Professor Randolph tactfully continued into the building, granting them a relatively private reunion.

He indulged in the overwhelming urge to pull her close. The touch of her temple against his cheek, her body pressed to his, chased away the shadows of anxiety still hovering from the long night. "I know you are all right, but tell me anyway."

"I am perfectly well now that you are here. What about you?"

"The same." Conscious of the myriad details still demanding his attention, he reluctantly released her. "I have just spoken to our driver. He will conduct you, Jane, and Bingley to your parents' house as soon as Mr. Jones considers them fit to travel. How are they?"

"Sleeping now in our coach. Not very peacefully—coughing a lot. But on the whole unharmed by the fire, thank goodness. And thanks to you."

"It is you they have to thank. You discovered the fire in time." A few minutes more and the couple certainly would have perished—the blaze had already spread from the hearth to the foot of their bed when he'd entered their chamber.

"How bad is the damage?"

"The master suite and the room adjacent—the Parrishes' chamber—are lost. Furniture, clothing, everything. The floor joists are holding at present but need replacement as soon as possible. The flames burned through the ceiling and into Mr. Kendall's room above. They did not, however, reach his trunk, which appears to have never been unpacked. Our chamber and the rest of the rooms on the first and second floors of that wing suffered extensive smoke damage. Everything needs cleaning and airing."

Though much work lay ahead to repair and restore Netherfield, they had been very fortunate. Fire constituted a great house's worst enemy; it all too often consumed entire mansions. Darcy lived in constant dread of one overtaking Pemberley. He chased the horrible thought from his mind by attempting to wipe a smudge from Elizabeth's brow, but wound up adding more soot from his fingers. His own appearance must be frightful. "Are the Hursts and Mr. Kendall here as well?"

"Resting in their respective carriages."

"I imagine Kendall is eager to depart for his own home. If you do not think it too great an imposition on your family, the Hursts and Parrishes should accompany you to your parents' house. I realize your mother and Bingley's sisters hardly seek out each other's company, but under the circumstances I think they will be more comfortable at Longbourn until Netherfield is set back in order."

"You mean they will be out of the way. I don't know whom I pity more—them or my mother. I, however, won't be there to observe the sport, because I intend to stay right here with you."

She could not be dissuaded, and he had to confess that his efforts to sway her resolve were halfhearted at best.

The family party departed for Longbourn in time to arrive for a late breakfast. Bingley accompanied them only to see Jane safely delivered into her mother's care and the papers Darcy had rescued last night consigned to Mr. Bennet for safekeeping. He then returned to Netherfield. Though he trusted Darcy to handle matters, he said he did not want to impose on their friendship by letting him shoulder the full burden of overseeing all the work involved in cleaning up the mansion and restoring household operations. His health, he asserted, was much improved over the day before.

Professor Randolph accompanied the Parrishes to Longbourn. Since Caroline's apparent suicide attempt, he had been meeting with her daily. He recorded his observations and had already posted two letters to his colleague in America, but given the distance, no one expected a response from Dr. Lancaster anytime soon.

Mr. Kendall remained at Netherfield, claiming that the sky continued too threatening to trust the roads all the way to London. Though it did appear that the storm had only suspended, not ended, Darcy suspected Kendall's true purpose was to perform further snooping while the household was in an advantageous state of chaos.

He caught the businessman twice loitering outside Bingley's former chamber. The first time Kendall scurried away without comment in an unconvincing pretense that he'd just been passing by, but on the second occasion Darcy's sudden emergence from the chamber took him by surprise. Kendall stood so close to the door that Darcy wondered if he'd had his ear pressed against it. "Might I assist you in some matter?"

"I would like to examine the extent of damage within."

"Why?"

"My chamber sits directly above. I wish to assure myself that the floor won't collapse beneath me when I go up there to retrieve my things."

Darcy's first impulse was to deny the request, but he quickly reconsidered. Perhaps Kendall's conduct inside would betray a familiarity with the room that he should not possess. He pushed the door fully open. "By all means."

Kendall shouldered his way past Darcy and headed straight toward the hearth. Flames had weakened the thick oak floor beams around it, but to Darcy's disappointment, they held under Kendall's weight.

"Have you learned the fire's cause?" Kendall scanned the room, taking in each piece of furniture. His gaze rested longest on the scorched splinters of a Chippendale chair and what appeared to be the ashy remains of a dress.

"No," Darcy lied. The proximity of the gown to the hearth led him to believe a stray spark had ignited the muslin as it lay draped on the chair, but he saw no reason to share that information with Kendall.

"Well, often these things go undetermined." He studied the bedstead, which had been almost completely consumed by flames after Darcy rescued the sleeping couple from it. "Looks like Bingley was lucky to get out of here alive."

"His wife, also."

Kendall's attention turned to a blackened portable writing desk Bingley had given Jane as a wedding gift. Darcy had given a matching one to Elizabeth so that the sisters, who would be geographically separated by their marriages, could remain close through frequent correspondence.

"Mmm? Oh, yes, Mrs. Bingley. Their marriage is off to a dramatic start, isn't it? As is the Parrishes', from what I hear."

Darcy's tolerance was approaching its limit. "Have you completed your inspection? The servants await my instructions for restoring this room."

Kendall glanced at the ceiling for the first time since entering the chamber. "I'm satisfied that I won't be dropping in unexpectedly."

Darcy suspected, however, that an intentional visit was planned. Though Bingley's papers were securely stashed at Longbourn, he nevertheless charged his own valet with the task of keeping an eye on the businessman.

The day passed in a blur of activity. That evening, Bingley returned to Longbourn to be with Jane. Darcy and Elizabeth would have spent the night at Longbourn as well, to free Netherfield's overworked staff from attending to their needs, but he didn't dare leave Kendall unsupervised. He and Elizabeth, therefore, retired to a new chamber in another part of the house, near Kendall.

She had already bathed when he entered, and sat before the fireplace drying her hair. The smell of rosewater was a welcome change from the odor of smoke and burned wood that had filled his nostrils all day.

"I had fresh water drawn for you." She rose to greet him with a kiss. "And Lucy brought up a cold supper for us." She gestured toward a small table set for two.

He glanced at the tub, looking forward to washing away the grime of the past twenty-four hours. "Where is Lucy now?"

"Asleep in her room, I hope. I told her to get some rest. Your man is off keeping watch over Mr. Kendall. So if you need assistance with your bath, I'm afraid it will have to come from me." She cast him a playfully wicked smile. "Do you want to bathe or dine first?"

"If you are assisting me with my bath, I think we had better dine first."

After quickly washing his hands and face in the water basin, he fell to the meal like a starving man. It wasn't much—cold roast beef, bread and butter, vegetables—but he hadn't realized how hungry he was until he started eating. Elizabeth, too, eagerly approached her food. She had spent the day as busily employed as he, overseeing the near-legion of servants sent from throughout the neighborhood to help with cleanup efforts. She'd proven herself a capable commander, organizing her troops into an efficient workforce that had accomplished more in one day than Darcy ever thought possible. He had observed her with pride; her skillful handling of the crisis showed she would make a fine mistress of Pemberley. Not that he had ever doubted her.

Halfway through their supper, she became pensive. "I have been wanting to ask if you determined what caused the fire."

He released a frustrated breath. Despite his suspicions, he'd found nothing to link Kendall to the blaze.

"Poor luck and a stray spark, I'm afraid." He withdrew a handful of silver buttons from his pocket and set them on the table. "I found these and some charred scraps of fabric near the fireplace, amid the remains of a chair. The buttons are from one of your sister's dresses, are they not?"

"They are. I remember her sewing them on it herself." She frowned. "But I can't think what that dress would have been doing draped on a chair. She hasn't worn it since we arrived from London."

"Perhaps her maid set it out for the morning?"

"Perhaps."

"You sound unconvinced."

"When I last checked on Jane, shortly before Bingley joined her, there were no clothes lying about the room. I find it unlikely that her maid would risk disturbing the couple to set out clothes Jane might not even wear the next day, depending on her state of recovery."

"It's easy enough to ask her when she returns with Jane."

"We should. There are also other members of this household whose movements last night invite further consideration."

"Do you speak of Mr. Kendall?" Maybe his wife knew something that could substantiate his suspicions.

"He's one of them. When I roused everyone to warn them about the fire, he was fully dressed—from cravat to boots! Whatever was he doing completely attired at half-past four in the morning?"

"Did he offer any explanation?"

"He claims he fell asleep in his clothes, but every instinct says he's lying. Do you not agree?"

"I do find it an unlikely coincidence that he would fall

asleep in his clothes two hours before he has to rise and flee a burning house in the middle of the night," Darcy said. "Particularly after making threats against Bingley earlier in the day and skulking about after the rest of the household has retired. But there is no proof that he entered their room. Jane and Bingley recall nothing."

"Nevertheless, I have a bad feeling about him."

"Kendall has that effect on most people."

"He has that look in his eyes—that same hardness of expression I saw in the cutpurse who accosted Caroline Parrish. Cold calculation, divorced from all principle or proper feeling."

"One cannot, however, convict him on impressions alone."

"He has to be up to something. Why else is he still here? We all went through a harrowing ordeal last night. Netherfield is not a comfortable place to be at present—the servants are preoccupied with cleaning and repairing the damage, the house still smells of smoke, his host is not even in residence. Good heavens, we have family connections inducing us to stay, and *I'm* eager to return to my own home."

"We desired that before the fire. But for a series of accidents, we would be at Pemberley now."

She pushed the food around on her plate, her appetite apparently having waned. "The situation was easier when I could just resent Caroline's bad luck. But with all that happened to Jane and Bingley yesterday, it now seems the universe is scheming against the Bingley family in general." Her fork stopped suddenly. "Or someone else is."

"What do you suggest?"

"Darcy, I dreamed about the carriage accident last night. Repeatedly."

It troubled him to see the lines of care that marked her face since the carriage accident. He wished he could somehow shield her, take the burden of worry for her sister entirely upon his own shoulders. "I am not surprised. It was a disturbing sight."

"No—I didn't dream about us discovering it. I saw it happening. I kept seeing a bolt or something fall to the ground, and then the wheel flying off. Are you quite sure it came loose by itself?"

"Not having inspected the coach before it left, I cannot tell you anything with certainty. But the vehicle could have been left vulnerable by negligent maintenance."

"Or sabotage."

"You suspect the accident was no accident?"

"It's possible, is it not?"

He considered a moment. Possible, yes. But probable? "Who would do such a thing? Who would have anything to gain?"

"Mr. Kendall. You told me he threatened Bingley yesterday with court action. If Bingley had perished in the mishap, could not Kendall file his claim against the estate? He then goes to Chancery with his false accounting records, and without Bingley there to refute them—"

"But Kendall did not arrive here until after we all departed for Longbourn."

"So it appeared. But we know the man prowled around Netherfield House for no good purpose last night. Could he not have done the same in Netherfield's outbuildings the night before, then timed his 'arrival' after seeing us all depart?"

He conceded the plausibility. Kendall could well have been in the area long before they would have been aware of him. Darcy already believed him capable of starting a fire to destroy the audit evidence and make good on his threat. Had he tampered with Bingley's carriage?

It was Darcy's experience that while many men might bluster out dire warnings, especially in the heat of an argument, most of them possessed enough conscience to stay on the decent side of the line between threat and action. Only a small number possessed the black state of mind and heart that enables one to commit wickedness against fellow human beings to advance one's own interests. Fortunately, Darcy had encountered few of them in his personal dealings—his rakehell brother-in-law Wickham was one of them—but they seemed to share a common pattern of behavior. They began with minor transgressions and escalated their misdeeds, each one making the next acceptable in their own minds until they arrive at a destination so foreign to civilized men that their broken moral compass can no longer lead them home.

Kendall, in his affairs with the Bingleys, had marked just such a course. Greed to larceny, larceny to extortion . . . extortion to attempted murder was not too great a leap. "If Kendall is capable of having set the fire," Darcy said, "he is capable of causing the carriage accident."

Their supper over, she rose and gathered their dishes back onto the tray. "You know . . . this would not mark the first time a Kendall was in the vicinity of a Bingley family misadventure involving horses."

"You believe the two episodes are related?"

"I didn't until just now. Think about it, though—we said from the start how curious it was that Caroline's riding incident lacked an obvious cause, and odd that Juliet Kendall invited her out to ride in the first place. The two had been estranged for a long time, and now Miss Kendall is frightfully angry at Caroline for 'stealing' Mr. Parrish from her."

"The servants said Miss Kendall never went near Mrs. Parrish's mare."

"It just seems rather convenient that the Kendalls have been in proximity of a good many recent Bingley catastrophes."

"I will grant you that. But I saw them nowhere in view when Mrs. Parrish was strolling down Bow Street, nor do I think Miss Kendall broke into the townhouse in a jealous pique to stab her with a carving knife."

"Mr. Kendall could have orchestrated those events. Mrs. Parrish was on some sort of mysterious business with that overstuffed reticule—who is to say that her errand did not involve him? Perhaps he sought to extort the money from her that he could not legally get from her brother."

"And when her mission failed, she tried to take her own life?" He took her face in his hands and kissed her forehead to soften his words. "My dear wife, I have long admired the liveliness of your mind, but I think it reaches too far this time. Logic does not support the connections you are trying to draw. Moreover, Mrs. Parrish's altered demeanor since the wedding presents a much stronger case for herself as the catalyst of her own misfortunes."

Elizabeth's expression grew troubled. "That supports a darker possibility."

"What might that be?"

"Mr. Parrish suspects his wife may have set the fire."

His brows rose. "He said so outright?"

"Indirectly. But his meaning was clear. He fears she is a danger to herself and others."

"Her injury upholds his misgivings. But the conflagration originated in Bingley's chamber, not hers. How could she have accidentally started it there?"

Elizabeth made no answer, only met his gaze. Her eyes held sadness, pity, resignation.

Darcy shook his head. "I cannot believe Caroline Parrish would deliberately harm her brother, even in . . . an altered condition of mind."

"Perhaps Bingley was not her target."

"I cannot believe she would harm your sister, either."

"She has never cared for Jane."

The assertion was true—as Caroline Bingley's unwilling

confidante when they first met the Bennets, Darcy knew only too well her opinions about every member of the family. Miss Bingley had never considered Jane Bennet good enough for her brother. Yet Darcy could not see supercilious snipes leading to such extreme physical expression. Mrs. Parrish was far more likely to assassinate another woman's reputation than her person.

"Perhaps she did not care for the dress."

"Sneaking into someone else's room in the middle of the night to destroy an unbecoming gown seems rather excessive fashion monitoring," she said. "I think even Beau Brummell would draw the line at that."

"Brummell would impale the wearer with his wit."

"So would the Miss Bingley we once knew."

He was forced to concur, not liking the unpleasant possibilities he was starting to entertain. While he doubted Caroline Parrish capable of deliberately trying to injure others, he could envision a scenario in which madness led her to damage property—and in which carelessness led to casualty. That potential made her more dangerous than Lawrence Kendall, for one could not anticipate her behavior.

"Mr. Parrish is wise to raise his vigilance," he said at last. "We should as well."

"Agreed. We shall keep a close eye on Mrs. Parrish when she returns." She released a sigh. "I suppose that happy task will fall largely to me, as I seem to encounter her more often than anybody."

"You *are* her most particular friend these days. Will you walk arm-in-arm during your next moonlight promenade?"

With a saucy look, she returned his impudence in equal measure. "Just to be safe, darling, I shouldn't wear the olive morning coat in her presence anymore if I were you. It is your least flattering."

Nineteen

"I was never more annoyed!"
Caroline Bingley to Darcy, Pride and Prejudice, *Chapter 6*

"Vulgar woman. Insipid girls. Deadly conversation. It is good to be home."

Elizabeth overheard Caroline's voice as she passed the music room. After four days at Longbourn, the family party had returned to Netherfield about an hour ago. Jane reported that upon hearing Netherfield was once again ready to receive them, the Bingley sisters had ordered their coaches with alacrity. Elizabeth wondered that Mrs. Hurst hadn't campaigned for a temporary return to the house in Grosvenor Street rather than stay with the Bennets, but Jane said the townhouse had been shut up when the Hursts left for Netherfield.

Major repairs to Netherfield's east wing were under way and would continue for a long time to come. But the staff, aided by every servant who could be spared from regular duties in houses throughout the neighborhood, had worked tirelessly to restore the rest of the home to a habitable state so that their mistress and the others could return. Elizabeth and her sister were grateful for the generosity of so many nearby families, especially since results varied according to who had performed which tasks. Those undertaken by Jane and Bingley's newest employees exhibited more zeal than skill: Smoky rugs looked like they'd been flogged rather than merely beaten; soot-stained walls had been scrubbed hard enough to reveal plaster beneath the paint.

"Thank heaven for Frederick and Louisa," Caroline continued. "I should have suffocated otherwise. And to be indebted to Mary Bennet for the clothes on my back until new ones can be made—it is simply mortifying! Why must she alone among my acquaintance approach my height?"

Elizabeth steeled herself against the insults to her family. In a way, she welcomed them—Caroline sounded more like herself than she had in weeks. If her visit with the Bennets had somehow provided the push she needed toward recovery, perhaps they would all be able to return to their own lives before too much longer. Provided, of course, that no more "accidents" befell anyone.

A series of notes issued from the pianoforte, an étude she recognized as a right-handed exercise. Mrs. Parrish yet wore a bandage on her left hand; her husband said the burn was healing slowly.

"I can't think how Charles and Darcy tolerate their new connections. They make the dullness of Mr. Hurst positively alluring."

Elizabeth chuckled softly. She'd no idea Caroline shared her opinion of Louisa's husband. But to whom was Mrs. Parrish speaking so candidly?

She ducked her head through the doorway, her mind rapidly assembling some excuse for the intrusion. But instead she found herself masking the surprise that had surely flashed across her face upon discovering the room's occupant.

Caroline Parrish was alone.

"Mrs. Darcy, would you be so kind as to join me and Mrs. Parrish in the drawing room?"

At Professor Randolph's request, Elizabeth slid a bookmark into the second volume of *The Italian* and rose from her seat in the conservatory. "Is something amiss?"

"Nothing of great consequence. It's only that this is the time of afternoon when I always meet with Mrs. Parrish to take notes for Dr. Lancaster. Usually Mr. Parrish joins us, but I can't find him, and I thought there should be a third person present for the sake of propriety. I'd ask Mrs. Hurst but I'm told she's napping, and Mrs. Bingley—"

"I'm happy to help you, Professor."

A smile conveyed his gratitude. "I'm sorry to disturb your reading. By all means, bring the book with you."

"You needn't apologize. I was beginning to think a warm fire preferable to views of the bleak landscape outside." Indeed, the only things green or cheerful about the conservatory today came from within the room. On the other side of the glass, thick grey clouds hung low in the sky, and the temperature had plummeted since morning.

They found Caroline pacing in the drawing room. She greeted Elizabeth's entrance with a look of uncertainty. "My husband is not coming?"

"I could not locate him." Randolph ushered her to the sofa. "Mrs. Darcy has consented to play chaperone."

Elizabeth held up her novel. "I will just sit in the corner with my book so as not to intrude on your privacy." She settled into a wing-backed chair and opened the volume.

"Mrs. Parrish, how are you feeling today?" Professor Randolph sat at the desk and withdrew a small notebook from one of his breast pockets.

"My hand hurts." She pulled at the bandage. "This is wound too tight."

"I'm sure Mr. Jones applied it properly when he saw you

this morning." Randolph dipped a quill into the inkpot and jotted a few words. "How are your spirits?"

"How should my spirits be? I have just spent two days with the—" She caught herself. "Away from here. All my clothes were destroyed in the fire. I am reduced to wearing borrowed cast-offs from Jane's sister until my London *modiste* can produce new gowns. And everywhere I go, the staff whispers about me. How would *your* spirits be?"

Elizabeth read the same paragraph for the third time and still comprehended none of it. She gave up trying to fool herself into thinking she would attend Mrs. Radcliffe's words instead of Mrs. Parrish's, but upheld the pretense of reading for Caroline's benefit.

"Have you suffered any headaches today?"

"None but this interview."

"That's a good sign—the spearmint leaves must be helping." Randolph entered a few notes.

"What is it you're writing about me?"

"Only what you've just told me."

She stomped over to him and seized the notebook. "'Headaches improved, but out of sorts,'" she read. "Really? Is that your impression?" She transferred the notebook to her left hand and snatched the pen with her right. She dipped it into the ink hastily, scattering drops of ink onto the desk as she withdrew it. Then she scrawled something onto the page.

"There—" She shoved the notebook and quill back at Professor Randolph. "Forward *that* observation to your colleague!"

As Caroline abandoned him to pace around the room, Randolph read the words. He colored, cleared his throat, and turned to a fresh page in the notebook.

She picked at her bandage again, this time unraveling the gauze. She then tossed the dressing into the fire. "I am taking off this bloody thing!"

"Mrs. Parrish—"

"Shocked you, did I? Well, I will say it again. Bloody! Bloody-bloody-bloody-bloody-bloody-bloody-bloody! I'm bloody tired of everyone in this bloody house treating me like a bloody invalid!" She tugged on her wedding ring but could not slide it off her still-swollen finger. "My hand hurts. But that is all. I am fine. I am fine!" She burst into tears, great gulping sobs that wracked her whole frame. "I am fine. . . ."

Professor Randolph returned the quill to its stand and closed his notebook. He met Elizabeth's troubled gaze and released a sigh. "Of course you are, Mrs. Parrish."

He withdrew his pocketwatch, muttered something under his breath, and glanced at Mrs. Parrish. He stared at her a long moment, then returned the watch to his waistcoat without opening it. Indeed, there seemed little point in consulting the time—Elizabeth doubted the interview had lasted five minutes.

Caroline quieted, apparently having pulled herself together. Elizabeth offered to escort her to her chamber. With a nod, she accepted.

As she rose and reached for Elizabeth's arm, her ring scratched Elizabeth's skin. Elizabeth bit her lip to keep from crying out. Good Lord, but those stones were sharp! The scratch didn't bleed, but did leave an inch-long welt on her arm. A month ago, she might have thought the accident deliberate. But in Caroline's current state Elizabeth doubted she was sensible of half her actions anymore.

Mrs. Parrish came down to dinner that evening for the first time since leaving London. Her husband, his face drawn with anxiety, watched her every move and never left her side. The man looked exhausted. Elizabeth wondered if he'd allowed himself any sleep since the night of the fire.

Caroline sat between Mr. Parrish and Professor Randolph. Mr. Kendall, still hanging around Netherfield for reasons the

Darcys could only guess at, sat opposite. He lounged in his seat with the ease of someone actually welcome among the party, which he decidedly was not. His contemptuous presence smothered any gaiety that might have been felt upon the eve of the family's homecoming. Had he conducted himself thus at Pemberley, Elizabeth suspected Darcy would have shown him the door long before now regardless of the weather or any other excuse the brute could devise. But Bingley, lacking the firmness to oust even an uninvited guest from his home, and worn down by recent events, tolerated his continued imposition with forced civility. The others followed his lead.

Tonight, however, Kendall's insolence exceeded all previous displays. No sooner had the soup been served than he commenced offering backhanded compliments to his hosts. The main courses saw him expanding his veiled insults to include additional members of the group. During dessert, he stared at Caroline until she became so disconcerted that her fork clattered against the plate each time she lowered it.

Finally, she gave up eating altogether. "Have you something you wish to say, Mr. Kendall?"

"I was just noticing how your color has faded since the London season. Perhaps it is too much bloodletting." He cast a pointed look at her scarred wrists. "Someone should question your physician."

"Maybe other leeches are to blame."

Beside her, Parrish took her hand in his in a gesture of support. His wedding ring caught the flickering light of the candelabras. "Don't let him provoke you, dearest."

She winced and brought both hands to her temples.

"Caroline?" Bingley's voice held concern.

"I fear another of my headaches is coming on." She rose to leave. When Mr. Parrish began to join her she motioned him back to his seat. "Stay. I'll be fine."

Parrish looked as if he very much wanted to follow, but

heeded her request. As the door closed behind her, Kendall shrugged. "Pallor. Headaches. It would seem that marriage does not agree with her."

Parrish locked gazes with Kendall as the rest of the company waited in strained silence to see if he would rise to the ill-mannered gentleman's bait. They stared at each other a long moment, and Elizabeth sensed some unspoken communication was taking place. Ultimately, Parrish placed his napkin beside his plate, rose, and bowed to Jane. "Excuse me, Mrs. Bingley. I am going to check on my wife." He departed without another look at Kendall.

Elizabeth admired his restraint. Kendall's presence in the house was unpleasant to all, but it must be particularly awkward for Mr. Parrish in light of his previous relationship with Kendall's daughter.

Bingley's face flushed with uncharacteristic ire. "Mr. Kendall, I must insist that while you are a guest in my home, you treat my family with respect."

"Respect your family!" He laughed, a short burst that sounded like nothing so much as a donkey's bray. "Do you speak of your mad sister or her fickle husband? I'm a betting man, Bingley, and I bet Mr. Parrish won't stick around this family for long."

Kendall's gaze swept the company, coming to rest on Mr. Hurst. A glint entered his eye. "Not like the steadfast Mr. Hurst here. Nothing's more important than family in times of adversity—right, Hurst?"

Startled by the direct address, Mr. Hurst nearly spilled his wine. "Er—right."

"How about it, Hurst? Care to lay a wager with me regarding your new brother-in-law?"

"I—uh—" Hurst's pasty face reddened. Perspiration dotted his forehead. "No, thank you," he said hoarsely. "I'm not much of a gambler."

"Indeed? I thought I'd heard otherwise. I must be mistaken." Kendall hefted his bulk to a standing position. "I think I'll retire early this evening. The servants were unbearably noisy this morning."

"Perhaps you would find it more comfortable to return home and conduct any remaining business with Mr. Bingley via post," Darcy suggested.

"If this damnable weather would cooperate, that is precisely what I would do. Unfortunately it lingers, therefore so must I." As Kendall sauntered through the door, the wind howled outside.

Another storm was rising.

Twenty

Mrs. Hurst . . . had married a man of more fashion than fortune.

Pride and Prejudice, *Chapter 4*

The snow everyone anticipated did not come. Instead it rained: huge, angry drops that froze as soon as they reached the ground. Elizabeth woke to a world encased in ice. Sunlight glinted off the crystals, lending an ethereal sparkle to the landscape that would have been beautiful had it not also provided Mr. Kendall an excuse to trespass upon Netherfield's hospitality and patience still longer.

"There will be no traveling today, I fear. For Mr. Kendall or anyone else." Elizabeth left the window but did not succumb to the temptation of crawling back into her snug bed. Instead, she padded across the cold oak floor to the armoire and selected her warmest gown from among those Lucy had laundered after the fire.

"Can we not find him a pair of ice skates and send him off?" Darcy fastened his shirt and sat to pull on his boots. "I do not think I can tolerate his company at one more meal without developing indigestion."

"He was insufferable at dinner, was he not? Spewing

venom at everybody. I thought Mrs. Parrish might be reduced to tears for the second time in a day."

"He seemed to be seeking a fight from any quarter. Had I my fencing gear handy, I might have obliged him."

"I would like to watch you fence sometime, but against a more worthy opponent. Let Mr. Kendall exhaust his quarrel-someness on lesser men—Mr. Hurst, perhaps. He seemed to pay that gentleman extra attention last night."

"Yes. I do not think Hurst saw it coming." He approached the mirror to fold his cravat.

"His invitation to wager struck me as odd." So had Hurst's reaction to it—the suggestion seemed to have made him nervous. "It reminded me of Lord Chatfield's remark about Mr. Hurst. What was it the earl said?"

"That Hurst's name appears often in White's betting book."

"He also mentioned losses at cards. Yet Mr. Hurst asserted that he wasn't much of a gambler."

"Elizabeth, I have seen *you* lose at cards in your own mother's drawing room. Does that mean I married a gamester?"

"My surrender of a few shillings has never become an item of public conversation."

"Idle gossip."

"The earl hardly impresses me as a scandalmonger. Does he you?"

He met her gaze in the mirror, then returned his attention to the cravat. "No," he admitted.

"Then perhaps the rumors have substance after all." Though if they did, what would it matter? So Mr. Hurst wasted his money on speculation. He could afford it, could he not?

Perhaps he could not.

Elizabeth's mind leapt. When the Hursts had first entered Hertfordshire, general knowledge had set their income at two thousand a year, derived from his own inheritance and Louisa's settlement invested in the five percents. If he had lost more than his finances could bear, how would he pay off his creditors? What did indolent gentlemen do to generate income, other than sit around waiting for some wealthy relative to—

She caught her breath. No. Surely her imagination ran wild. Didn't it?

It must.

Maybe not?

Darcy's question about Jane and Bingley's recent "accidents" came back to her. *Who would have anything to gain?* Her pulse quickened. "What would happen to Bingley's fortune if he and Jane died without heirs?"

"According to the will he drew up upon his inheritance, it would be divided evenly between his sisters. Though, of course, as they are married women, that money would fall under their husbands' control," Darcy said. "Now that he has wed Jane, he might change the terms to provide for your sisters as well, but to my knowledge he has not done so yet."

"And if Caroline also met an untimely, childless end along with them?"

"Then the Hursts would—" He regarded her incredulously. "Surely you do not suggest that Hurst is behind the Bingley family's recent troubles?"

"If he *is* hurting for money—"

"Elizabeth—"

"—an 'unexpected' inheritance would solve his financial problems."

"Elizabeth!" He regarded her in horror. "Consider what you are saying! To accuse a respectable gentleman, without anything remotely resembling evidence—"

"Now that I think about it, he did answer his door awfully fast the night of the fire. Especially for a man who never moves quickly for anything except the sherry decanter. He could not have been sleeping when I knocked." Not wanting to wait for Lucy to help her dress, she slipped into her gown and slid her arms into the sleeves. She was suddenly impatient to begin her day.

"This is absurd. I refuse to participate in this conversation further." He put on his coat.

"If Jane and Bingley are in danger, we must consider all the possibilities."

"All the reasonable ones."

She crossed to him for aid in buttoning the back of her dress, lifting her braid to grant him better access. "At least let us learn more about Hurst's finances. If you could write to Lord Chatfield—"

"You wish me to *what*?"

"There can be no harm in a discreet enquiry."

"No harm except destroying a man's reputation."

"Mr. Hurst is managing that well enough on his own if rumors are already circulating."

"Then we should not make matters worse." He fumbled with the small buttonholes. "How many buttons does one dress need?"

"Explain to the earl that it's precisely out of concern for Hurst's reputation that you wish to know specifically what is being said about him. That you worry your friend is the victim of unsubstantiated gossip."

"This pursuit is a waste of time."

He reached the top button. She turned and caught his hands in hers. "Darcy," she said softly, "I fear for my sister's life. Please—indulge me in this."

He looked away and uttered a sound of exasperation. She brought one of his hands to her face and cupped it against her cheek. His fingers were stiff at first, but she leaned into his palm, and eventually the muscles relaxed.

He once more met her gaze, his reflecting resignation. "You know I can deny you nothing."

"Ouch!"

Elizabeth dropped her embroidery hoop and sucked a small drop of blood from the finger she had just pricked. The stitchery had been going poorly, even for her, whose skill with needle and thread was passable but far from extraordinary. She had not the patience of Jane, the discipline of Mary, or the compulsive ostentation of the Bingley sisters that enabled them to devote endless hours to producing elaborate designs that garnered praise from even casual observers. While she admired their efforts, Elizabeth took a utilitarian approach to her own needlework, preferring to spend her leisure hours reading, in conversation with others, or outside enjoying fresh air and exercise.

Today, however, the weather kept her indoors, her housemates had scattered to engage in other pursuits, and nothing in Netherfield's library could hold the interest of a mind preoccupied with recent events. Too preoccupied, apparently, for she had carelessly stuck herself while sewing a simple backstitch.

She looked at her finger. The tiny wound was barely visible but still stung, encouraging her to indulge in the alreadyexistent inclination to abandon the project and find something else to do. When she went to secure the needle, however, she discovered that it had slipped off the floss. A scan of her empty lap revealed that it had fallen farther afield.

"God bless it!" She rose and examined the sofa. No luck. She dropped to her hands and knees. Where was the troublesome thing?

While she thus pawed the carpet, inevitably someone entered the drawing room. "Mrs. Darcy, might I be of service?"

She recognized the voice even before glancing up, thankful to see Mr. Parrish's amiable face. If she had to be caught in such an undignified position, she would rather have it witnessed by him than Mr. Kendall or one of the Bingley sisters. "I've lost my needle."

"It can't have strayed far." He knelt and ran his fingers over the rug. "I'm amazed you women keep track of these things as well as you do. I'm sure I'd lose them left and right, only to locate them in some unpleasant manner hours later."

"I hope to spare anyone in our acquaintance such a pointed discovery."

"Oh, I don't know about that. Perhaps we should invite Mr. Kendall to join us. In his stocking feet, of course."

She returned his grin. "Of course."

His smile faded. "I hope I don't misrepresent myself, Mrs. Darcy. It is not in my nature to wish ill on anyone. At least, not any decent person."

"I understand. Mr. Kendall was most ungentlemanly last night."

"Caroline was beside herself after dinner. It nearly broke my heart, for I knew myself to be Kendall's true target. Why could he not confine his attacks to me? I can ignore them." He returned his attention to the rug. "I bear him no real animosity. I know he lashes out at a woman I love, to defend a woman he loves. He wants to punish me for a perceived slight to his daughter. I just wish he would finish his business with Bingley and depart."

You and everyone else, she wanted to say. "I have not yet seen Mrs. Parrish this morning. I hope she is better?"

"Sadly, no. She had seemed to be improving since the fire, hadn't she? At least, I thought so—though maybe I saw what I longed to see. But Kendall's offense last night has set her back again."

"Temporarily, I am sure."

"I'm not so certain. She remains distraught. His observations struck a heavy blow to her vanity at a time when she's already so fragile." He studied her as if trying to decide upon some matter. Then he cleared his throat. "Mrs. Darcy, I would do anything to restore my wife to herself. I—I wonder if you might help me."

"I will do what I can."

He relaxed and ventured a half smile. "I hoped you would say as much. I have, well, a rather bold request. Might I be so forward as to ask for a lock of your hair?"

The petition rendered her momentarily speechless. She knew not what to think. Even Darcy had never solicited a lock of her hair. "My—my hair?"

"Oh—not for myself," he said hurriedly. "I wish to place it in a locket to give to Caroline."

Necklaces, rings, even embroidery made of hair were common enough gifts between loved ones. When Elizabeth was ten, she and her sisters had given their mother a bracelet fashioned from their locks for her birthday. She was not, however, close enough to Caroline Parrish to feel moved to bestow a similar present upon her. Indeed, something within her rebelled at the very idea.

"I'm asking her family as well," Parrish continued. "Some of them have already agreed."

The inclusion of others made the entreaty less strange but brought her no closer to acquiescence. "Forgive me, Mr. Parrish, but I fail to comprehend how such an ornament can heal what ails her."

His face reddened. He looked apologetic. "You'll probably consider this balderdash. But I've become desperate enough to try a custom I once overhead a woman describe as I walked in the French Quarter. She was telling her friend that a good-luck charm created from the hair of someone dear can ward off harm by encircling the wearer with the protection of friends. I don't necessarily believe there's any truth in it, but I figured it couldn't hurt."

Elizabeth had never heard of the superstition but esteemed

Mr. Parrish for his willingness to try a foreign practice if it meant helping his wife. She doubted Darcy would display so broad a mind. "I don't find it silly at all," she said.

His features relaxed. "You agree, then?"

She hesitated. Admire him she might, but if Parrish sought to include her in the experiment, he mistook the intimacy of her acquaintance with his wife. They were not friends; indeed, before her engagement to Parrish, Miss Bingley had been her open antagonist. Despite present circumstances, Elizabeth doubted anything of hers would hold value for Caroline.

"I'm afraid I must decline," she said.

His face fell in disappointment. "Won't you reconsider?"

She almost assented rather than subject herself to his despondent aspect a moment longer. But she listened to instinct. "I want very much for Mrs. Parrish to enjoy the protection you describe. Fill the locket with strands from her family—they will hold more meaning for her than any I can offer."

He turned away from her, busying himself with the carpet once more. "I beg your pardon, Mrs. Darcy. You've been generosity itself since this ordeal began. I see that in this I've asked too much."

Guilt gripped her. "Mr. Parrish, I—"

"Look! Here it is—your needle." He handed her the instrument. "Now at least one crisis is ended." She immediately withdrew the housewife she kept in her sash pocket and inserted the needle into the small notions case for safekeeping.

As she watched him leave, she nearly called him back. Was she being selfish? What harm would it do to accede? Yet cooperating felt wrong somehow, as if contributing her hair to the locket would not help Caroline's recovery but hinder it. Moreover, she knew Darcy would not approve. He would dismiss the custom as nonsense and consider it an affront that

Parrish had requested so personal a token from his wife, even on another's behalf.

No, 'twas better not to participate. But the part of her that wanted to believe in simple superstitions and Professor Randolph's mysterious articles truly hoped the charm would work.

Twenty-one

"*You are considering how insupportable it would be to pass many evenings in this manner—in such society; and indeed I am quite of your opinion.*"
Caroline Bingley to Darcy, Pride and Prejudice, *Chapter 6*

*M*r. Morris wants a commitment, and I can't say I blame him. It will cost a fortune to repair the fire damage." Bingley descended the stairs more quickly than he had in almost a se'ennight. Darcy took the brisk gait as a happy sign that his friend had fully recovered from his recent accidents.

"Yes, but it does not have to be your fortune," Darcy replied. "You planned to quit Netherfield soon anyway. A long-term lease is not in your best interest."

"He asks for three years. Perhaps I can talk him into a twelvemonth." They rounded the banister and headed toward the billiard room.

"Even if you can persuade Mr. Morris to accept a shorter term, why subject yourself and Jane to the noise and discomfort of a house under repair? Have you given my proposal further consideration?"

"I have. But who knows when the right estate will present itself for purchase? Meanwhile, we can't just move into Pemberley with you indefinitely."

"Why not? We certainly have the space. And our wives would be delighted." Darcy longed to be home. Not since before his parents' deaths had Pemberley held such expectation of domestic felicity as it did now that Elizabeth would be returning with him. Adding Bingley and Jane to the family party created a still happier prospect.

"But Caroline seems no closer to recovery."

He sobered. "Yes, there is that." The same fire that motivated his invitation to Bingley made him reluctant to extend the invitation to the Parrishes. He felt compassion for Caroline and sympathy for her husband. But until she either recovered or was absolved of all suspicion in his own mind of having caused the Netherfield fire, he would not risk her setting Pemberley ablaze as well. "How does the sale of Mont Joyau proceed? Might Parrish purchase an estate here in England soon?"

"I don't know. I suspect the situation with Caroline has distracted him from other matters."

They reached the billiards room, where Darcy had intended to press his case over a friendly game. They found the table already in use, however, by Mr. Hurst and Mr. Kendall. Bingley apologized for their intrusion, whereupon Mr. Hurst assured them that the match was nearing conclusion.

"Your shot, Hurst," Kendall prompted.

As Hurst leaned over the table and slid the cue between his fingers, his hand trembled. The shot slipped, sending the white ball straight into a pocket without touching the other two.

Kendall made no attempt to suppress his smug smile. He potted the red ball on his next shot. "Game over."

Hurst's face lost some of its color. "Come—let's play again. Same stakes."

"Perhaps later. These gentlemen wait for the table."

Hurst glanced from Kendall to them and back. "Of course." With still-unsteady hands, he replaced the cue on the wall rack.

"It is nearly dinnertime anyway." He passed Mrs. Nicholls in the doorway.

"Mr. Bingley, sir? Mrs. Bingley wishes to see you. She's in the dining room instructing the staff on Christmas preparations."

"Thank you, Nicholls. Tell her I'll be there directly." He turned to Darcy. "I can't imagine this taking long."

"I'll wait."

Kendall chuckled as the door closed behind Bingley. "You pups obviously haven't been married long. When a woman wants to discuss holiday preparations, plan to devote your whole afternoon to it. But don't expect to see any of your suggestions actually adopted."

"Thank you for the marital advice."

He gestured toward the table. "He'll be a while. Shall we have a game of carambole in the meantime?"

Unable to quickly devise a polite excuse, Darcy agreed. He did, however, decline Kendall's suggestion to "make things interesting" with a wager. He suspected the only safe bet involving Kendall was that the man cheated at billiards the same way he cheated in business.

Kendall positioned the balls. "Married life treating you well, Darcy? It's been what—over a fortnight now?"

"Twenty days."

"Ha! Still counting each day, are you? Your lady must be keeping you well satisfied."

Darcy stared, shocked that even Kendall would display such vulgarity as to allude to the intimacy he shared with Elizabeth. That he indeed enjoyed a state of connubial bliss beyond his bachelor imaginings was beside the point.

Kendall lined up his opening shot. "Parrish, on the other hand, probably regrets his choice of a wife. That woman is one cold fish."

Though he was inclined to agree, Darcy felt called upon to

defend his friend's sister. "I think you criticize her unfairly because of another young lady's disappointed hopes."

"If you speak of my daughter, the only person suffering disappointment is Frederick Parrish. I don't regret for a moment discouraging his addresses toward her."

"I understood it was he who cried off."

"Hmmph. So he'd like everyone to believe."

Darcy leaned on his cue stick as Kendall attempted the next shot. "You harbored some objection to Mr. Parrish?"

"The rake was far too forward. Hadn't even declared himself, and he asks her for a lock of her hair!" Kendall missed the shot. "Made me wonder what else he might be asking her for. I demanded its return and told the whelp to go sniff around some other girl's skirts. He certainly lost no time finding a replacement. An inferior one, but she seems to suit his purposes."

Darcy regretted ever having agreed to the game, wishing he had chosen rudeness over subjecting himself to Kendall's conversation. Juliet's father was probably just trying to save face, to preserve his daughter's reputation by injuring Parrish's. By claiming for himself the responsibility of ending the courtship, Kendall could prevent other potential suitors from pondering what faults Juliet possessed that had caused Parrish to reject her. But why the defensive father felt the need to harangue Darcy over the business, he knew not.

As Darcy prepared to take his turn, a muffled cough issued from the other side of the door. "Come in, Bingley. You will not disturb my shot."

The door remained shut. Kendall opened it and stuck his head into the hall. "No one here." He shrugged. "Must have been a passing servant."

Must have been. Darcy wished it had signaled the arrival of anyone else in the household—anyone with an errand requiring him to abandon this game. But unfortunately, no convenient rescue appeared forthcoming. He leaned forward and made the shot.

"I suppose you consider Parrish a good catch for Bingley's sister." Kendall's statement seemed timed to distract Darcy, but he nevertheless scored. "What do you think of him?"

Darcy really hadn't given Parrish much thought at all. Since his engagement to Elizabeth, his own affairs had been foremost in his mind, with the Bingley family's recent troubles occupying the rest of his attention. Whether Parrish had been too ardent a suitor with Miss Kendall neither concerned nor interested him. Though the American might exhibit a little less polish when compared to his English counterparts, over-all his conduct had been what Darcy would expect of a gentleman. Which is more than he could say for Kendall, and why he had no inclination to discuss his perceptions of Caroline's husband with him.

"I am pleased to know him."

"You might change your mind upon closer acquaintance."

First marital guidance, now social counsel. Darcy had heard as much of the man's smug blather as he could tolerate for one afternoon. "Is there some point you wish to make, Mr. Kendall?"

They were interrupted by the entrance of the very person under discussion. Mr. Parrish popped into the room. "Darcy, I just saw Mr. Morris arrive. I thought Bingley might wish you to join them."

Bingley probably did, but Darcy would seize upon the opportunity to escape Kendall regardless. "Thank you, Mr. Parrish. He comes to discuss plans for demolition work in the east wing. Have you and Mrs. Parrish retrieved all that you care to from your former chamber?"

"I believe so."

"If not, have the servants do it today. Morris may choose to begin as early as tomorrow."

Kendall observed their exchange with quiet interest. Darcy replaced his cue stick on the rack.

"Do you concede?" Kendall asked.

"The game is yours." Though he had been winning, Darcy was happy to forfeit the victory along with Kendall's company. Had he accepted Kendall's proposal of a wager, he would have gladly relinquished that, too.

"How about you, Parrish? Care to play?"

Parrish appeared even less inclined to subject himself to Kendall's society than Darcy. "Billiards is not my forte."

"No, you excel at other games, don't you?"

Parrish stared at him a long moment. "Yes, I do," he said finally.

They left Kendall in the billiards room alone. "My courtship with Juliet is ended," Parrish said to Darcy as they walked. "I've married someone else. I wish Mr. Kendall and his daughter would just reconcile themselves to that."

Darcy thought of the wrath he himself had incurred when he'd disregarded someone else's unofficial "understanding" and chosen to marry Elizabeth over his cousin Anne. His aunt, Lady Catherine, was still so affronted that, despite Mr. Collins's speculations to the contrary, he doubted she'd forgive him to the end of her days.

Hell hath no fury like the parent of a woman scorned.

Elizabeth retraced her steps, trying to recall where she'd left her bonnet. She had brought it with her when she came downstairs that morning in anticipation of taking a walk directly after breakfast. Jane, however, had distracted her by soliciting an opinion of the garland that had just been hung on the staircase in the hall. One end of it drooped drunkenly, its tail dangling to drape a suit of armor in an evergreen boa.

"Is it very noticeable?" Jane had asked. "The servants have

been working so hard to put the house back in order. I hate to criticize them about Yuletide decorations."

"Jane—it's noticeable."

Then it had been on to the parlor, where holly hung so thick that its pointed leaves threatened to draw blood from all who entered. "I said I thought a little holly might be nice. . . ."

"Apparently, a little more is nicer still. I hope you made no similar suggestion about mistletoe, or we're all in trouble."

Jane's eyes had grown wide. "I have not yet seen the drawing room!"

They had found that room converted into a bower capable of staining even Cupid's cheek with a blush. Now, as thick clouds gathered and threatened to cut short her walk, Elizabeth headed back there in hopes of finding the door frames clear and her bonnet lying in the only remaining place she could think to look for it.

She heard Professor Randolph's voice coming from the room and recalled that this was his usual meeting time with Mrs. Parrish and her husband. She opened the door quietly, intending to duck in, retrieve her bonnet, and exit without disturbing them. When she entered the room, however, she stopped suddenly.

Randolph and Caroline were alone. And they were engaged in no ordinary interview.

Twenty-two

"Disguise of every sort is my abhorrence."
    Darcy to Elizabeth, Pride and Prejudice, Chapter 34

*C*aroline lay on the sofa, arms crossed over her chest, head tilted back, eyes closed. Small bluish green leaves were scattered on her forehead. Professor Randolph stood over her, chanting foreign words and pressing some sort of object into her left hand.

From where she stood, Elizabeth could not identify the item. It was small and round, and flashed in the strong late afternoon sunlight penetrating the south windows. Nor could she identify the language he spoke—it sounded like none of the Romance languages she'd heard.

Utterly absorbed in his ritual, Randolph didn't notice her entrance. He continued his chant, moving the object to Caroline's chest, her forehead, her lips. His voice, lower than usual, rose and fell in volume like the swell of waves against the sand. All the while, Caroline lay still. Unnaturally still.

A cloud passed over the sun. Goosebumps raced across Elizabeth's skin. The chant seemed to swirl around her, its cadence dulling the edges of her consciousness. Lethargy took hold of her body; her limbs weighed more than she could lift.

What was happening to her? To Caroline? She forced her jaw to work, her tongue to speak.

"Professor?"

He whirled around. "Mrs. Darcy! I did not hear the door."

She blinked. Her mind was clear, her body perfectly normal once more. Had she only imagined the previous sensations? Regardless, she had not imagined Randolph's actions. "What are you doing?"

He palmed the mysterious object and brought his hand to his hip. "Doing? Oh—the song? That was a canticle from ancient times, said to bring peace to troubled minds. A lullaby, if you will. Mrs. Parrish said she has not been sleeping well."

"It did not sound like a lullaby."

"Yes, well . . ." He cleared his throat. "I'm afraid you have found out my secret, Mrs. Darcy."

Startled by his directness, she held her breath and waited for him to continue. Her heart pounded so hard she thought its beat would drown out his admission.

"I am an exceedingly poor musician."

And an even worse liar. "Where is Mr. Parrish? Does he not usually join you when you meet with his wife?"

"He was unavailable. I could find no substitute, and the hour grew late."

She pointedly eyed his hand. "What is that you hold?"

"Nothing, madam." He turned up two empty hands as proof. "What do you think you saw?"

He must have slipped the item into his trouser pocket. "I know not."

"Perhaps it was a trick of the light."

She studied his face, a mask of pretended innocence. "Yes—I am certain it was indeed some sort of trick."

She entered the room further, wanting a better look at Mrs. Parrish. As she approached, she noticed bluish green sprigs on the floor that matched the leaves on Caroline's forehead. It looked like rue from the herb garden. The sprigs formed a circle around the sofa; another sprig rested in a small bowl of water on a side table. "What is the rue for?"

"Another cure for headaches." Mumbling something under his breath, the professor knelt to retrieve the sprigs from the floor. When he had gathered them all, he set them on the table. "After last night, I thought Mrs. Parrish needed something stronger than spearmint."

She removed the leaves from Caroline's forehead herself. Mrs. Parrish still did not move. Her continued stillness alarmed Elizabeth as much as Randolph's equivocation. "I have never heard of a physician using rue in this manner."

"Rue has many uses in folk medicine. It is believed to aid the mind."

"As I recall, it didn't do Ophelia any good." Distrust made her reluctant to return the leaves to him. She instead withdrew her housewife and dropped them inside, watching for his reaction. He said nothing, only met her gaze with a look that indicated he understood her motive perfectly. If only she could comprehend his.

The room grew dimmer as frozen droplets pinged against the glass. The sound captured his attention. He stared through the windows at the incipient storm. "Winter announces its arrival."

His statement reminded her that it was the twenty-first of December—the winter solstice, a date he had mentioned the last time they had discussed herbalism. What was it he had called the art? *A little bit medicine, a little bit magic.*

What was this man truly about? As she studied him, his features seemed to shift in the grey light, recasting themselves into something not quite of this world. An overwhelming urge to flee seized her. But before she could act on it, Mrs. Parrish stirred. Caroline winced and brought her hand to her temple; her eyes fluttered open. When her gaze lighted upon Elizabeth and the professor, she bolted upright and swung her legs to the floor.

"What is going on? How came I to be lying here?"

"You nodded off, Mrs. Parrish." Randolph walked to the wine decanter and poured a draught. "Here—sip this. How do you feel? You complained of a headache earlier."

Caroline accepted the glass. "It's better. Not gone, but better."

"I am glad to hear it." Randolph turned to Elizabeth. "See, Mrs. Darcy? Naught is amiss. You needn't concern yourself— or anyone else—with what you observed. Or, rather, thought you observed. Moreover, I'm sure Mrs. Parrish wishes her interviews with me to remain confidential."

"Of course."

"I assure you, Mrs. Darcy—I am only trying to help Mrs. Parrish."

She forced a smile. "Pray, forgive the intrusion. I came in here seeking my bonnet, but now that the weather has turned I believe I'll instead walk in the gallery. Would you care to join me, Mrs. Parrish?"

"What time is it?"

Randolph withdrew his pocketwatch from his trousers. "About half-past three."

Elizabeth started, but quickly recovered her composure. The watch—she recalled the strange markings on it that she'd noticed at Lord Chatfield's dinner party. Was this the object she had just seen him using? Didn't he usually keep it in the fob pocket of his waistcoat? Sure enough, that was the pocket to which he returned it.

Caroline declined Elizabeth's invitation, citing a desire to take her time changing her gown for tea. Elizabeth was just as happy to escape her company without leaving her alone with the professor. The three of them exited the room together. In the hall, where garland now drooped on two sides, they

parted. Mrs. Parrish and Professor Randolph headed upstairs.
Elizabeth headed straight for Darcy.

She shivered. Darcy's embrace, strong as it was, could not
suppress the dread that suffused her.

What had she witnessed? More than Randolph's weak
explanation suggested. She had not merely fallen prey to a
trick of light; her ears had not mistaken a lullaby for something more potent.

Professor Julian Randolph. Who was he, really? She had
liked him, found his eccentricity charming. He was different
from anyone else in her acquaintance and she considered his
uniqueness refreshing.

Now it alarmed her.

What did any of them actually know about him? That he
studied the supernatural and drifted from job to job. What
manner of man was he? He claimed to be motivated by academic enquiry, but did he have an ulterior purpose for his
specialty? Was he some sort of practitioner of the dark arts?
Elizabeth had heard of such people—in stories. Not in real
life. But folklore sprang from grains of truth. If, in fact, individuals existed who could manipulate unseen forces, and if
Randolph were such a man, what power did he hold? And to
what purpose did he use it?

As shadows overtook the sitting room, Darcy led her to the
chaise longue and pulled her down beside him. "Elizabeth, I
have been waiting patiently for you to speak, but you are
starting to worry me."

She tucked her head in the crook of his neck. "I've just had
the most strange encounter with Professor Randolph. I
believe we have been deceived in his character."

"I am sorry to hear it. He seemed an honest fellow, if misguided. Tell me."

She related the incident—the mysterious object, the rue, the chanting, the dissembling. "How stupid does he think I am?" she asked at the conclusion. "He was doing *something* to her, Darcy. Casting a hex or laying a curse or practicing God-knows-what ritual."

"What he was *doing* was muttering a string of nonsense and touching a pocketwatch to her. Mrs. Parrish seemed unaltered by the event?"

"To all outward appearance."

"Then it sounds as if he did not actually harm her."

"This time. But he meets with her every day—he has unlimited opportunity to attempt again what I interrupted this afternoon."

"Then he has had ample opportunity before today. Yet Mrs. Parrish does not seem to be suffering the effects of any spell."

"Doesn't she? She has not been herself since—well, since Randolph stood up at her wedding. What if her behavior is not caused by nerves at all, but some sort of supernatural influence, directed by him?"

"With the help of a timepiece?" Darcy shook his head. "Elizabeth, Randolph can no more practice magic than I can. If he could, would he not use it to generate wealth? Or at least remain employed?"

She wasn't ready to give up her theory of Randolph's mystical connections, but let it drop for now. Surely, however, Darcy could not deny the alarming nature of whatever she had observed in the drawing room. "You cannot believe his actions benign?"

"I believe them mundane. His charms cannot really work. But if he *believes* they can, he might attempt to use them. Or if Mrs. Parrish believes in them, she might be susceptible to suggestion. We must, however, ask ourselves to what purpose Randolph abuses his knowledge of the supernatural. What has he to gain from manipulating Mrs. Parrish?"

What indeed? She burrowed against him once more, wishing they were anywhere but Netherfield, discussing anything but Caroline Parrish. Caroline's crisis was an inconvenience to all: Darcy and her, Bingley and Jane, the Parrishes themselves— all of them were trapped in a state of suspended animation, unable to truly begin their new lives as married couples until the situation reached a resolution. All hoped Randolph's correspondence with his American colleague would yield a cure. But the recent bad weather had made posting letters to London, let alone abroad, difficult—Darcy's enquiry to Lord Chatfield had just gone out this morning. Who knew when they might hear from Dr. Lancaster? Meanwhile, the questionable professor was the closest thing to an expert they had at their disposal.

Perhaps that was it.

Elizabeth caught her breath. Darcy had joked about Randolph using his supernatural expertise to find employment, but in effect Caroline's "nervous condition" had created a living for him—secured him a place in Parrish's daily life, his home, his gratitude. Randolph had said he hoped for Parrish's patronage; Caroline's illness had given him just that. "Perhaps Professor Randolph seeks to make himself indispensable to Mr. Parrish."

Darcy's eyes flashed immediate understanding. "The poor scholar has enjoyed a comfortable life since Mrs. Parrish fell ill. Her condition earned him an invitation to Netherfield."

"Which not only provides him free bed and board, but puts him in close quarters with you and Bingley—two more potential benefactors. And Bingley is so generous, and easily guided . . ."

"Mrs. Darcy, I do believe you may be on to something."

She left Darcy to change for tea. Encountering Mr. Parrish in the great hall, she begged a word with him as they climbed the staircase together.

"You, Mrs. Darcy, may have two or even three," he said gallantly. "I am your humble servant."

"I have a question concerning your friend Professor Randolph. I wonder how well you know him?"

"We met about a year ago. He's a fine fellow—a bit odd, maybe. But kind, and generous with his time and knowledge."

"You trust his assessment of Mrs. Parrish's condition?"

"Indeed, yes. He has proven himself invaluable since Caroline . . . fell ill."

They paused at the top of the stairs. "Perhaps too valuable," Elizabeth said.

"I beg your pardon?"

"Did you miss their session today?"

"No, I was present. For most of it, at least—I left while Randolph was finishing up his notes. I had a letter to write to my solicitor." His brows drew together. "Why do you ask?"

"I happened to enter the drawing room while they were still together and found him engaged in strange behavior—scattering rue and reciting some sort of chant as Mrs. Parrish slept. He also seemed to be using his pocketwatch somehow—surely you have seen it, the one with the runes inscribed? I wasn't sure if he did so with your knowledge."

His expression darkened. "No, he did not. What sort of chant? What were the words?"

She shrugged. "A foreign tongue."

He stared at her, incredulous. "I can't believe Randolph would—" A muscle in his jaw tensed. "I trusted him!"

"The professor assured me he was only trying to help Mrs. Parrish."

In the space of a heartbeat, his expression changed from angry to panicked. "Caroline—how was she? How did she respond?"

"She seemed all right. Better, in fact—she indicated her headache had subsided."

"Well," he said with forced brightness, "I'm glad of that." But anxiety soon overtook his features once more.

Elizabeth regretted having told him—or at least, having added to the burden of cares he already bore. "I'm sorry for alarming you. And I certainly don't wish to make you doubt your friend. I just—I thought you should know."

"I thank you. It is good to know that Caroline and I have a true ally in you. Please—may I have your assurance that if you witness anything else unusual concerning Randolph, you will tell me immediately?"

She promised. Outside the wind moaned as it pelted sleet against the windows. A draft caught her, chilling her through her thin muslin gown.

Surely that's why she shuddered.

". . . think you're doing. Whatever it is had better stop right now." Mr. Parrish's voice, though hushed, was forceful enough to carry from the hallway through Elizabeth's cracked door. She paused, her hand on the latch, reluctant to interrupt his argument with Professor Randolph to continue on her way to tea.

"But we never—"

He cut off Randolph. "No excuses. No discussion. We had an arrangement, and it didn't include you muttering mumbo-jumbo around Caroline without my knowledge. You are not to meet with her again unless I am present. Is that understood?"

"Understood."

"I don't know what game you play, but it ends now." Parrish brushed past Randolph, nearly knocking him down. He stopped just long enough to help Randolph regain his balance, then continued toward the stairs without another word.

Twenty-three

"*Without scheming to do wrong, or to make others unhappy,*
there may be error, and there may be misery."
Elizabeth to Jane, Pride and Prejudice, *Chapter 24*

*I*t is abominably rude of them to keep us waiting." Mrs.
Hurst gestured toward the empty seats. Mr. and Mrs.
Parrish, Mr. Kendall, and Professor Randolph were all absent
from the dinner table. "Charles, let us start on the soup."

The rest of the party—namely the Darcys, the Bingleys,
and the Hursts—had gathered in the dining room fifteen
minutes earlier, though to hear Louisa one would think it had
been an hour.

Actually, so incessant had been Mrs. Hurst's discourse on
tardiness that to Elizabeth the brief period felt like an hour.
She would sooner listen to the sleet pelting the window glass.
Bingley had tried to divert his sister to another topic of conversation, while Jane, Elizabeth, and Darcy made occasional
nods and polite listening noises. Mr. Hurst sat in stupid
silence, exerting himself only to raise his glass in a mute
demand for more wine. His hand shook so much that the
housemaid, instead of giving the glass back to Mr. Hurst after

refilling it, set it back on the table lest she take unfair blame for an accidental slosh on the tablecloth.

Jane nodded her permission to the servants to serve the soup. No sooner did a footman bring the tureen to the table than Mr. Parrish entered.

All gasped at his appearance.

Three deep scratches ribboned his face, including an ugly gash perilously close to his right eye. The bleeding had stopped, but the fresh wounds yet shone.

"Good Lord!" Louisa blurted. "What happened to your face?"

"I had a little accident."

Bingley jumped from his seat. "Was Caroline with you? Where is she?"

"She will not be joining us this evening." Parrish slumped into his chair. His whole countenance expressed defeat.

Bingley regarded Parrish uncertainly. No other information appeared forthcoming. He addressed the nearest housemaid. "Go to Mrs. Parrish's room and enquire whether she needs anything."

"Don't bother, Bingley. She's sleeping now."

Jane waved her hand, dismissing the servants. "Mr. Parrish? Will you now relieve our anxiety?"

Parrish hesitated. "This is not an easy thing for me to say." He closed his eyes and ran a hand through his hair, gripping the locks at his crown. "I believe Caroline's condition is worse than we imagined. Indeed, I fear her mind too disturbed to recover."

Mrs. Hurst issued a small mewing sound. "My poor sister!"

"Dear Caroline." Bingley slowly sank back down onto the chair. "What leads you to say so?"

"Less than an hour ago, she attacked me."

The table erupted in exclamations. Mrs. Hurst denied it

was possible; Jane thought perhaps Mr. Jones ought to be summoned. Bingley looked as though he were going to be sick. Mr. Hurst swallowed more wine.

When Caroline's aggrieved family had quieted, Parrish continued. "I entered our chamber to dress for dinner. She was unusually agitated—pacing, talking to herself. When she saw me, she flew across the room at me in a frenzied rage and struck me repeatedly. I was so shocked that I scarcely defended myself. I called out for help and fortunately her lady's maid heard me. We managed to subdue her."

He stared, unseeing, at a spot on the tablecloth as if trying to reconcile himself to the image of his wife having completely lost control. "The whole while, she looked at me as if she didn't even recognize me." He met Bingley's gaze. "Me—her husband! I gave her some laudanum to calm her down. I didn't know what else to do."

"None of us would have been prepared for such a scene," Jane said. "You handled it as well as could be expected."

"Thank you, Mrs. Bingley. I wish your kindness could relieve the heaviness of my heart. She rests now, but what new trouble will confront us when she wakes? She has become utterly unpredictable—God help her, she has become violent!" He glanced at each of them one by one. "You are her family. You love her as I do. What is to be done?"

Elizabeth wished she had an answer for the unfortunate Mr. Parrish. Every attempt to check Caroline's advancing illness had proven futile. Apparently, even the locket he'd petitioned the family for help to create—as unlikely a source of aid as he'd conceded it to be—had failed . . . if he'd followed through on it at all. She couldn't recall having seen Caroline wear such an article since Parrish had requested the locks of hair. He must have given up on the far-fetched idea.

"Whatever we do, it must be done quietly," Mrs. Hurst

declared. "I cannot bear the thought of my poor sister becoming an *on-dit* at Almack's."

Parrish nodded. "We must protect her as much as possible," he said. "But not just from gossip—from herself. And . . ." His voice broke. "I'm afraid we must protect others from her. Removing to Netherfield has not had the effect we'd hoped. We must consider a more drastic alternative."

"Do you speak again of taking Caroline to America?" Bingley asked.

"I think she is even less capable of such a journey now than she was before," Darcy declared.

"I agree. How I wish a retreat to my home could cure what ails her! But no—unfortunately, I fear we must investigate another type of home for her."

"You mean an asylum." Louisa made the statement without emotion.

Parrish let silence serve as his affirmation. Outside the wind howled its own protest.

Elizabeth's mind revolted at the notion. She bore no love for Mrs. Parrish, but cringed at the image of her in such a place. The hospitals, with their inhuman conditions, were holding cells, not places of healing, a last resort for families who had given up not just hope but also conscience. Once Caroline entered, she would be lost to them forever.

"Surely there exists a less extreme solution?" Darcy asked.

"If I could think of a better plan, I'd offer it." He threw out his hands in despair. "This is not the marriage I envisioned when I took my vows less than a fortnight ago. I married Caroline for better or worse, in sickness and health, and I meant those words when I spoke them. Sickness has come. Worse has come. And I remain steadfast. But I cannot allow her to endanger all of you any longer. We cannot wait until she assails someone with a more deadly weapon than a wedding ring. Or until the next house burns all the way to the ground. Or until she . . . finishes what she attempted back in London." His voice shook. "Standing by her doesn't mean turning a blind eye to peril. It means making decisions in her best interest even if doing so breaks my own heart."

Elizabeth wondered anew how Caroline had managed to win such devotion. For a time no one spoke. All were visibly moved by his passion—except for the red-faced Mr. Hurst, who appeared only marginally aware of what was being discussed.

"You are her husband. It is your choice," Bingley said finally. "I will support you in whatever course of action you deem best."

"As will I," said Mrs. Hurst. Jane concurred. Mr. Hurst downed another glass of wine.

Affecting as Parrish's speech had been, Elizabeth was yet troubled by the idea of committing Mrs. Parrish to a mental hospital. She wondered that no one but Darcy had offered the slightest resistance. Back in London, when Randolph had suggested sending Caroline to Louisiana, the entire family had engaged in considerable debate. Yet now that an even worse fate was contemplated, no one voiced an objection. She could only surmise that in Jane and Bingley's case, the ordeal of the fire, not to mention their carriage mishap, had worn down their ability to cope with other matters. The Hursts' complacency she attributed to the laziness and selfishness that motivated most of their decisions.

In Elizabeth's opinion, what Caroline needed most was to escape Professor Randolph and his "help." His motives were suspect, his methods objectionable. Whether he possessed real power or only delusions of it, his attention seemed of little benefit—and perhaps considerable harm—to Mrs. Parrish. Free of his proximity, how rapidly might she improve?

"Maybe Mrs. Parrish could take up residence in a quiet

cottage with a full-time companion?" Elizabeth suggested.

"All of us together have been unable to chaperone her here at Netherfield," Parrish replied. "How could a single companion—along with myself, of course—keep up with her?"

"Multiple companions, then," Darcy said. "Well-trained nurses devoted to her care—and supervision."

Parrish shook his head dismissively, but then paused as if reconsidering. "A secluded cottage . . . The idea does bring a feeling of peace with it, doesn't it? And with the right sort of help . . . Perhaps—perhaps—Mrs. Darcy, you are invaluable! I shall start looking for just such a place directly."

They were joined presently by Professor Randolph, who apologized profusely for his lateness. "I lost track of the time," he explained.

How could he, Elizabeth mused, with that pocketwatch he constantly employed? At least his ability to influence Mrs. Parrish with it would soon come to an abrupt end.

"No matter, Professor," Jane assured him. "Dinner has been delayed anyway."

He took his seat and nodded at the others in greeting. When his gaze landed on Parrish, he started. "Good heavens, Mr. Parrish! Are you all right?"

"Caroline has suffered a setback."

His shoulders sagged. "I thought I'd observed some improvement of late." He began to rise. "I will go speak with—"

"That won't be necessary."

Randolph sat back down. "But if I could meet with her yet this evening—"

"She rests. In the morning, I intend to search for a quiet cottage for us to retire to, one without the distractions of Netherfield."

"Indeed?" He pushed his spectacles to the bridge of his nose. "Well, I can certainly post my observations to Dr. Lancaster from one location as well as another."

"I appreciate your offer to continue meeting with Caroline, but I think she needs solitude."

"Surely her withdrawal from society should not include me?"

"You have your next expedition to think about."

"A delay is of no consequence if by postponing those plans I can be of service to Mrs. Parrish."

"Your service is no longer required."

Elizabeth inwardly applauded Parrish. Apparently, she and he were of like mind where the eerie archeologist was concerned.

Randolph seemed about to protest further, but then thought better of it. "I see." He cleared his throat. "Yes—well, then." He glanced nervously around the table, conscious that all eyes were upon him. "As soon as the storm breaks, I'll return to London."

Twenty-four

> "When persons sit down to a card table, they must take
> their chance of these things,—and happily I am not in such
> circumstances as to make five shillings any object."
> Mr. Collins to Mrs. Philips, Pride and Prejudice, *Chapter 16*

London
21 December, 18——

My dear friend,

I confess myself surprised by your ignorance of the tales circulating about Mr. Hurst, for I know you to be far better acquainted with
him than I. Perhaps that intimacy is precisely why the story has not
reached your hearing. Or is it that the new bridegroom has ears
only for the sound of his lady's voice?

Regardless, I am happy to oblige your request for information.
The report first came to me by way of a peer whom I consider a
reliable source. I have since heard it repeated by others, leading me
to believe it has attained the status of common knowledge amongst
the regulars at White's.

As you know, Hurst has long frequented the club's card rooms.
During this past season, Beau Brummell himself, short a fourth for
whist, invited Hurst to join a high-stakes game. Hurst, cup-shot and

*not nearly the player he thinks himself, lost famously. But he was
flattered by Brummell's notice and bitten by the gambling bug.
In a vain attempt to court the Beau's favor, Hurst returned nightly for
more high-stakes cardplay. Brummell, of course, has no use for one as
dull as Hurst and never repeated his invitation to the bow window, but
Hurst found other high-flyers willing to endure his company for a
chance to take his money. When Hurst began voweling his debts, he
found himself unwelcome among the green baize brotherhood and
took to entering wagers in the betting book. Even in this form of speculation, however, few will now accept a challenge from him.*

*Bearing in mind your desire for discretion, I have taken the lib-
erty of making a few cautious enquiries into the extent of Hurst's
losses. General consensus estimates his debts in excess of eighty
thousand pounds. At least a dozen gentlemen held IOUs bearing his
signature until last month, when Mr. Lawrence Kendall (you will
recall him from our last dinner party) bought up the notes, relinquished by most at reduced value in despair of ever collecting the
full sum from Hurst.*

*That is all I know of the matter. Do return to London soon with
your charming wife. Lady Chatfield and I were both taken with Mrs.
Darcy, and hope to enjoy the pleasure of your company often. I am
yours, etc., etc.—*

James, Lord Chatfield

Elizabeth handed the letter back to Darcy. "Eighty thousand pounds! Can he ever hope to make good half that sum?"

"If he depletes his own inheritance and Mrs. Hurst's settlement entirely, he will still fall short of the full debt." Darcy
refolded the letter and put it in his breast pocket. It had
arrived in the morning post; once everyone else had left the
breakfast parlor, he'd lost no time sharing its contents with
Elizabeth. He had thoughts of his own about the news but
was eager to hear her opinion.

"And Mr. Kendall now his chief creditor!"

Darcy found that bit of intelligence equally shocking—and alarming. Hurst would almost be better off dealing with a moneylender. At least they would know such a man's motivation. "Kendall's interest in Hurst's financial affairs can have no good purpose."

A servant entered to clear the breakfast dishes. Darcy rose. "Come, let us walk." The cough he and Kendall had heard outside the billiards room yesterday had reminded him that no room of a great house was truly private. Moreover, he had not seen Kendall since their game ended; Darcy's valet had lost track of him, so nobody knew where the weasel skulked. If he and Elizabeth kept moving as they talked, no one could overhear more than a brief snatch of conversation.

They headed for the staircase. Weak daylight struggled through the windows, casting a dreary pallor over the hall. Last night's storm had abated, but ponderous clouds blotted out the sun, and an atmosphere of gloom pervaded the entire household.

"What do you think Kendall wants?" she asked in a loud whisper.

"To use his power over the Hursts to force Bingley's hand. He has already threatened Bingley with public scandal in the form of a court battle if he does not comply with his demands. The ability to ruin Hurst provides still more artillery in the war he seems bent on waging against the family."

"Charles won't surrender his rightful inheritance, Caroline stole his daughter's beau, and now Louisa's husband owes him a fortune. No wonder he won't leave Netherfield—maintaining all his grievances against the Bingleys keeps him too busy to travel." She stopped at the first-floor landing and looked down the passage to the blackened east wing. "Perhaps very busy indeed."

He caught her meaning. "The link to Hurst provides yet more reason to suspect Kendall of orchestrating the family's recent troubles. Though yesterday he gave me to understand that it was he, not Parrish, who ended the courtship with Miss Kendall. He accused the American of being far too forward in his attentions."

"Regardless," Elizabeth said, "Mr. Kendall has a connection to every branch of the Bingley family, and doesn't wish any of them well. Do you think he pressures Hurst for payment yet?"

Darcy recalled Kendall goading Hurst at dinner two nights previous, and their talk of stakes in the billiards match he and Bingley had interrupted. "He plays some sort of cat-and-mouse game with Hurst. I do not believe the rest of the family knows of Hurst's debt. In addition to demanding payment, he may also be threatening to expose Hurst to his wife or to Bingley."

They turned their footsteps toward the west gallery. Like most of Netherfield's furnishings, the majority of the artwork there belonged to the landlord. But a few Bingley portraits, including one of the late Charles Bingley, hung on the walls. Elizabeth studied the painting of Bingley's father. "Kendall cannot touch Bingley's estate to collect Hurst's debt, can he?"

"Legally, no. But Bingley could decide to settle the debt to protect the family honor."

"And so Kendall gains Bingley's fortune after all. Assuming Bingley acts to save his sister from disgrace, which, given his nature, is entirely probable. But for argument's sake let's say he does not—is there no other way Kendall can get at Bingley's fortune through Hurst?"

"Only if Hurst somehow gained possession of it first. If the money came to him as a gift, for example—"

"Or as an inheritance."

All feeling within him resisted even contemplating that possibility. Yet circumstances forced his reason to acknowledge it. Jane and Bingley had almost perished in the fire, and the blaze's origin was starting to seem less and less accidental. Darcy had questioned Jane's maid upon her return to Netherfield, and learned that she had not set out the silver-buttoned gown or any other that night—which meant that either the injured Jane had risen in the middle of the night from her laudanum-induced slumber to pull it from the armoire, or someone else had.

"If Jane and Bingley passed away," he said, "the Hursts would inherit half the family fortune."

"And with Caroline out of the way, they would inherit it all."

They moved on, through the newly relocated family quarters. Darcy could scarcely believe they discussed something so appalling as a murder plot against his oldest friend, let alone one that encompassed two women as well. "I think last night proved Mrs. Parrish is the cause of her own misfortunes."

"An advantageous coincidence for Kendall. If she manages to do herself in, she spares him the trouble. And if she doesn't, the death of a madwoman can easily be made to look accidental."

Darcy thought the connection too tenuous. He had to concede Kendall possessed sufficient intelligence and deviousness to contrive such a scheme, but did he possess the subtlety to execute it? Beyond that, no evidence existed to suggest that Caroline was in danger from anyone other than herself. "We may be confusing the matter by trying to include Mrs. Parrish in the design. Even if the Hursts inherit only half of Bingley's estate, it is still a sizable sum."

"Large enough to satisfy Kendall's greed?"

"Large enough to satisfy Hurst's debt."

"And provide Kendall the triumph of gaining at least part of his late associate's fortune."

Her line of reasoning was logically sound, but unsupported. "My dear, we can never prove Kendall's guilt with circumstantial facts alone. We cannot verify that Kendall was in the neighborhood before Bingley's carriage accident, nor that he was anywhere but his own room when the fire started. So unless someone comes forward who saw him in a place he should not have been—"

"Or unless he had help. Could Kendall have coerced Hurst into collusion?"

"Hurst is a weak man. But I cannot reconcile myself to the idea of him deliberately harming Bingley."

"Yes—it would require him to get up off the sofa." They mounted a side staircase. "I have never observed anything in his conduct that would indicate affection or regard for Bingley, let alone Jane. Meanwhile, Hurst has never known want or even had to contemplate supporting himself. The threat of losing everything could well induce him to take actions he otherwise would not, especially with a bully like Kendall directing him."

She lapsed into silence as they walked down the second-story hall, until they had passed Kendall's new chamber and approached the center staircase. "In fact," she continued, "as much as we dislike Mr. Kendall and would love to blame him for all our friends' adversity, it is not inconceivable that Hurst acts alone. He fancies himself more intelligent than he really is—that's how he got himself done up in the first place, thinking he could outplay his whist opponents and devise witty wagers."

They found themselves back on the first floor again, and wandered into the damaged east wing. It was eerily quiet in this part of the house, and cold, the whole wing having not been heated since the fire. Although servants had made temporary repairs to shore up the walls and ceilings in the burned-out rooms, Mr. Morris had decided yesterday to begin the formal restoration work after the new year. Until then, the wing stood dreary, drafty, and deserted.

She paused in front of what remained of the master suite. Behind her, the door stood ajar. "Murdering Bingley and Jane provides an oh-so-clever solution to Hurst's problems. We have trouble imagining him capable of it not because he has too much honor, but too much cowardice. Their deaths make his life easier—and ease motivates Hurst above all else—but he hasn't the fortitude to witness it happening. So rather than risk a direct confrontation, he resorts to indirect means like tampering with carriages. He couldn't even cause his victims immediate harm while they lay defenseless in a drugged sleep—instead, he set fire to Jane's dress across the room and made his exit before the flames reached them."

Darcy had spent far more time in Hurst's company than had Elizabeth. Her assessment of him was based on a few weeks' total exposure, spread over more than a year, with little direct interaction. Yet she had captured his character with accuracy. Hurst was lazy, unresourceful, disengaged from the family. Were Darcy suddenly stripped of his fortune, he would find some honest means of supporting his wife and any children God blessed them with, even if it meant lowering himself to earn a living as a common farmer. He could not say the same of Hurst. His way of life threatened, unable to imagine another one, and unwilling to expend any effort toward his own maintenance, Hurst must be in a panic. And men in a panic made bad choices.

Repugnant as the idea was, he had to consider both Hurst and Kendall as suspects. But suspects in what? He had no proof that the Bingley family's troubles were anything other than a string of unfortunate, but unrelated, accidents.

"I should speak more with Hurst and Kendall before we explore this any further."

"Then take care that you do it before somebody winds up dead."

As they turned to head back to the main part of the house, a draft from the master suite caught Darcy's neck. He approached the gaping door, intending to pull it closed. Instead he stopped short.

"We're too late."

Twenty-five

"Importance may sometimes be purchased too dearly."
Elizabeth, writing to Mrs. Gardiner,
Pride and Prejudice, *Chapter 26*

*S*omeone had decided to free them all from Lawrence Kendall's company.

Darcy tried to block his wife's view of the violent spectacle, but she disregarded his attempts and pushed the door fully open. Mr. Kendall's unmoving form lay facedown on the floor. A dark red circle stained the upper left side of his back.

He caught her hand and tried to draw her away from the room. "Elizabeth, this is not a sight for—"

She shook off his grasp. "I'm hardly going to succumb to an attack of the vapors." Despite her bravado, she entered the room slowly and stopped about three feet from the body.

He followed. It was even chillier in the room than it had been in the hall. A grey film coated the windows, further darkening the cloudy light that filtered in and lent an ashen hue to Kendall's already pale form.

They stood in mute shock for he knew not how long. Much as he'd despised Lawrence Kendall, he would not wish such a fate on anyone. His wife shuddered, whether from cold or horror he could not tell.

"How long do you suppose he's been lying here?" she finally asked.

He knelt for a closer look. He had seen death before; it had come early for his parents, earlier still for three infant siblings between him and Georgiana. It had arrived violently for a rash Cambridge schoolmate who had insisted on proving his honor in a duel. That display had been the worst, a ghastly spectacle the likes of which he'd thankfully never borne witness to again. Until today.

Kendall's blood had congealed into a thick paste, though for a fatal injury, the inch-long wound had produced less than he would have expected from someone who had bled to death. Shielding his actions as best he could from Elizabeth, he rolled the body halfway over to check for additional wounds. Kendall's flesh was icy to the touch, his limbs stiff. No other wounds presented themselves, but his sides were swollen with fluid, and blood stained his mouth and cravat. The attack must have pierced his lung, causing him to bleed within and drown in his own blood.

Darcy elected not to share that gruesome detail with his wife. He released his hold and let the body roll back into the position in which they'd found it. "I would say he has lain here for hours, at least. Perhaps since last night." He rose and took her hand once more. "Come, Elizabeth. This is no scene for a lady's eyes."

"We just found someone dead! What ladylike pursuit would you have me go undertake? Shall I stitch a sampler?" One hand rose to her throat. "My God, Darcy—there is a murderer at Netherfield. A murderer! And it isn't Mr. Kendall! We've speculated for days about all these strange goings-on, but I don't think I truly believed it possible until this moment that there's a killer among us. A man is dead, by the hand of someone we know! What do we do?"

"Bingley will summon the constable." For whatever good that would do. If London's charleys were barely competent, country lawmen were worse. Darcy doubted the ability of any constable to adequately investigate a crime with no obvious solution. Meanwhile, a killer freely roamed Netherfield's corridors—a killer in the guise of a friend.

Elizabeth stared at Kendall's corpse. "He never came to dinner. I wonder if he was dead then?"

"No one regretted his absence"—Darcy had actually been relieved by it—"so he could easily have been missing since dinner without anyone thinking or caring to look for him. And nobody, even the servants, has reason to come to this part of the house."

He scanned the floor, seeking evidence of what had happened in Kendall's final moments. The businessman lay sprawled—had not survived the strike long enough to crawl toward help as his lung filled with blood. He'd been stabbed from behind, with a knife, Darcy presumed. By whom?

Scraps of wood and other debris lay strewn throughout the chamber, but no obvious clue presented itself. The weakened floorboards creaked under his weight as he looked about. He hesitated to wander too far into the room, lest he disturb the layer of dust and soot that had settled on the floor. He and Elizabeth had already left a trail of footprints from the door to Kendall's body, Elizabeth's obscured by the sway of her gown's hem. Their tracks added to the swirling mass of impressions already surrounding the body, and prints from Mr. Morris's inspection yesterday. He did not want to create more tracks before the constable arrived.

He noticed, however, a set of fresh footprints that led to Jane's writing desk. In size and stride length, they matched a faint older set Kendall had left when he'd nosed about the room with Darcy a few days earlier. Perhaps Darcy's comment to Parrish that demolition work was about to begin had inspired one last search of the desk before it was destroyed.

Another fresh set of prints, spaced farther apart, extended about halfway into the room. The trail mixed with Kendall's prints, then doubled back to the door. Kendall's body had fallen facing away from the desk, his head nearest the door. "He was struck as he was leaving."

She shuddered and hugged herself. "Do you think he saw his attacker?"

Darcy studied the footprints further. "I believe Kendall returned here to break into the desk. The killer could not have sneaked in after him, because the creaking floorboards would have betrayed him. So the murderer either was hiding in the dark when Kendall entered, or Kendall was aware of his presence. They may have arrived together, or the attacker may have come in later, but Kendall would have heard him enter."

"You're sure it's a 'him'? Kendall wasn't the only man attacked last night. Caroline Parrish—"

"A large man stabbed in the back?" He considered the possibility a moment, then shook his head. "Mrs. Parrish does have a questionable history with knives, but I doubt this her work. A woman's hemline would have left traces in the dust, and yours are the only such marks. Her feet would have made smaller prints. Plus, according to Parrish, she was sedated last night. I think it is safe to say that a man did this."

"Which means the killer is Bingley, Parrish, Randolph, or Hurst. We can eliminate Bingley—the very thought that he could have killed anybody, even Kendall, is ludicrous. Parrish was busy dealing with his wife and has the scars to prove it. That leaves Randolph, who was very late coming to dinner, and Hurst, who was foxed before the soup was served."

"Randolph has no motive. He is probably the only person

at Netherfield without a connection to Kendall." He sighed heavily, disliking the logical conclusion to which that fact led. "So Hurst becomes our chief suspect."

"Kendall's death does solve his financial problems. And with the convenience of one quick strike—far more efficient than eliminating his wife's entire family." Her gaze flickered to the corpse, then away again. The spectacle obviously distressed her. It distressed *him*, for heaven's sake. He wished she would allow him to lead her away and return to pursue his investigation alone, but knew he could not fight her resolve.

"Stabbing is a more direct method than I would have given Hurst credit for," she continued, "but striking his victim from behind is cowardly enough. Then afterward he drinks himself into oblivion."

Elizabeth's line of thought echoed Darcy's own. Hurst possessed a pocketknife. He had cause. And Kendall, cockily pulling Hurst's strings like a marionette, could have himself provided the opportunity for Hurst to act, could have brought him up to this deserted place to issue more threats or coerce him into searching for Bingley's records. Then desperation had at last forced the lazy man to act.

Hurst, the murderer. Reprehensible thought! But a reasonable explanation of events.

He studied again the confusing mass of footprints surrounding Kendall. A trail of them seemed to circle the body. Upon closer examination, he realized that they paralleled a dark outline on the floorboards that had previously escaped his notice in the dim light. The line appeared to have been made by scraping a charred piece of wood across the floor. Straight lines within the circle formed a star, with Kendall at its center.

Elizabeth followed his observations. "That is most curious. Where did those marks come from?"

He shook his head in ignorance. "I cannot imagine why

Kendall or Hurst would trace such a pattern on the floor, either before or after the murder."

"The design looks familiar—I've seen it before." She frowned. "Though I cannot remember where."

He approached the body once more. Kendall's arms shot out from his sides; his fingers combed the dust. An unexpected but genuine surge of pity passed through Darcy. What an undignified way to die!

Kendall's right hand caught Darcy's attention. Scratches covered the back of it. Darcy bent for a better look, and discovered that the same symbol etched on the floor had been carved into Kendall's skin. He hadn't noted the mutilation immediately because unlike the back wound, these scratches had not bled.

Something shiny was trapped under the palm. He bent down and lifted Kendall's hand, tried to pry stiff fingers away from the round article. A thin chain slid down. Darcy used it to tug the object out of the dead man's grasp. He gasped in recognition.

So did Elizabeth. "Professor Randolph's watch."

Twenty-six

"People themselves alter so much, that there is something
new to be observed in them for ever."
Elizabeth to Darcy, Pride and Prejudice, *Chapter 9*

*A*fter examining the murder scene, the constable commenced his interviews. Elizabeth, to her satisfaction,
was allowed to observe. Darcy had questioned the propriety
of her being present during the examinations, but she had
insisted on staying, particularly for Randolph's interview. She
had spent more time in conversation with him than had anyone else at Netherfield excepting Mr. Parrish, she had argued,
and thus could better judge his truthfulness. Darcy had reluctantly consented, but only after exacting a promise from her
to remain unobtrusive.

She now sat off to one side, next to Mr. Bingley, who was in
attendance as master of the house but otherwise content to
let Darcy and the constable conduct the interrogation. She
studied Professor Randolph as he answered the constable's
enquiries. What was it the archeologist had said at dinner to
excuse his tardiness? *I lost track of the time.* He must have lost
track of his pocketwatch as well by then—after having used it
shortly before tea, during his "meeting" with Mrs. Parrish.

That meant the murder had occurred sometime between half-past three and half-past seven.

Professor Randolph answered the lawman's questions patiently at first, but became increasingly agitated as the same queries were repeated. "I don't know how my watch came to be in Mr. Kendall's possession. . . . No, I didn't give it to him or anyone else. . . . I haven't been in that part of the house since the fire. . . . From tea until dinner I was in my chamber, drafting a monograph—I can show you the manuscript pages, if you like. . . . Yes, I own a pocketknife, but so do many gentlemen . . . I told you, I didn't kill him!"

The constable then brought up the pattern on the floor and Kendall's hand, which matched the engraving on the front of his watch.

"It's called a pentagram," the professor said.

"A symbol of the devil, isn't it?"

"No!"

"I hear you study that hocus-pocus stuff. Did you cast some sort of hex on Mr. Kendall before you killed him?"

"I didn't kill him!" Randolph looked at the others pleadingly. "Mr. Bingley, Mr. and Mrs. Darcy—I swear to you, I didn't have anything to do with this."

When the circular line of questioning yielded no new information in more than fifteen minutes, Darcy interceded with a subtle hint that the constable complete his interviews with the rest of the household. The constable, intimidated by Darcy, complied with the suggestion. He dismissed Randolph and requested that Mr. Parrish be summoned.

Randolph paused on his way out. "Please, may I have my pocketwatch back?"

The constable looked to Darcy. "I don't see why not. That is, I don't think I need it anymore. Do I?"

"Perhaps I should take it for safekeeping. We can return it to Professor Randolph when this matter is resolved."

"Just what I was thinking, sir."

Randolph glanced from the constable to Darcy, then to Bingley, and finally to Elizabeth. He appeared unwilling to leave the timepiece behind, but unable to do anything about it. He left, but accosted Elizabeth immediately when she went in search of Mr. Parrish.

"Mrs. Darcy, may I—may I please have a word with you?"

Her pulse quickened. She could be standing with a murderer right now. Probably was. She looked about for someone to help her disengage from Randolph's conversation, but the hall was deserted. She forced her voice to remain calm. "What is it, Professor?"

"My pocketwatch—I need it. Is there any way you might prevail upon your husband to give it back to me?"

"Mr. Darcy has his own mind. You shall have to ask him yourself."

"He does not respect me. A petition from me will not move him."

"Then you must wait until he is ready to surrender it." She tried to walk past him, but he stayed her with a hand on her arm. His touch sent a chill racing up to her shoulder.

"There isn't time to wait!" His eyes burned with intensity. "If you will not give the watch to me, can you get it to Mrs. Parrish? Urge her to carry it on her person. For her own protection."

"Protection from what?"

"From the forces at work upon her."

Another chill passed through Elizabeth. She had thought Professor Randolph deceitful and calculating. But now she wondered if he was actually mad. The fervor of his gaze frightened her. "What forces?"

"The forces that prey upon her mind. The watch—it's an amulet—it can help her. You are her friend, yes? You do want to help her?"

Elizabeth wanted nothing more than to escape Randolph's presence. "I'll see what I can do." Again she tried to move past him, and again he restrained her.

"You must! You must make sure Mrs. Parrish receives it. But without her husband's knowledge. He cannot know! He won't allow her to keep it. He no longer trusts me."

Neither did she.

"Mr. Parrish, how well did you know Mr. Kendall?" the constable asked as Parrish took a seat. Darcy relaxed in his own chair, expecting this interview to proceed uneventfully.

"I met him in London last season, when I became acquainted with his daughter, Miss Juliet Kendall."

"Were you and he on good terms?"

"I bore him no ill will." Parrish spoke slowly, appearing to choose his words deliberately. "London society being what it is, assumptions were made about my intentions toward Miss Kendall—assumptions that were unfounded. When I offered my hand to the woman who is now my wife, the misunderstanding may have led to some injured feelings on the part of the Kendalls."

"And how did you get along here at Netherfield?"

"Except for encountering him at meals, I left him to himself." He shrugged. "I am a newly married man, sir. My attention has been elsewhere."

The constable nodded knowingly. "When did you last see Mr. Kendall alive?"

"At breakfast yesterday. He was just finishing up when I came downstairs."

Darcy frowned. That wasn't correct. "What about later? In the billiards room?"

"Oh, yes! The billiards room. Thank you, Darcy—I was there so briefly, I'd forgotten about that." He leaned back and crossed his legs. "I last saw Mr. Kendall yesterday afternoon, playing billiards. When Darcy and I left the room, he was alone."

Kendall had been so full of spite, Darcy didn't know how Parrish could have forgotten his rudeness so quickly. Perhaps the power of Kendall's verbal assaults diminished with repetition.

"How did you spend the rest of the day?"

"Mostly with Caroline. I spent part of the afternoon writing a letter."

"Do you have any idea who might have killed Mr. Kendall, or why?"

Parrish shook his head. "Mr. Kendall was not a likable man. He was rude and insulting. I don't think anyone here harbored the slightest fondness for him. But you don't slay someone for uncivil behavior. The *ton* takes care of that well enough."

"I imagine so. Mr. Parrish, how did you come by those cuts on your face? Were you in some sort of fight?"

Parrish shifted in his seat. Darcy couldn't blame him. What man wanted to admit that his wife had physically assaulted him? Or that she was mad?

"My—" He cleared his throat. "My wife accidentally scratched me with her wedding ring. She's not yet used to wearing it." He looked to Bingley and Darcy as if beseeching them not to betray the full truth.

"Those are pretty big scratches."

"It's a pretty big ring."

"When did this happen?"

"Yesterday evening, before dinner."

"And if I ask your wife, she'll confirm this?"

"Of course."

Mrs. Parrish was summoned. As they waited, Parrish asked whether the constable had many questions for Caroline.

"She's been unwell today. I hope your enquiry won't tax her too greatly?"

"Of course not, sir. I'll be quick about it."

Bingley led Caroline into the drawing room. She appeared sleepy and slightly disoriented. Parrish immediately crossed to her and helped her to a seat beside him on the sofa. He took her left hand in both of his.

"Darling, this man is concerned about the marks on my face. I told him about that silly little accident yesterday when you happened to scratch me. Remember?"

Caroline nodded.

"I assured him the injury wasn't intentional."

"No," she said groggily.

"Mrs. Parrish, may I see your ring?"

Caroline appeared not to have heard the constable. Parrish lifted her hand and held it toward him.

"That's indeed quite a ring." The constable peered at it closely. "Hmm—looks like there are even a few bits of skin still caught in there. You need to be a little more careful, Mrs. Parrish, or your husband'll have to buy you smaller jewels in self-defense."

Parrish laughed politely, then turned serious once more. "As you can see, my wife is still very tired. May I escort her back upstairs now?"

"Certainly."

He rose and assisted Caroline in doing the same. As they headed toward the door, the constable stopped him with one last question. "Mr. Parrish, you don't by chance know what a pentagram is, do you?"

Parrish furrowed his brows. "That's some sort of star symbol, right? Has something to do with witchcraft? Professor Randolph no doubt knows. I'd ask him more about it."

"Thank you. I will."

———

Hurst entered the drawing room and went straight for the sherry decanter. Darcy intercepted him. He wanted at least the start of the interview to be conducted while Hurst was still sober.

"Allow me, Hurst." He lifted the carafe and, with slowness visibly excruciating to the other gentleman, poured half a glass of wine. He did not immediately hand it over. "Please, have a seat."

Hurst regarded Darcy uncertainly, then glanced to the other men. Elizabeth he ignored entirely. "What's this? What's going on here?"

"Nothing alarming, Hurst," Bingley reassured him. "The constable just has a few questions for all of us about last night. He's trying to figure out what happened to Mr. Kendall, and he's hoping one of us saw something that can help him piece it all together."

Hurst remained standing. "I don't know anything about it. Didn't even know the man, except for meeting him during his visit here."

Darcy handed him the sherry. "Did you not play billiards with him?"

"Once."

"What did you talk about?"

Hurst drained the glass. "Fox hunting. Shooting. He did most of the talking. Kept rambling about flushing prey out of their dens, or something or another. You know I'm not much of a sportsman, Darcy. I just let him go on."

Darcy looked to the constable, preferring to let the official take over the questioning so as not to put himself in the role of Hurst's antagonist.

"When did you last see Mr. Kendall?" the constable asked.

"In the billiards room. He was with Darcy when I left."

"And where did you go?"

"To my chamber."

"How long did you stay there?"

"All afternoon. I—I took a nap." He swallowed hard, sending his Adam's apple bobbing. "Might I have another glass of sherry?"

"We're almost finished. Can you think of anybody who might have wished Mr. Kendall dead?"

Beads of perspiration formed on his forehead. "No, not a one."

The constable's gaze flickered to Hurst's waistcoat. "I'm told you carry a pocketknife. Is that true?"

Hurst's eyes narrowed. "Yes—lots of gentlemen do. What of it?"

"May I see it?"

Grumbling, Hurst produced the pocketknife. The constable opened it. The blade was clean. It extended three inches, and was perhaps half an inch wide at its base.

The constable folded the knife and returned it. "Mr. Hurst, do you know what a pentagram is?"

"A what? No. I haven't the foggiest." He handed his glass back to Darcy with a shaking hand. "Are we done now?"

"Yes, Mr. Hurst. Thank you."

The normally sluggish Hurst could not leave the room fast enough.

That night, Darcy entered his chamber, and his wife's embrace, like a man seeking sanctuary. Whatever trouble surrounded them, Elizabeth's presence brought peace to his world. How he had lived without her in the days before they met, he could scarcely remember.

She gently directed him to sit down while she rubbed the tension out of his shoulders. "Tuppence for your thoughts."

He groaned. With her hands on his back, he ought to be able to banish all unpleasantness from his mind, but he could not. Pieces of the day kept intruding, nagging him to ponder them until he knew what had happened to Lawrence Kendall. "I cannot figure out what Randolph's watch was doing in Kendall's hand, or why that symbol was used. Setting those details aside for the moment, Hurst emerges as the most likely suspect. He's the only one with a clear motive, and his claim that he passed the *whole* afternoon napping is hard to believe— even for Hurst. Circumstantial evidence points to him.

"Yet the watch puts Randolph in the room at the time of the murder, and who else knows about symbols like that?" he continued. "And he, too, owns a knife. The physical evidence implicates the professor. But why would he kill Kendall?"

"Other than general principle?" She massaged the corded muscles of his neck.

"There is no connection between the two of them. At least, none that I can see."

"That's because you are looking with your eyes. I think the connection is in Randolph's head."

He frowned. "What do you mean?"

"I believe Randolph is a fanatic, bent on using his supernatural knowledge toward some ill purpose. He begged me today to obtain his watch from you and get Mrs. Parrish to wear it on her person, without her husband's awareness. He claims it will help her, but I think that watch is the root of all her problems. It's cursed somehow, or he has used it to curse her. It bears the same pentagram symbol that was on the floor and carved into the corpse—I shudder to contemplate what diabolical ceremony he conducted on Mr. Kendall at the time of the murder."

This again? As much as Darcy respected his wife's mind, he could not understand her willingness to entertain such preposterous notions. She was a smart woman, gifted with wit perhaps greater than his own. Yet she allowed herself to indulge in ideas that held no more credibility than faerie stories. "I would like to curse *him* for putting these thoughts in your head."

"Mr. Kendall was killed on the same day that I interrupted whatever ritual Randolph was performing on Caroline. A day that seems to hold meaning for him—the winter solstice."

"I agree that he may have tried to invoke some mystical effect with that symbol, perhaps even related, in his own mind, to the date. But attempting and doing are two different things, and I do not believe him—or anyone—capable of magic."

Her hands stilled. "I am quite serious. There is something unnatural going on at Netherfield. I can feel it." She came round to face him. "I—I sense things sometimes. Indistinct impressions. Randolph—when he spoke to me today, it was as if an alarm sounded within me. We should not dismiss his studies as nonsense. He possesses some power—some knowledge."

"He possesses a watch that was found in a place it should not have been."

"And why would Kendall clutch it in his dying moments if Randolph hadn't been using it somehow at the time of the murder?"

Darcy pondered a moment. Why indeed? "Kendall was struck from behind. To me, that indicates that he did not grab the watch to interrupt some ritual. Rather, it was already in his hand as he was leaving. But even if Randolph was futilely trying to conduct sorcery, what killed Kendall was a knife wound."

Elizabeth's expression grew cold. "You will not believe me." She crossed to the window and gazed into the darkness, her back to him. It was the first night of the new moon, and the blackness outside Netherfield's walls matched the gloom within.

"Elizabeth, if Randolph could command the kind of power you think him capable of, why would he resort to killing

Kendall with a physical weapon? Would he not instead slay him with a lightning bolt or something?"

"Do not mock me."

"Elizabeth—"

"I am not some simpleminded country girl. I may not have had an education equal to your own, and as a woman, I cannot move about in the world like you, but that doesn't mean I don't know how it works."

He crossed to her, put his hand to her shoulder. "Elizabeth—"

She shrugged him off. "Do you think I cannot distinguish between reality and fantasy?" She turned to face him. "Do you think I am that foolish?"

He had hurt her. Without meaning to, he had hurt his wife, and he wasn't sure what to do to make it right. He could not believe in the ridiculous, and he would not lie to her by pretending to. "I do not think you are foolish," he said finally. "Only misled."

"And I do not think you are arrogant." She blinked back angry tears and turned again toward the window. "Only blind."

The amulet called to her from across the room.

All right—it didn't call, exactly. It lay silent in the top drawer of the highboy where Darcy had placed it. And it was a watch, not an amulet. Just a watch.

Yet it arrested Elizabeth's attention like no object ever had.

She sat upright on the bed, hugging her knees, staring at the drawer. Darcy had departed the room for the moment, summoned by Bingley on some late errand just as he'd been about to retire. He'd left Randolph's timepiece behind.

Deliver the watch to Mrs. Parrish without her husband's knowledge, the professor had exhorted. For what purpose—fair or fell? What did the supernaturalist think or hope it could do?

She crossed the room and slid open the drawer. The watch

rested in the corner, its chain pooled around it. Despite Randolph's claims, it appeared innocuous—a simple timepiece, albeit one with unusual markings. She grasped the fob and slowly pulled it out of the drawer.

Firelight danced across the silver as the watch gently swung like a pendulum from her fingertips. She detected a faint humming noise—surely deriving from its movement, nothing more. The sound distracted her, and the sway made it further difficult for her to study the engraving. The five-pointed star and its surrounding circle remained fixed, but a shape within the star seemed to change in the uneven light. It looked to her like a man, standing with arms and legs spread to the sides. She tried to focus but the image would not hold still. It shifted—one moment visible, the next not.

She grasped the watch itself to stop its swing and get a closer look. But as she touched it, intense heat seared her hand. She let go. It dropped back into the drawer, which she quickly shut. She then darted just as quickly away from the chest to stand, heart hammering, near the fireplace.

The heat had lasted but a moment—gone so fast that she wondered if she'd only imagined the sensation. It left no burn or other mark. But she could still feel the weight of the watch in her palm.

She shuddered, anxious for Darcy to return. She needed his presence to chase away the shadows that now seemed to dance on every surface in the room.

What, oh, what had Professor Randolph brought to Netherfield?

Twenty-seven

"There was truth in his looks."
Elizabeth to Jane, Pride and Prejudice, *Chapter 17*

$\mathscr{I}$ demand an explanation."

"I will do my best to oblige you."

Juliet Kendall ignored Bingley's gestured invitation to take a seat. She instead remained standing in the middle of the drawing room where Darcy and Bingley had found her pacing upon their entrance. Cloudy late-morning light filtered through the windows, softening but not flattering her sharp features.

Upon learning of her father's death, Miss Kendall had taken advantage of the morning's break in the weather to swoop down upon Netherfield, talons glinting as she hunted for information. The gloomy sky threatened more snow—and with it, the extended stay of yet another unwelcome Kendall. What was it about this family that procured them weather favorable for travel *to* Netherfield, but turned it to prevent their departure?

Darcy did not envy his friend the ordeal of this meeting. What little they had to tell her—that her father's business dealings and conduct had ultimately made him reprehensible enough that no one had realized his death for hours and the killer could be one of several people—would not be pleasant for her to hear, and would no doubt elicit a response equally unpleasant. Darcy would sooner debate with Elizabeth the likelihood of Randolph's occult powers.

"My father was murdered under your roof. I want to know by whom."

"As I wrote in my letter, the local authorities are still investigating the matter."

"Yes, I have already met with the constable. He believes Professor Randolph was involved. Where is he? I demand to speak with him."

Bingley sent for the professor. As they awaited him, Miss Kendall repeated her questions, as if asking them enough times would somehow yield an answer where moments before none existed. The constable, it seemed, had spared her the more gruesome details of the crime, and Darcy and Bingley endeavored to keep those facts secret. Other information they truly did not possess.

Miss Kendall grew increasingly irritable. "Did no one see anything?" she asked for the fourth time. "Hear anything? A man died among you, and no one noticed?"

Bingley cleared his throat. "It is a large house. . . ." He glanced to Darcy with an expression of entreaty.

"I assure you, Miss Kendall, that we are doing all we can to learn what happened," Darcy offered.

She ignored him. "Mr. Bingley, this is your house. Until the murderer's identity is ascertained, I hold you responsible for my father's death."

"You have my most sincere condolences—"

"I don't want condolences. I want answers. And then I want someone's head on a platter."

After fifteen excruciating minutes, the servant returned. "Mr. Bingley, sir, I cannot find the professor."

"Where have you looked?"

"Throughout the house."

"Check the grounds. Perhaps he has gone for a walk."

More time passed. Eventually Miss Kendall's shrill voice lapsed into hostile silence. At last the servant reappeared, but with disappointing news. The search had turned up no Randolph.

"His trunk is still here but his greatcoat and traveling clothes are gone," the footman reported. "So is one of the horses."

Randolph had fled during the night. To escape the consequences of his crime? Though Darcy still struggled to pinpoint a motive for the professor to kill Kendall, evidence against Randolph was mounting. He silently berated himself for his stupidity—why had he not taken steps to have the archeologist watched more closely after the murder?

Miss Kendall regarded Bingley accusingly. "You *are* going to pursue him, aren't you?"

"I—well, of course. We'll send a rider out toward . . ." He looked to Darcy for guidance. "He said at dinner the other night that he would return to London?"

"Yes, but that was before the murder was discovered and he became a suspect. As he left his trunk here and disappeared without taking leave, there is no reason to believe he still intends to go there." Darcy frowned as he considered the possibilities. A lone rider on horseback, Randolph could be headed anywhere. Perhaps a port city, seeking passage to America? "Let us summon Mr. Parrish. They are friends—or were. Perhaps he can guess where Randolph might go. The professor may have even spoken to him before he left and dropped some hint."

Parrish came at once. He hurried into the room, his countenance anxious. "Bingley? Your servant said you needed me urgently." He stopped short upon sight of the lady present and regarded her warily. "Miss Kendall." He bowed. "I did not know you were at Netherfield."

"I have only just arrived."

He took a step toward her. "I am sorry for the loss of your father. He—"

"Save your pretty words, Mr. Parrish. Perhaps your wife wants to hear them. I don't."

Bingley cleared his throat. "Mr. Parrish, the professor has left Netherfield. We wonder if perhaps you know where he went."

Parrish blinked. "Randolph is gone? I had no idea. He said nothing to me about it." He sank into a chair, his face clouding with chagrin. "He said a couple days ago he would leave, but to depart so abruptly, without telling anyone . . . Surely you don't think it was he who—" He cut his words off as he glanced at Miss Kendall. "Yet it must have been. The symbols that were found—it all points to him, yet I didn't want to believe it. Randolph, the murderer!"

"We do not know with certainty that Randolph is guilty." Darcy wished fervently that Parrish hadn't brought up the pentagrams before Miss Kendall. He hadn't even known that anyone beyond himself, Elizabeth, and the constable knew that the symbols had been found on and around Kendall's body. He supposed he had the servants to thank for that.

"What symbols?"

"There were some markings on the floor." Darcy sought to redirect her attention. "Miss Kendall, did your father know Randolph well or have cause to associate with him often? Perhaps he considered financing the professor's upcoming archeological dig?"

"My father would never have speculated on such a losing enterprise as backing that man's pursuits," Juliet said. "Professor Randolph always gave me the shivers. He is an oddity."

"I thought him a harmless eccentric." Parrish shook his head in disbelief. He rose and walked to the window, stared at the light snow that had started to fall. "But the unusual nature of his studies must have worked upon his mind in insidious ways. I wonder if he even realizes what he has done."

"He damn well better." Miss Kendall's use of profanity shocked Darcy. The more time he spent with Lawrence Kendall's daughter, the more he thought Parrish got the better end of the deal when he instead married Caroline Bingley—mad or not.

Parrish turned back toward the room, meeting each of their gazes. "Bingley, Darcy—Miss Kendall, you most of all—I'm sorry. This is my fault. I brought Randolph among you."

"No man is responsible for the actions of another," Bingley said. "Especially actions so unpredictable."

Parrish released a heavy sigh. "Nevertheless, in trying to help my wife I brought harm to others. What kind of madness has gained hold of Randolph's reason, and how long has it gripped him? What dark gods does he think he serves? The carriage accident, the fire—I now wonder how many of our recent misfortunes can be laid at Randolph's feet?"

He left to check on his wife, leaving the others in contemplative silence.

Madness. Darcy had ascribed that possible motive to Caroline Parrish, but had not truly considered it where Randolph was concerned. Elizabeth, however, had—she'd suspected the professor of fanaticism. Though she thought he'd used supernatural means to aid his crime, a hypothesis Darcy still could not seriously entertain, a misguided attempt to appease imaginary powers could explain actions that reason could not. Perhaps the connection between Randolph and Kendall amounted to no more than Kendall presenting himself as a convenient victim for some dark rite.

Were that the case, Randolph was a very dangerous man—unpredictable and violent. Though they must initiate pursuit to save others from his demented zeal, Darcy was glad the madman no longer roamed Netherfield's environs freely.

At least, he hoped the lunatic had indeed fled.

Suddenly, he needed to assure himself of Elizabeth's whereabouts.

"Mrs. Nicholls, fire me if you want, but I won't do it! I won't be in there with her by myself—not with her cutting up her own husband with that ring he give her! Her sister sat with us yesterday while I did her toilette, but I can't find her today and I'm not walking in there alone! Not with all the goings-on round here and her acting so crazy!"

Elizabeth paused at the head of the stairs, surprised to find the housekeeper and Caroline's maid openly arguing in a public part of the house. They stood in the corridor that led to the new family quarters. Though they did not shout, their voices carried in the empty hallway.

"Nan, I can't spare anyone else right now just to—" Mrs. Nicholls broke off as she spotted their audience. She colored. "Mrs. Darcy. Excuse us, ma'am. We should be holding this discussion elsewhere."

Elizabeth sympathized with the maid. A murder in the house, Mr. Parrish attacked, Caroline sinking into madness, Randolph doing God-knows-what . . . the carriage accident, the fire . . . Netherfield was hardly an ideal place to be employed at present. "Perhaps I can help. You seek Mrs. Hurst?"

"She kept Mrs. Parrish company while Nan attended her yesterday." Mrs. Nicholls crossed her arms over her chest and glared at the maid. "But she hardly need be troubled again—"

"I can come." Elizabeth had been seeking something to occupy herself anyway, and had been avoiding Darcy since their argument the night before. She was also anxious to see whether Caroline's condition had improved—or worsened—since Randolph was relieved of his pocketwatch.

"Ma'am, please don't inconvenience yourself. Nan can—"

"It's no bother." She walked to the Parrishes' door and knocked softly. "Mrs. Parrish? It's Mrs. Darcy. Your maid is here to attend you, and I wondered if I might come in?"

She heard movement within. A minute later, Caroline answered the door in an extreme state of dishabille. Her hair had come loose from its braid overnight; long strands stuck out from her head in all directions, while what remained of the plait hung lopsided behind her left shoulder. Her dressing gown was tied haphazardly and parted to reveal an unevenly buttoned nightdress. She wore no slippers to protect her feet from the cold wood floor.

Mrs. Parrish seemed, however, oblivious to the appearance she presented. She stared through the servant, but blinked as her gaze drifted to Elizabeth. "Come in," she said. She pushed the door open farther and ambled to her vanity, leaving Elizabeth and the maid to enter and close the door themselves.

Caroline sat down and stared at her reflection. She fingered a tortoiseshell comb but didn't lift it. Her burned left hand continued to mend, the swelling having subsided, but still glowed an angry red. The bright pink scars on her wrists offered a hideous counterpoint.

Elizabeth drew a chair near the dressing table and sat beside her. "How are you this morning?"

She made no answer. Nan stepped behind her, removed the tie that had so poorly secured her braid, and reached for the comb. Caroline seized it and handed it to her, causing the maid to flinch at the unexpected movement. Nan stepped back and accepted the comb with a pincer grasp, eyeing Caroline's wedding ring cautiously.

"I thought I might take a walk in the gallery today," Elizabeth continued as the maid combed Caroline's hair and swept it into a chignon. "Would you care to join me?"

"Perhaps." The word seemed almost a heavy sigh, as if it had required great effort to utter.

Nan picked up several hairpins and started to secure the knot. When she ran out, Caroline handed her three more. Once again, the maid flinched as the oversize ring neared her.

Elizabeth took pity on the maid. "Mrs. Parrish, that heavy ring cannot feel good on your injured finger," she said. "Shall we remove it while your hand heals? We can give it to your husband for safekeeping."

Caroline's half-focused gaze met Elizabeth's in the mirror. She nodded her assent. With slow, deliberate movements, so as not to startle or threaten her, Elizabeth reached for her hand. Her skin was cool, except for the injured area around the ring, which emitted heat. How agonizing the burn must be still! No wonder Caroline seemed preoccupied—in constant pain, she probably could not think of much else.

Elizabeth gently tugged on the ring. She expected the gold to also be very warm, having absorbed the skin's heat. To her surprise, she found the band ice-cold. Unfortunately, it resisted removal.

Elizabeth hesitated to apply more force, but Caroline nodded again. She pulled more firmly. This time the ring loosened, but the movement made Caroline wince in obvious suffering.

"I'm sorry," Elizabeth said. "I'll stop—"

"No," she whispered hoarsely. She extended her arm fully, spread her fingers wide, and squeezed her eyes shut.

Sorry she ever suggested this, for it troubled her to see even Caroline Bingley in such distress, Elizabeth grasped the ring tightly. She pulled once more, rotating the band in hopes it would slide more easily. Mercifully, the ring at last slipped off.

She found the ring no more attractive up close than she

had when viewing it on Caroline's finger. She noticed an inscription on the inside: *Deux coeurs, une pensée.* Two hearts, one thought. A pretty sentiment, but Elizabeth still preferred her own, simpler, wedding band.

"There." She set it on the vanity. "Maybe now your burn will heal more—"

Caroline seized her hand. Gripping hard—surely a painful effort given her injury—she met Elizabeth's gaze directly. Her eyes had lost their cloudiness; indeed, she regarded Elizabeth fiercely. "He—"

"Darling! I'm so relieved to see you safe!" Mr. Parrish came bounding into the room. Startled by the sudden intrusion, Caroline dropped Elizabeth's hand and jerked back. "You, too, Mrs. Darcy," Parrish continued. "Have you heard the news? Randolph has disappeared! Heaven only knows where he is or what he might—"

He spotted the ring. "What's this?" He grabbed Caroline's wrist and, in one swift movement, swept the ring from the vanity top and back onto her finger. "My dear wife, I understand you have been a little forgetful of late, but your wedding ring isn't something that ought to be left lying around."

Pain flashed across Caroline's face—from the haste with which Parrish had restored the ring or the humiliation of being reprimanded before others, Elizabeth could not tell. The maid scurried out. Elizabeth wished she could escape the embarrassing scene as easily.

Caroline said nothing in her own defense. She stood still, her gaze on her husband, the distracted look back in her eyes. Elizabeth wondered if she'd only imagined the fleeting moment of lucidity.

"Forgive me, Mr. Parrish," Elizabeth said. "Removing the ring was my idea. It seemed to make the maid nervous. Every time Mrs. Parrish moved her hand—" She stopped, not wanting to add further tension by reminding him of his own injuries inflicted by the ring. The scarcely healed cuts lent his handsome countenance a piratical aspect.

Too late. "What, the little baggage thought her face would end up looking like mine? Caroline is so mad the servants fear her?" His jaw muscles flexed in anger. "She may be ill but she is still my wife! I gave her that ring—I alone have the right to remove it."

She bowed her head. "I apologize. I should not have presumed—"

Mr. Parrish took a deep breath and slowly released it. "No, Mrs. Darcy. It is I who should apologize. Pray forgive my outburst just now. It is only that . . ." He seemed to search for words. "The ring symbolizes the promise I made to Caroline on our wedding day."

With the thumb and fingers of his right hand, he absently stroked his own ring, the companion to Caroline's. "Perhaps it is foolish of me to place such heavy significance on so small and light an object. But so long as she has the ring with her, I am with her, and in this difficult time, it's important to us both to remember that."

"I am lucky to have you, Frederick," Caroline said softly.

He stroked her cheek. "And I, you, dearest." He turned back to Elizabeth and shrugged. "You have been more fortunate than us in the early days of your marriage. Perhaps you cannot understand."

Pity moved her. He was right—she and Darcy *were* fortunate. Their little quarrel the night before amounted to nothing when compared with the trials the Parrishes faced. "I do understand," she said.

Caroline sank back to the vanity bench. Parrish sat down next to her and drew her to his side. She leaned into him.

Elizabeth left in search of her own husband.

Twenty-eight

"There is a stubbornness about me that never can bear to be frightened at the will of others."
    Elizabeth to Darcy, Pride and Prejudice, *Chapter 31*

*E*lizabeth sent her maid for Darcy, with the message that she awaited him in their chamber. She regretted their fight and wanted to smooth things out, but in a place where they were assured of privacy. No one else need inadvertently learn they'd quarreled, let alone over what.

Professor Randolph and his powers—real or not—continued to occupy her thoughts. That watch was more than a simple timepiece, of this she was certain. He'd used it somehow with Mrs. Parrish, and again with Mr. Kendall. She recalled the image of Randolph standing over Caroline, pressing it into her hand, and shuddered. Would Caroline have met the same fate as Kendall if Elizabeth hadn't happened to walk in?

She glanced to the highboy. Did the watch yet rest in the top drawer, or had Darcy removed it that morning? Something told her it remained there, and she crossed the room to confirm her intuition. Sure enough, it lay right where she'd dropped it the night before. Apparently, Darcy thought it impotent enough to leave unattended.

She wanted to touch it—to pick it up, to feel its weight in her palm again. Why? Every reasonable thought told her to leave it alone. It was dangerous. Cursed. *Why not just stick your hand in the fire while you're at it?* Yet instinct urged her to reach for it.

She did.

The silver again felt warm to her touch but did not sear her this time. Again, she wondered if she'd only imagined the previous sensation. She pushed the drawer closed and carried the watch to the window, to better study it.

She popped open the case to examine the characters inscribed within. Randolph had said the strange symbols belonged to an ancient alphabet, but they bore little resemblance to English words. Opposite, the clock face was intriguingly designed. The hands were, quite literally, hands—shaped to resemble slender arms with pointing index fingers. The numbers were absent, replaced by images of the moon in successive phases, with the full moon at twelve.

The watch's back side held the same pentagram symbol as the front. Even in daylight, the image of a spread-eagled man seemed to appear and disappear at its center. Who was the figure? Some dark pagan god Randolph had tried to invoke?

A noise at the door startled her. She slipped the watch into her pocket and turned to face the door.

Darcy entered. He closed the door behind him and paused, regarding her uncertainly. Once, there had been many such awkward moments between them, when prejudice and lies and pride and misunderstandings had clouded their vision of each other and themselves. But then they'd found their way to each other, and not since then had such tension hung between them as it did now.

"Eliz—"

"Dar—"

They spoke in unison, then stopped. She offered a half smile and saw relief enter his eyes. They were in accord once more.

After they embraced, she told him of the scene she'd witnessed between the Parrishes. "I felt sorry for her when Mr. Parrish got so angry," she said, "and then I felt sorry for them both. The strain of recent weeks . . ."

"Yes, one can readily excuse a brief show of temper on Mr. Parrish's part."

"Still, to insist on his wife continuing to wear her wedding ring." She fingered her own shiny band. "I can understand its significance to Mr. Parrish, but Caroline seemed to very much desire its absence for a while."

Sliding Caroline's ring from her finger had caused obvious pain, yet she had encouraged—indeed, silently begged—Elizabeth to remove it. The metal, further weighted by the oversize gem, must irritate the damaged skin beneath. Elizabeth recalled how, the night Caroline had suffered the injury, she had also encouraged its removal despite the agony caused by each attempt.

How had she suffered the burn, anyway? Now that Professor Randolph was implicated in other recent terrifying events, Elizabeth reconsidered her suspicions from that night. Had Caroline set the fire, or merely been injured by it? She posed the question to Darcy.

He shrugged. "With Kendall dead and Randolph gone, we may never know exactly what happened that night. It still might have been an accident—though one wonders how that dress came to be where it was—just as Mrs. Parrish's injury may well have been accidental. Perhaps her nightdress caught fire and she hurt herself trying to put out the flames. That could explain how she came to be wearing servants' clothes instead of her own."

Darcy's theory made sense on the surface, but something nagged at the fringes of her consciousness. She tried to imagine

Caroline batting at a flaming nightgown. "Were that the case, would she not have suffered burns elsewhere on her person?"

"I suppose so."

Elizabeth continued to envision other scenarios. "And if she tried to smother flames elsewhere, or started the blaze herself . . ." The mental pictures still didn't look right. Something wasn't fitting together. Something she couldn't quite— She recalled Caroline scrawling her retort in the professor's notebook during their interview.

"Darcy, is Mrs. Parrish right-handed?"

He mused a moment. "Yes, she is." He caught her line of reasoning. "Yet she injured her left hand—and only her left."

"Is that not curious?"

He concurred. "One would think she'd use her dominant hand out of instinct in such a situation."

"Instead, she uses her off-hand. Why?" Another image flashed through her mind. "Professor Randolph was holding his watch to Caroline's left hand when I walked in on his ritual."

"I have given up trying to explain Randolph's behavior."

Her thoughts tumbled forward. "She fairly exploded at Randolph the day I sat with them. At the time, I believed her complaint was of the bandage, but now that I look back on it, I think she was trying to remove her ring."

Darcy made a reply, something about Mrs. Parrish attempting to ease her discomfort, but Elizabeth's mind raced too fast to hear him. She recalled her mother's visit upon their arrival at Netherfield, and Caroline half-removing her ring then. That had been before the fire, before her burns.

She remembered Caroline holding up her left hand when she appeared, ghostlike, on the balcony; Caroline showing off the ring at her wedding breakfast . . . the last time Mrs. Parrish had truly seemed herself. She recollected the way the ring had radiated intense cold when she herself had removed it this morning—the same way Professor Randolph's watch was unnaturally warm to her touch.

Her heartbeat accelerated. "Darcy, there is something baleful about that ring."

A sigh was his only reply. But his expression revealed his thoughts. Once again, he did not believe her.

"Caroline has not been the same since she started wearing it."

"Elizabeth," he said gently. "If gaudy, overpriced jewelry caused madness, all the *ton* would be afflicted. Mrs. Parrish's problems derive from more than a simple object."

She bristled at his facile dismissal. "A simple object she's been trying to remove almost from the day she started wearing it."

"She has an injured hand. It chafes."

"Maybe she injured her hand *because* of the ring. It caused her to be careless. Or—" her thoughts leapt—"she injured herself on purpose, for an excuse to remove it."

Darcy closed his eyes and rubbed his temples. "Elizabeth . . ."

"Perhaps she scratched Mr. Parrish with it for the same reason. So he would take it from her."

"Now you have strayed into absurdity. If Mrs. Parrish is that desperate to remove her wedding ring, why does she not simply take it off herself?"

"Because she doesn't want to wound her husband's feelings. Or—" The image of Professor Randolph intruded her thoughts once more. Somehow, she knew with certainty, the supernaturalist was involved. "Perhaps she physically cannot."

"If you could slide it from her finger, what prevents her?"

"Randolph. He charmed or cursed it somehow, as part of whatever plot he's working against the Parrishes." At his scornful look, she pressed. "Consider, Darcy—he stood up with Mr. Parrish at the wedding. The ring was probably in his possession before the ceremony. He had ample opportunity to work his dreadful sorcery upon it."

He looked heavenward, like a man praying for patience. "Elizabeth, I will not give credence to these preposterous notions. A man has died, and his suspected killer's whereabouts are unknown. There is too much at stake to waste further time in fanciful conjecture."

His words stung. He'd spoken to her as if reprimanding a child. That she loved him made his disbelief all the more painful. She knew she was right, knew there was more to Caroline's condition and Kendall's murder than cold facts. Why could he not set aside his deuced pride and trust her instincts?

She shook with frustration, anger, hurt. "Darcy, I need you to believe me in this."

"I cannot."

She swallowed hard and willed her voice to steady. "Then I guess there's nothing left to say."

She walked past him, silently begging him to stop her. But he let her pass unchecked, and did not even turn around to see her close the door. He must have heard it, though, for she applied enough force to rattle the frame. Then she headed down the hall, back to the Parrishes' chamber.

If Darcy would not save Caroline from that ring, she would.

Twenty-nine

"Handsome men must have something to live on, as well as the plain."

Elizabeth, writing to Mrs. Gardiner,
Pride and Prejudice, *Chapter 26*

*D*arcy stayed in the room but a minute following Elizabeth's decisive exit. He did not want to argue with her. Truly he did not. Clashing with his wife left his stomach knotted. But these ideas! How could he, or any reasonable man, be expected to take them seriously? How could she?

If the truth were ever to be discovered, it would be through deduction, not intuition. A review of the facts, not *I sense things sometimes*. How could he take "I sense things sometimes" to the magistrate as evidence of guilt? *Arrest this man—he attacked his victims with a ring and a pocketwatch*. He'd be laughed out of the county.

No, reason and logic would prevail. And it stood to reason that a man with his hands in as many pockets as Lawrence Kendall would keep some record of his affairs. He'd produced papers enough where Bingley was concerned—perhaps he possessed other documents that would reveal a clearer link between him and Randolph.

To Darcy's knowledge, no one had yet gone through

Kendall's personal effects. Now that his daughter had arrived, those items would soon be transported out of his reach. He had better examine them now, before Juliet Kendall ordered them packed up and loaded onto her coach. If she had not already.

He passed no one in the hall on his way to Kendall's chamber, to his satisfaction. He could not bear another spat with Elizabeth just now, and in his present mood had no patience for anyone else. He arrived, however, to find Kendall's quarters occupied.

Juliet Kendall sat at the desk. In her hand she held a closely written page, one of a sheaf of papers spread before her. Damn! She had beaten him to Kendall's documents; he would never see them now. He braced himself for her vitriol.

She glanced up to see who had interrupted her reading. "Mr. Darcy," she acknowledged. Her voice was uneven, her expression stricken.

The strain of her father's death must be wearing on her. Though it seemed ungentlemanly to press that advantage, he tried to rapidly devise a strategy that would persuade her to let him see Kendall's records. Ultimately, he assured his conscience, he was only trying to help her by identifying her father's killer.

"Miss Kendall." He bowed. "Forgive my intrusion. Are you finding everything all right?"

"I am finding more than I expected," she replied. "Including this." She handed him a letter.

New Orleans
1 September 18——

Dear Sir,
    After a perilous Atlantic crossing, I reached Louisiana and have spent the past three weeks performing the enquiries you entrusted to me. Your suspicions are confirmed: Mr. Frederick Parrish is not the man he claims to be.

The local authorities were unfamiliar with him by the name Par-
rish, which I presume he adopted when he arrived in London. But
when I showed them the likeness you had the foresight to commission
without his knowledge, they recognized him immediately as Jack Dia-
mond (also assumed to be an alias). Diamond is a drifter; no one quite
knows where he came from before arriving in New Orleans. In the
twelvemonth or so he spent here, he earned his living as a pickpocket
and a swindler, with a talent for confidence games. His disarming per-
sona fooled everyone; it was not until he killed the son of a wealthy
plantation owner in a knife fight that his true nature became known.

Diamond disappeared from the area about a year ago and has
not been heard of since. Many thought him dead. He had made lots
of enemies, including several prospective grandfathers—if you
understand my meaning.

Mont Joyau ("Mount Jewel"), Parrish's alleged estate, does not
exist. The painting in his drawing room is a copy of one commonly
for sale in the French Quarter; the artist tells me it is inspired by
several nearby plantations but depicts none in particular.

As for Mr. Parrish's associate, Julian Randolph, I have learned
little. He did hold a legitimate university post at one time but was
dismissed for unspecified reasons. He is known to frequent pawnbro-
kers' shops. I will endeavor to learn more of him before returning to
England. I have booked passage on the Seahawk, which sets sail one
fortnight hence.

> *I am, sir, your most obedient servant—*

By the time he finished reading, Darcy gripped the letter so
tightly it crumpled on one side. Parrish—or Diamond, or
whatever the scoundrel's name was—had deceived them all.
All except Kendall, who had been smart enough to have his
daughter's suitor investigated. Would that he and Bingley had
been so wise! Distracted by their own marital preparations,
they had accepted the "gentleman" at his word and allowed
Caroline to marry a dangerous fortune hunter.

Kendall, meanwhile, had reveled in their ignorance. In fact, he'd been so full of his own superiority at knowing what they did not, that he was unable to completely contain himself. He'd dropped smug hints about Parrish's character—at dinner, during the billiards game—which they'd all interpreted as mere sour grapes over the broken courtship.

He glanced to Miss Kendall. "Did you know any of this?"

She shook her head. "When my father forced Mr. Parrish to end our courtship, he implied that he had disparaging information about Frederick. I tried to hint as much to Caroline. That's why I asked her to go riding that day—I started thinking about the times we'd played together as girls and felt I owed her that much. But I never imagined this. Merciful heavens! Thievery, seduction, murder—what crime has he not committed?"

They could probably add involvement in Kendall's death to the list. Given Kendall's goading comments to Parrish and the hints he dropped to everyone else, Parrish must have known Juliet's father possessed this information. Kendall's continued presence at Netherfield therefore posed a threat to whatever plans Parrish had for Caroline, and the risk of exposure would be too great for Parrish to tolerate long. Kendall could even have been blackmailing Parrish. Given the businessman's dealings with Hurst, it would come as little surprise, and would explain why he had brought the letter along with him to Netherfield.

Was Parrish responsible for other events as well? The carriage accident? The fire? Darcy would have to reconsider all of his previous theories. But now he hadn't the time. He had to warn the others of Parrish's duplicity. He shoved the letter back into Miss Kendall's hands. "Show this to Mr. Bingley."

"Where are you going?"

He hurried out the door, his heart hammering. Frederick Parrish was capable of anything, and he held the trust of the entire household.

Including Elizabeth.

Thirty

"There is but such a quantity of merit between them; just enough to make one good sort of man; and of late it has been shifting about pretty much."

Elizabeth to Jane, Pride and Prejudice, Chapter 40

$\mathcal{F}$or the second time that morning, Elizabeth knocked at the Parrishes' chamber. This time it was Mr. Parrish who answered. He had removed his coat and cravat; the top buttons of his shirt were open. He appeared dour, as if his earlier displeasure yet lingered.

"I am glad to find you still here," she said. He held the door open but a little, so that she could not see inside. "Is Mrs. Parrish within?"

"She is resting."

Elizabeth hesitated to disturb her, but thought the errand should not wait. "I believe I may have important intelligence to share with you both."

His brows rose. "Indeed?" He studied her face for a moment before opening the door wider and stepping back a pace. "Come in."

She noticed as she passed him that he wore some sort of medallion around his neck beneath his shirt. It appeared to be fashioned of braided hair, in several hues, knotted together.

She recalled the amulet he had proposed making for Caroline and wondered if he wore a similar article.

Caroline was abed, sitting up with pillows propped behind her. Though she opened her eyes upon Elizabeth's entrance, they stared vacantly, as if not recognizing the visitor. Her hands lay motionless in her lap.

Elizabeth shivered. It was cold in here; the fire sputtered in the grate. Outside, heavy flakes of snow had begun to fall rapidly, casting the room in dimness. She wondered that Mr. Parrish hadn't asked a servant to bank up the fire.

She walked toward the bed and greeted Caroline, but received no response. The wedding ring remained on Mrs. Parrish's left hand. It looked innocuous enough. But as Elizabeth neared the ring, the skin on the back of her neck prickled, and a sense of foreboding settled upon her.

Parrish closed the door. "What is this news?"

"I think I know what ails Mrs. Parrish."

He started in surprise, then recovered himself. "Truly? I am all attention."

She took a deep breath, anticipating the incredulous reaction she'd received from Darcy. If her own husband didn't believe her, what chance did she have of convincing Parrish that the very ring he'd given his wife as a symbol of his affection was the source of all her problems? But the longer she stood in proximity to the ring, the more certain she became that her intuition was correct.

"Please do not accuse me of reading too many novels," she said, "but I believe the ring you gave Mrs. Parrish bears some sort of curse."

He laughed. But it was not a merry sound, nor one of casual dismissal. It was a sinister cackle. His countenance changed, the characteristic openness suddenly replaced by a hardened mask. "Why, Mrs. Darcy, you are more intelligent than even I gave you credit for."

Dread swept her. He knew. The ring was cursed, and he already knew.

"Too smart for your own preservation."

In an eyeblink, he had a knife in hand, pulled from his boot before she realized he'd reached for it. The blade glittered in the weak firelight.

She instinctively retreated a step, evoking more laughter from him.

"That's right—back up. Closer to my helpless wife."

She glanced at Caroline, who lethargically observed them as if watching a theatrical. "What have you done to her?"

"Improved her disposition. Don't you agree?"

"I concur with Mr. Kendall. Marriage does not seem to agree with her."

"Take care, Mrs. Darcy. Or you'll meet the same fate he did." He spun the knife in his hand. "Only Kendall never saw it coming."

The knife—Kendall had died of a knife wound. Parrish must have been involved in Randolph's ritual. "You killed Mr. Kendall?"

"Does anyone else in this house have the guts?"

"Why?"

"The greedy bastard was trying to blackmail me. I told him to go to hell. Then I sent him there."

Still gripping the knife in his right hand, Parrish brought his left forward. He grasped his own wedding ring between thumb and forefinger, and twisted it round. "Caroline, help Mrs. Darcy find a seat while I decide what to do with her."

Caroline rose easily from the bed, in full possession of her physical faculties. She grabbed Elizabeth with surprising strength, forced her into a chair, and held her arms immobile.

"Mrs. Parrish—*Caroline*? How can you help him do this?"

Mrs. Parrish either couldn't hear her or ignored her.

"Caroline belongs to me." Parrish cackled again. "Her

wedding vows included a promise to obey—didn't yours? Tsk! Terrible oversight on your husband's part. I'll have to give him the name of my jeweler."

His gaze never leaving Elizabeth, Parrish crossed to a chest of drawers and removed a fistful of neckcloths. Pressing his knife to the base of Elizabeth's throat, he instructed Caroline to bind her ankles and wrists to the chair. Elizabeth breathed shallowly through her nose, afraid the slightest movement would cause the blade to pierce her.

When she was bound, he held the knife away a few inches and ordered Caroline to gag her with the last cravat. "I really quite liked you, Mrs. Darcy. You were the only person in this whole vapid house with sufficient wit to challenge me." He tossed the blade in the air, spinning it end over end, then reached up and caught it squarely by its handle. "Don't attempt anything stupid, and I might let you live."

Her heart pounding so loud that it nearly drowned out his words, she nodded.

He snickered. "Why don't I trust you?" He handed the blade to Caroline. "Slice her if she moves."

He crossed to the armoire with rapid steps, withdrew a valise, and set it open on the bed. From various drawers he pulled clothing, money, documents—and a dagger with a jagged blade twice the size of the one Caroline held.

A knock at the door interrupted his packing. He gestured for Caroline to hold her knife against Elizabeth's throat once more. Unreleased breath filled her lungs. Staring at the dagger Parrish gripped, she at once prayed it was Darcy who stood outside, and prayed it wasn't.

Parrish approached the door. "Who's there?"

"Mrs. Darcy's maid, sir. By chance is she with Mrs. Parrish?"

He opened the door a crack. "Mrs. Darcy isn't here. I haven't seen her all morning."

"Yes, sir. Sorry to disturb you."

He shut the door without response.

Lucy! Elizabeth silently willed her faithful servant to get as far away from this chamber of horror as possible—yet to somehow know she needed help.

Pressed against the wall outside Parrish's room, Darcy met Lucy's gaze. She shook her head and shrugged—she had not been able to see inside.

Damn.

He jerked his head toward the stairs. As prearranged, the servant left to summon assistance.

Parrish's lie that he hadn't seen Elizabeth all morning further strengthened Darcy's suspicions that she was in fact within. If this was what his wife meant by intuition, he was starting to put some stock in it. He only hoped the instinct that told him she yet lived was also accurate. He deeply regretted their quarrel, that their last moments together had been laced with tension and unhappiness. Dear God, if he could but hold Elizabeth safe in his arms once more, hear his name on her lips, he'd patiently listen to every far-fetched notion she cared to utter.

Cold terror clawed his chest. He had never feared for himself the way he now feared for her. Parrish was a violent man without conscience, and Elizabeth was within striking range. Common sense told him to wait for help, but he dared not allow another minute's delay.

He cocked the pistol he had borrowed from Bingley's desk. Bracing himself for whatever he might find on the other side, he swung wide the door and burst in.

"Mr. Darcy. I wondered when you might join us."

Parrish calmly greeted Darcy's dramatic entrance. Standing in the center of the chamber, he gestured with a wicked-looking dagger toward the side of the room. "As you can see, your wife has already made herself comfortable."

Elizabeth was bound and gagged, and—Darcy's jaw dropped—held at knifepoint by Caroline Parrish.

"Mrs. Parrish?" Darcy struggled to comprehend the scene. He could not believe Caroline would act in collusion with the ruffian.

"Put down that pistol before someone gets hurt. My wife is a most attentive hostess, I assure you."

Darcy instead aimed the weapon at Parrish. "I know Caroline Bingley. She would not harm Elizabeth."

"Caroline Bingley might not. But Caroline Parrish will if I ask her to. She'll do anything I command. Imagine that—a wife who does her husband's bidding! Perhaps yours would get into less trouble if she followed suit."

Parrish was bluffing. Had to be. Darcy had known Caroline for more than a decade, and while she did not harbor any great affection for Elizabeth, physically harming another person was not in her nature. He held the pistol steady.

"Don't believe me?" Parrish slowly brought his hands together and twisted his ring. "Caroline, run that blade down your own cheek."

Caroline lifted the knife. In a motion too swift for Darcy to prevent, she scratched the side of her face. A thin ribbon of blood welled and dribbled down her cheek. She returned the blade to the base of Elizabeth's throat.

"If a woman as vain as my wife will disfigure herself at my command, do you doubt what she'll do to your precious Elizabeth?"

Darcy, nauseated by what he'd just witnessed, stared at Parrish. What kind of monster was he? And what sort of domination did he hold over Caroline? He looked at Parrish's ring. He'd fingered it before issuing the vile order. Glancing back at Caroline, he noted that she still wore her own wedding ring. Was it possible that Elizabeth was right?

Could the rings possess some mysterious power?

Parrish laughed, a malevolent, sickening sound. "Realization dawns on stuffy English intellect. Your wife caught on much faster than you. Now, speaking of the little lady—if you love her, put the pistol down."

Slowly, Darcy set the pistol on the floor.

"Fool."

Thirty-one

"How is such a man to be worked on?"
Elizabeth to Darcy, Pride and Prejudice, *Chapter 46*

*E*lizabeth ignored the lump in her throat, not daring to swallow it. The tip of Caroline's knife pressed into her flesh. Perspiration trickled down her throat. Or was it blood?

Parrish kicked the pistol toward Caroline. "Here, darling— I think even you can figure out how to use this." The weapon scudded across the floor, coming to rest near Elizabeth's foot. Elizabeth, hoping to kick it under the bed, strained against the bond at her ankle, but it held fast. Caroline set her knife on the night table and picked up the gun.

"If either of them tries anything, shoot the other," Parrish said.

Elizabeth hadn't known such wickedness existed in the world. She dared not look at Darcy. He'd already relinquished his weapon because of her; she did not want him to see the terror she felt for him and herself. Nor did she want Parrish to know that in threatening him he'd found her greatest vulnerability.

Her mind raced, trying to devise a way to help her husband.

She couldn't speak, couldn't move . . . much. She tested her wrist constraints. The left secured her tightly to the chair arm, but she found the right just loose enough to allow slight movement. If she proceeded very slowly, so as not to draw Caroline's notice, perhaps she could reach her pocket—and the housewife inside. What she hoped to accomplish with sewing notions she knew not, but attempting to reach a pin or needle seemed more useful than doing nothing.

"Parrish, there is no reason anyone has to get hurt." Darcy held his hands before him in a show of cooperation. "Let my wife go, and we can settle this like gentlemen."

"Like gentlemen?" Parrish snorted. "And just what does that mean? Shall we repair to the drawing room for tea? I've endured enough foppish English manners. I've got you and your wife at gunpoint, man—let's drop the phony civility."

Darcy straightened and took a step toward Elizabeth's side of the room. "All right, then. Tell me what it is you want."

Elizabeth worked her fingers closer to her pocket. They reached its edge.

"First, I want you to stop moving toward your wife. Do you think I'm stupid? There—" With the dagger, he pointed to the other side of the room, near the sputtering fire. "I want you there."

Darcy moved where he indicated. Just a couple feet from the flames, his form cast long shadows on the floor.

To keep both eyes on Darcy, Parrish now had to stand with his body turned away from Elizabeth. She dipped her fingers inside her pocket. They brushed something, but not the expected housewife—a chain . . . Professor Randolph's watch. She nearly cried in frustration. Of what possible use was that watch right now? She pawed it until it slid into her palm. Perhaps she could move it out of her way and yet reach the housewife.

"Second," Parrish continued, "I want money. Lots of it."

"How much?"

"How much do you have?" Parrish ran a fingertip along the flat of the blade. He cocked his head as if an idea had just occurred to him. "More to the point, how much is your wife worth? She'll be taking a little trip with me, you see, until a generous sum finds its way to us. I'd planned to just bring Caroline—we never had a proper honeymoon, you know. But adding Elizabeth could make things far more . . . exciting."

Elizabeth fought down the bile that rose in her throat at Parrish's indecent suggestion. Darcy made no reply, but she could see from the tightening of his jaw that Parrish had baited his anger.

"I can hardly wait to find out, Darcy—is your wife as spirited by night as she is by day?"

Darcy's gaze flickered to Elizabeth. She could read in his expression that he wanted nothing more than to silence Parrish's offensive utterances. His hands clenched into fists. But the villain's order to Caroline prevented action—Darcy might risk harm to himself, but never to her.

Loud footsteps clattered in the hall, heading toward the chamber. Parrish looked at the door, then back at Darcy. "I won't be outnumbered." He leapt toward him, dagger poised.

Darcy sprang. But not forward—back, to the fireplace. He grabbed the poker and brought it up to block Parrish's attack. Steel struck iron as he deflected the thrust.

Caroline pointed the pistol at Darcy. Elizabeth struggled against her bonds, but to no effect. Caroline wrapped both hands around the handle and moved her finger to the trigger.

At Darcy's parry, Parrish retreated a step. He stood between Caroline and Darcy, blocking her aim. Darcy gripped the poker in his right hand like a fencing foil, his stance *en garde*. The two men circled. In another moment, Caroline would have a clear shot.

Elizabeth hurled her whole weight at Caroline, upsetting

both chair and captor. She knocked Caroline to the ground and landed on top of her legs. The pistol flew out of Caroline's grasp and skidded under the night table.

The fall knocked the wind out of Elizabeth. She labored for breath, helpless as a turtle on its back. Her right hand, yet grasping the watch, had slid from her pocket, but her bonds still held fast. She could do little against Caroline but try to maintain the pin, and nothing to help Darcy. From her present position she could barely see her husband and Parrish.

"Caroline, kindly kill Mrs. Darcy, will you?" Parrish lunged at Darcy, trying to stab him in the gut. Darcy parried the strike. The sound of clashing metal filled the air.

Caroline fought to free herself from Elizabeth's weight. She kicked and twisted, trying to move out from beneath the chair. She stilled, however, when she caught sight of the watch in Elizabeth's hand.

The watch! Perhaps it truly did hold power. If so, she could use it somehow. But did she dare? She didn't want to harm Caroline, only prevent her from acting on Parrish's orders.

Caroline resumed her struggle. She stretched her arm toward the night table, attempting to reach the pistol. Her fingers brushed the handle.

The chamber door flew open. Bingley rushed in—accompanied by Professor Randolph. Randolph carried a forked wooden rod.

"Bingley!" Darcy cried. "Help Elizabeth!"

Parrish fingered one of the knots in the medallion at his neck, his other hand still brandishing his weapon. "No—help your sister! Mrs. Darcy is attacking her!"

Bingley stood rooted to the floor, frozen with indecision, his gaze ricocheting from Darcy and Parrish to the women. Elizabeth didn't understand his hesitation. How could he possibly believe Parrish's claim? Could he not see that Elizabeth was bound to the chair?

Caroline managed a tentative grasp on the pistol, clawing it into her hand. Randolph hurried forward.

"Mrs. Darcy, the amulet—my watch—touch it to her!"

Why? What would it do? She longed to ask but the gag still silenced her.

Parrish kept his eyes on Darcy as the two yet faced off. "Bingley, now Randolph's trying to use his hocus-pocus on Caroline."

Bingley grabbed Randolph, preventing him from getting any closer to where the two women lay sprawled.

Randolph struggled against Bingley. "Mrs. Darcy! The amulet!"

"Caroline, shut him up!" Parrish snarled.

From her angle, Elizabeth could scarcely see Randolph, could not look him in the eye to judge his motives. What harm would the amulet inflict on Caroline? On herself, for using it? She clutched it in her palm. Did she dare trust the supernaturalist? Why had he returned to Netherfield? Wasn't he in league with Parrish?

Caroline had the pistol firmly in her grasp now. She twisted to take aim at the professor.

There was no more time to think. If Elizabeth was going to act, it had to be now. She pressed the amulet against Caroline's leg. And prayed she was doing the right thing.

Caroline's grip on the pistol relaxed. She lowered it to the floor.

Randolph fought to extricate himself, but Bingley's grasp was strong. "The amulet has reduced the ring's hold on her," the professor said to Elizabeth. "Ask her to free you."

With a howl of anger, Parrish suddenly abandoned his duel with Darcy and lunged at Randolph. Restrained by Bingley, the professor was helpless to defend himself. Just as Parrish was about to sink a fatal thrust, Darcy leapt for his legs. Parrish fell forward, the dagger still in his hand.

He rolled to his back and stabbed at Darcy. Darcy caught his wrist. Their arms shook with the strength of two matched forces in opposition. The blade inched closer to Darcy, coming but a hairsbreadth away from him.

Elizabeth stopped breathing. Her neck ached from the strain of watching from the poor angle, but she could not tear her gaze away.

Darcy never flinched. With slowness that seemed to last an eternity, he forced Parrish's hand back until it rested on the floor.

Elizabeth choked down a sob of relief.

Darcy disarmed Parrish, checked him for other hidden weapons, and—at Randolph's direction—removed both his wedding ring and the medallion he wore around his neck. With Bingley's help, he tied the knave's wrists to the bedpost. Parrish said nothing the whole time.

The moment Parrish was secured, Darcy hastened to Elizabeth. He tugged at her bonds until she was free and pulled her into his arms. "Elizabeth," he whispered fiercely, the single word at once an endearment, an apology, a promise. She understood it was all he *could* say. As he had once told her, a man who had felt less might have said more.

Her own heart was just as full. She tried to respond but discovered the gag had left her mouth too dry to speak. She settled for simply resting her head in the crook of his neck.

Randolph, meanwhile, seized Caroline's pistol and extricated Mrs. Parrish from Elizabeth's chair. Blinking, Caroline observed the scene groggily, like someone awakening from a long sleep. She glanced, expressionless, from Elizabeth to Darcy to Randolph. Her countenance turned icy when her gaze lit upon Parrish.

"Charles," she said wearily as she caught sight of her brother, "I don't feel at all well."

Elizabeth at last found her voice. "Professor Randolph, will Mrs. Parrish recover from her ordeal?"

"In good time," Randolph said. "But first, there is something else I must do."

Thirty-two

"Caroline is incapable of wilfully deceiving any one; and all that I can hope in this case, is that she is deceived herself."
Jane to Elizabeth, Pride and Prejudice, *Chapter 21*

*R*andolph still held the oaken rod he'd carried into the chamber; Elizabeth now recognized it from the London museum exhibit. Though she and Darcy had viewed the display of mysterious articles only a few weeks earlier, that day now seemed half a lifetime ago.

Taking Caroline's left hand, the supernaturalist touched the rod to her ring and uttered a command. The gem glowed momentarily, then dulled. "There," he said. "The bond is broken." He slid the ring from her finger and asked Darcy for Parrish's companion ring. Darcy hesitated, regarding him warily, but surrendered it.

Randolph withdrew two small silver candles from his pockets. As the assembly watched in disbelieving silence, he placed them before the fire and lit them. *"Ah-bro-GAH-tay."* He slipped Caroline's ring over the wick of one candle. *"Abrogate."* He dropped Parrish's ring over the wick of the other. *"Abrogate. As I will, so mote it be."*

He extracted a small leather pouch from one of his breast

pockets, and a thin silver stylus from the other. The stylus he used to lift the rings off the candles and place them into the pouch. He then extinguished the candles with his thumb and index finger. "These rings will never again be used for ill purposes."

"Where did they come from?" Elizabeth asked.

"Most recently, a pawnbroker's shop in New Orleans." Randolph tucked the pouch into his breast pocket. "You'd be surprised at the objects that find their way into such establishments. I spotted this pair and, based on appearance and the inscription, suspected they were a legendary set known as the Halbert Rings—the gift of a sixteenth-century French nobleman to his bride. It is said that the marquis loved his wife but was a jealous man, and feared being cuckolded as had so many of his peers. So he commissioned a pair of rings and had them enchanted by the village wisewoman to ensure his wife's fidelity. But the wisewoman dabbled with forces she did not fully understand and inadvertently invested the rings with the ability to bind one wearer to the other's will."

Darcy's face drew into a frown of suspicion. "If you were the one who found the rings, how did Parrish come to possess them?"

"I didn't have the money to buy them. I had just been dismissed from my most recent academic post and was seeking a new position. I had been keeping my eye on the rings for about a month when I encountered Mr. Parrish one day in the pawnbroker's shop. He noted my interest in the rings. I, taking him to be a gentleman of means, explained my professional curiosity about them in hopes that he might be prevailed upon to patronize my studies."

Randolph cast one of the candles into the hearth. The wax quickly softened and caught fire, brightening the dim room. "Mr. Parrish agreed to purchase the rings and keep them for me until I had the wherewithal to pay for them myself. He said, however, that he was leaving the country the next day and did not expect to return for some time. To my surprise and delight, he invited me to accompany him to England. He said he was intrigued by my studies and wanted to learn more about them. Perhaps, he suggested, he might consider financing my next expedition, or could introduce me to others who would.

"I could scarcely believe my good fortune! Indeed, I was so excited I didn't realize until later that I hadn't even learned the name of my new benefactor. Having no other prospects or connections, I packed my belongings and met him at the docks the next morning. It was then that he introduced himself to me as Frederick Parrish, owner of a sugar plantation."

The first candle having liquefied, he tossed the other into the blaze. It, too, was quickly consumed. "During the voyage, Mr. Parrish displayed insatiable curiosity about the rings—their history, what they did, how they worked. His enquiries then expanded to encompass other artifacts and enchantments. He proved a quick student, absorbing even the tiniest details. After so many years of having my work mocked and unappreciated, I was gratified by his abundant interest. I never realized that I was unwittingly helping him develop a most despicable plot."

"Would it have made a difference, Randolph?" Parrish snickered. "When we met, you didn't have a pot to piss in. You were at that pawnbroker's shop to sell one of your other pieces of junk just to pay your rent."

"That's true—I was," he told the Darcys. "Perhaps I didn't realize what was happening because I didn't want to. Once we reached London, Parrish established himself in the townhouse while I took a small room in Fleet Street. Concerned about the safety of my artifacts, I arranged for them to be displayed at the British Museum rather than store them in my room or accept Mr. Parrish's offer to keep them at the townhouse. He seemed quite put out by my decision, to the point where I feared losing his patronage.

"Mr. Parrish soon became the toast of the *ton,* and I benefited from his popularity. While he courted marriageable young ladies, I courted potential patrons. And so when he came to me with a lock of Miss Kendall's hair and asked me to teach him how to create a charm I'd told him about, to my shame, I complied rather than risk losing his favor."

Elizabeth recalled Parrish asking for a lock of her own hair. "What did the charm do?"

"If the lock is freely given, the charm blinds the giver to the wearer's faults," Randolph said. "It's not as powerful as the rings; it doesn't dominate another's will, merely discourages one from considering the wearer's statements and actions too critically. I believe Mr. Parrish fashioned a second charm—the medallion your husband just removed—from locks given by members of this household."

That explained the lack of resistance Parrish had encountered when he suggested institutionalizing Caroline, Elizabeth realized. He must have invoked the medallion that night, as he had with Bingley just now.

At Randolph's invitation, Darcy, still holding the medallion, cast it into the flames. The unpleasant odor of burning hair wafted through the room, but all were too interested in learning more from Randolph to leave.

"Did you not wonder why Parrish wanted to create such an item?" Darcy asked.

"I thought he only wanted to aid his suit and secure Miss Kendall's hand more quickly. By then, I had started to suspect that his financial resources were running low—he hosted fewer parties, spent more conservatively. He still talked about financing my expedition but never advanced any capital. I believed him simply strapped until the sale of his plantation was complete. Selfishly, I thought his marrying an heiress might restore his generosity, and I yet hoped some of it would fall my way."

Darcy squeezed Elizabeth's hand, then released her to approach Parrish. "When Mr. Kendall investigated you and ended the courtship, you had to find another heiress. And you had to act quickly, before Kendall exposed you to all of society."

Parrish looked at his wife in disgust. "Why else would I have settled for Caroline Bingley? She was an easy mark—licking her wounds over your engagement and unprotected by her brother's distraction over his. She would have given herself to anyone in breeches."

"Swine." Caroline pushed herself to her feet and went to stand before him. "I can't fathom how I ever believed your lies."

"Because you wanted to. Just like I tolerated your company because I wanted to—and because I didn't think I would have to endure it for long. But you just wouldn't die. You were too damned lucky! I send you out on Bow Street at midnight with a bulging reticule, and instead of a cutthroat, the Darcys find you. I send you down to the kitchen for some late-night slicing, and you take so long to bleed out that the cook discovers you in time. I couldn't get rid of you! So when Mrs. Bennet let slip how much money your brother really had, I figured I'd kill off your family first to gain a larger inheritance for my trouble—and do it before Bingley went and tied it all up in land." His lips curved into a smug grin. "Or rather, I'd have you do it."

"Monster! *You* directed me to loosen the bolt on that wheel." Caroline's voice shook. "*You* had me don servants' clothes and sneak into my brother's chamber to set the fire."

"And you couldn't even do those things right, you dumb—"

She slapped him. "And you!" She spun round to accost Randolph. "You stood by and watched him do it!"

"Indeed I did not, madam! I assure you, I had no idea he planned to use those rings until he produced them at the wedding ceremony. And even then, I didn't realize he intended to kill you. When you were found in the kitchen, I thought your spirit was acting toward its own destruction rather than allow itself to be subverted to Parrish's will." He turned to Elizabeth. "Mr. Parrish asked me to suggest taking his wife back to America, saying he thought her family would be more disposed to agree if the recommendation came from me. But the idea of consulting Dr. Lancaster was mine. I truly did want to help her! Later, I tried to use my amulet to weaken the ring's hold on her. That's what I was doing the day you walked in on our session."

"The day of the winter solstice?"

"A coincidence, that."

"I remember now," Caroline said vaguely, as if recalling a dream. "All along I could see what was happening to me, but as if I were witnessing it happen to someone else. At first, I didn't realize what was making me act so strangely. Frederick would suggest things, and I would just *do* them. After I went riding with Miss Kendall, I started to suspect something strange was afoot—Hecate shied from my touch all morning, and spooked when I laid my hand on her neck. The animal knew before I did that I wore an evil ring! But I was powerless to act in my own defense.

"Then Frederick's commands became more direct, and I noticed him manipulating his own ring when he gave them. I understood then. But the more I attempted to resist, the more mad I appeared to all of you. And the more time I spent in his proximity, the more the ring overpowered my will." She met Bingley's sorrowful gaze. "I am sorry, brother, for the injuries I did you."

He crossed to her and took her hands. "You could not help yourself."

"I tried! I tried to draw attention to the ring, but my efforts failed. Only once since my wedding day did I feel I had any control at all—after my last meeting with Professor Randolph. When I left, I felt strong enough to confront Frederick. I told him I knew what he was doing, and that I would reveal his treachery if he didn't remove my ring. He refused, and we fought. Then he drugged me, and when I awoke, I was weak again."

"Why didn't you simply remove the ring?" Elizabeth asked.

"I could not. I even burned my hand intentionally, hoping someone else would take off the cursed thing."

"I was also unable to slide it off," said Randolph. "It was magically bound to her. That's why I had to return to London for this rod—to break the bond."

Elizabeth frowned. "But I removed the ring myself, this morning."

Randolph regarded her in amazement. "You did? That's—why, that's extraordinary, Mrs. Darcy! In the long history of that ring, only the wearer of its companion band has been able to remove it without supernatural aid. You must—" His gaze flickered to the others present. He lowered his voice. "We must speak more at a later time."

Elizabeth held out the pocketwatch. "Meanwhile, you deserve to have this back. I'm sorry I withheld it from you."

To her surprise, he shook his head. "Keep it. Despite popular belief, the pentagram is not a symbol of evil, but of protection. That amulet kept you safe from harm today—may it continue to do so."

"It did not keep Mr. Kendall safe," she pointed out.

"Because it was planted in his hand after his death, just as the symbols were inscribed after the murder took place. Mr. Kendall was stabbed in the back by a common thief"—he cast a derisive look at Parrish—"who also snatched my watch right out of my pocket just after I tried to use it to help Mrs. Parrish. I didn't notice its absence until dinnertime, and it was the next day before I realized how I'd lost it." He addressed Parrish.

"You stole it before the murder. Did you intend to frame me then? Or merely prevent me from using the amulet again?"

Parrish shrugged insolently. A prod from Darcy opened his mouth. "The latter. Leaving it in Kendall's hand was a last-minute stroke of inspiration."

"When the watch was found, I knew the killer had tried to implicate me," Randolph continued. "And I knew the murderer must have been Mr. Parrish. He was familiar with my amulet, had seen it many times, but had taken little interest in passive, guardian magics—he wanted to learn only of devices that enable one to act upon others. Had I been a better teacher, I would have realized his malicious intentions sooner. But had he been a better student, he would have chosen a more appropriate symbol to aid his crime."

The sound of footfalls on the stairs soon led to the entrance of Miss Kendall and the constable. The snow-covered peace officer had not even paused to leave his greatcoat with a servant. "I hear you've found the murderer?" His eyes widened as they took in the image of Frederick Parrish bound to the bedpost. He turned to Darcy. "It was Mr. Parrish? Are you certain, sir?"

"Mr. Kendall knew that Parrish wasn't who he claimed to be," Darcy said. "He has no plantation in America, and he is wanted under the name Jack Diamond for murder and other crimes there." Darcy helped the constable handcuff Parrish. "Mr. Kendall threatened to expose you to us, did he not?"

"Kendall was a greedy bastard," said Parrish. "He got what he deserved."

"So will you."

When all the others had exited the room, Darcy drew Elizabeth to him and kissed her.

"I hope you will forgive me," he said. "Else it will be a long ride to Derbyshire."

"With sufficient atonement, I may be persuaded," she said lightly, her expression revealing that he'd already been acquitted.

"How can I make amends?"

She pretended to think a moment. "If you produce a nice enough gift on Christmas morning, perhaps I shan't make you ride the *full* distance in silence."

"But by Christmas morning we already will have made the journey." He smiled as her look of puzzlement was quickly overcome by one of hopeful anticipation. "Can you be ready to depart by this afternoon?"

"I am ready this instant."

Epilogue

> *"Mr Darcy sends you all the love in the world, that he can spare from me. You are all to come to Pemberley at Christmas."*
>
> Elizabeth, writing to Mrs. Gardiner,
> Pride and Prejudice, *Chapter 60*

*H*appy for all their domestic feelings was the day on which Mr. and Mrs. Darcy set off from Netherfield to spend Christmas at Pemberley. They had not an hour to waste, and exhausted the horses in the journey, but even the animals seemed relieved to reach home after so long a sojourn. Georgiana and the Gardiners met them with much elation, and all enjoyed a merry Yuletide free of the unpleasant people and events of recent weeks.

Mr. Parrish experienced the hospitality of the Hertfordshire county jail for months while he awaited trial. Although the paranormal details of his crimes were withheld from common knowledge, the miscreant's other acts proved sufficient to convict him in the court of public opinion well in advance of his appearance in the court of law. As word of his treachery spread, all the *ton* recalled having observed something untrustworthy in his aspect, questionable in his manner, dubious in his speech. Americans in general were declared uncivilized, and marriage to one the ultimate *mésalliance*.

Caroline remained at Netherfield to recover from her ordeal and petition for a divorce from her frog prince. The disgrace of her marriage chastened her little; free of the ring's effects, she was soon restored to her usual charming self, and took pleasure once more in derisive commentary on country society. Unfortunately, she was left to make her snide observations alone, as the Hursts departed for the Continent to live amongst other genteel expatriates fleeing high gambling debts. Louisa wrote to her brother with hints that a few extra pounds would greatly increase their comfort, and to her sister with suggestions that a French suitor might prove just the antidote for her American *faux pas*, but neither responded with enthusiasm.

Jane and Bingley, their house cleared of guests save Caroline, at last knew relative peace. Lest the newlyweds grow bored at Netherfield without murder and mayhem to fill their days, Mrs. Bennet's frequent visits and the servants' misguided eagerness worked in concert to keep life interesting. As soon as spring arrived, they undertook with alacrity the search for a new home.

Juliet Kendall enjoyed increased popularity following the Parrish scandal. In the convenient memory of the *ton* she was credited with having been the first to recognize the scoundrel for what he was. By the middle of the following season, she married a gentleman of moderate means who found her disposition bearable, and perhaps sweeter for the sizable inheritance that came with it. They settled in Sussex and never bothered the Bingleys again.

Professor Randolph managed to escape guilt by association with Mr. Parrish, and was generally considered another unfortunate victim of the rogue's duplicity. Aided by the patronage of Lord Chatfield, and Mr. Darcy's suggestion that he would do well to keep his specialty quiet, he secured a position as the British Museum's first resident archeologist.

He immediately commenced planning his next expedition, an investigation into several standing stone ruins in the north country.

Darcy, having witnessed with his own eyes the supernatural effects of the rings, was forced to concede to Elizabeth that there were things of this world that transcend the ability of science to explain. He continued, however, to believe in the superiority of reason over intuition. He also continued to train with his fencing master whenever business summoned him to London, in the unlikely event that he would ever again be called upon to defend himself with a fire poker.

Elizabeth met the demands of her new role as mistress of Pemberley with grace and aptitude. Her days were busy, but she took pleasure in the occupation. As time passed and the intrigue at Netherfield faded into memory, she could hardly believe herself that the eerie events she'd experienced had been more than a chapter in a gothic novel. She was content to set aside thoughts of plots and portents for more mundane concerns: the simple pleasures of home and hearth, and a new husband whose devotion to her was matched only by the affection she bore for him.

In quiet moments, however, she sometimes withdrew Professor Randolph's amulet and pondered his parting words to her. "I believe you have a gift," he had said. "A very powerful one. Should you ever choose to cultivate it, let me know."

Perhaps one day she would.